Meet Again

A MEET CUTE SERIES NOVEL

ABI SABINA

Copyright

©

2022 by Abi Sabina

Publication Date: May 5, 2022

Meet Again

All rights reserved

This book is a work of fiction. The names, characters, places, and incidents are products of the writer's imagination or have been used fictitiously and are not to be construed as real. Any resemblance to persons, living or dead, actual events, locales, or organizations is entirely coincidental.

The author acknowledges the trademarked status and trademark owners of various products referenced in this work of fiction. Any trademarks, service marks, product names or names featured are assumed to be the property of their respective owners and are used only for reference. There is no implied endorsement.

This book is licensed for your personal enjoyment only and contains material protected under the International and Federal Copyright Laws and Treaties. Any unauthorized reprint or use of the material is prohibited. No part of this book may be reproduced, stored in a retrieval system, or transmitted in any form, or by any means, electronic, mechanical, photocopying, recording or otherwise, without prior permission of the author. This book may not be re-sold or given away to other people. If you would like to share this book with another person, please purchase an additional copy for each recipient. Thank you for respecting the hard work of this author.

Cover design by Kat Savage

Editing by Rebecca Kettner, The Polished Author

DEDICATION

For N, a book you can read before you're 18. XO

GLOSSARY

THIS IS A LIST of Spanish words used throughout Meet Again with their English translation. It's a fun peek into Lex's Cuban background.

Spanish / English glossary:

- **Mi amor:** My love, sweetheart
- **Tostones:** Fried green plantains served as a side dish
- **Picadillo:** Ground beef cooked with a tomato-based sauce, tart vinegar, and sautéed onions and garlic. Usually serves with rice.
- **Crema de Vie:** A cuban twist on eggnog, usually spiked with rum
- **Su niña:** His little girl
- **Mijo/Mija (abbreviation of mi hijo/mi hija):** Used as a term of endearment by someone older which translates to my son/ my daughter, or my dear
- **Abuela:** Grandmother
- **Abuelo:** Grandfather
- **Pastelito:** Puffed pastry filled with different fillings: guava, guava and cream cheese, cream cheese, ground beef

1
LEX

I RUSH AROUND THE corner of the street, stumbling when my heel catches in a crack on the sidewalk. Grateful I didn't land on my face, I slow my pace and breathe out when I see the bright lights that read *Monroe's*.

It'd be my luck that the day I need to leave work on time, I get caught up with a parent. I'm ecstatic about the news she had to share. I'm not ecstatic about being late for my best friend's engagement celebration.

I stop outside of Monroe's, the restaurant we've always chosen for special moments in our lives, and run my hands down my dress while I take a deep breath to slow my racing heart. I don't want to arrive looking like I sprinted here.

When I feel myself relax a bit, I pull the heavy wooden door and enter. Deafening chatter hits me. Tables are full as I weave through them on my way to the backroom Hope reserved. I smile and wave at a few familiar faces as I pass their tables. As soon as I slip through the curtain separating the room from the rest of the restaurant, I see Hope dash toward me.

"You're thirty minutes late." Her eyebrows lift as she points to the clock on the opposite wall from where we stand.

"I know, I know. I'm so sorry." My eyes round. "Forgive me?" I clutch my hands and give her my best puppy-dog face.

Hope sighs and shakes her head. "Of course, you're forgiven. You're my best friend, but you'll have to make it up to me." She swings her arm across my shoulder and smiles before leading me toward the bar.

"I'll do anything." I smile at her. I want nothing more than for this time in her life to be unforgettable.

We reach the bar, and she steps to the side, smiling. "Anything?" Her eyes light up as I turn to look at her.

"You're my best friend. You know I have your back."

"Good because—"

"You've got to be kidding me." I interrupt her when my eyes land on the one person I could live the rest of my life without seeing. And he's approaching us with Toby, Hope's fiancé.

I scowl, my eyes dancing between Hope's apologetic expression and the two men.

"Good to see you, too, Lex." Hudson looks me over with his hands in his pockets and smirks.

I roll my eyes at his aggravating voice and stare at my best friend. I refuse to acknowledge him.

"Remember when you said you'd do anything for me a few minutes ago?" Worry fills her expression.

"Toby and I have been talking, and we don't want separate bachelor and bachelorette parties. We want to combine them and have a destination event. We'll still have girl time while the guys do their thing," she rushes out to explain. "Since you and Hudson are maid-of-honor and best man, you'll both be organizing this."

My face falls. My heart pounds at the thought of having to spend any time with that man. She says it as if it were no big deal.

"Hope, please tell me this is a joke." I don't shy away from my reaction to the news.

"Not a joke," Hudson says, and I shoot him a glare.

"It's not." Hope widens her eyes at Hudson and looks back at me. She gingerly grabs my elbow and steers me away, looking over her shoulder with a tight smile. "I know this is hard, and I wouldn't ask if it weren't important."

"I know you wouldn't, but this goes beyond my maid-of-honor duties." I cross my arms.

"Planning my bachelorette party is maid-of-honor duties." She raises an eyebrow.

"Can't I plan our side of it, and we just show up at the same place? Where do you want to go?"

"Winford in Vermont. You know how much Toby and I love skiing. It's where we went on our first trip, too, so it's special to us." She smiles wistfully.

Nodding, I can't help but smile. "I know." I squeeze her arm.

"So you'll do this?"

I close my eyes for a moment and take a deep breath. Could I spend time with the man who broke my heart and pretend it doesn't affect me? Seeing the hope in her eyes, I silently nod.

"But that doesn't mean I'll be nice to him." I point my finger at her.

"He deserves it," she says with conviction.

"Let's grab something to drink," I suggest, hoping it will help quiet my racing thoughts.

"All squared away?" Toby asks when we return to the bar, his eyes moving between us.

"Great," Hope smiles.

"Champagne." Toby grabs a glass and hands it to me.

I ignore the man standing in front of me while I take a sip of the fizzy drink. Hudson Remington is a man I stopped giving my attention to a long time ago. Just because his best friend is getting married to my best friend means nothing. Soon, he'll go back into the memory box hidden in my closet that I pretend doesn't exist.

Hope and Toby talk while Hudson and I remain quiet. His gaze burns into the side of my face, making me uncomfortable. I need space. Zoning out on the conversation, I scour the room for an escape from this current circle I'm standing in. Meeting Ellie's eyes, I release tension from my tight shoulders.

"Excuse me," I look at Hope. "I'm going to say hi to Ellie." I walk toward our friend.

She smirks and watches me approach, her eyes briefly glancing back toward where I came from.

"Hey."

"Hi. Did I just witness a civil reunion?" She shifts her weight, placing her empty champagne glass on the high-top table beside her.

"Ugh," I shake my head, failing to hide my emotions. Why is it that everyone can always read my mood? I wish I was one of those people who were stoic and emotionless. A statue. Yes! Being a statue would be ideal in this very moment. A gift. I'd pay big bucks so no one can see how this moment is affecting me.

"It was expected, considering you're both a big part of the wedding party."

"I know, but I was hoping I could extend it a bit longer." In reality, I was aware that this would happen soon. I'd have to confront Hudson, but my heart will never be ready for that.

"Anyway, why were you late?"

"Yeah, what reason would keep you away from my engagement party?" Hope sneaks up on me, and I jolt.

"I'm so sorry," I tell her again. "Sarah was cast in a local musical as one of their jazz dancers. Her mom stayed a bit longer after her class to tell me the news." Sarah is one of my best students and has worked her behind off. She deserves this opportunity.

"That's amazing." Hope beams.

"Wow, congrats!" Ellie hugs me.

Laughing, I shake my head. "It's all on her. She's extremely disciplined and has been endlessly practicing to get the role."

"But you're her teacher," Hope points out.

"Your humility doesn't have to extend to such an extreme, Lex," Ellie adds.

"Yeah, yeah." I roll my eyes and look away. I love dancing. My dream was always to open my own studio and share my passion with other people, even if not everyone thought that dream was good enough.

My eyes connect with Hudson's. I stare for a moment too long. His hair is perfectly combed, and his five o'clock shadow makes him look more grown. Gone is the boyish charm he carried years ago. He's matured.

I look away as sadness fills my chest.

"Ellie loves the idea of the destination party instead of individual bachelor parties." Hope smiles.

"I'm not against it. I just don't want to have to interact with Hudson." I twirl my flute between my fingers.

"I'm sure it won't be too much," Ellie naïvely says.

I remain quiet and nod. When a man in a suit comes to talk to Hope, she nods and excuses herself to find Toby.

"I'm so happy for them," Ellie sighs as she stares at the couple.

"Me too." Despite everything, I'm overjoyed for my best friend. She deserves her happily ever after.

"We'll be sitting for dinner," Hope announces to the group. "Please take a seat."

"Great, I'm starving." Ellie rubs her stomach.

MEET AGAIN

On cue, her stomach growls. We look at each other and boisterously laugh as we take our seats. When I look across the table, Hudson is watching me.

"Wonderful," I mumble as I place my napkin on my lap.

"I'm starting to feel like this hostility is personal." He doesn't remove his eyes from me. He's acting as if he doesn't have a clue what this moment means to me. He may be able to pretend everything is peachy, but it's not. Too much sits between us.

"You're picking up on that now?" I tilt my head.

A hand squeezes my leg under the table. I look to my right to find Hope silently pleading to keep the peace. I don't want to ruin her evening, so I look at Ellie.

"How's the farm going?" Ellie's family owns a dairy farm right outside of town.

"Great. We've got an important order, which will help us a lot."

"That's great. I'm sure it's a relief." Ellie's family has had some years better than others, and they've been struggling with commercial competition increasing, but those big companies don't value the purest form of products.

"Have you thought about finding an investor so you can expand the farm?"

My eyes snap across the table to Hudson.

"My family doesn't need an investor." Ellie crosses her arms defiantly.

"Not everyone wants help from some suit with a wad of cash," I shoot back. It's just like him to stick himself without asking.

"You didn't mind at one point."

"And I was an investment you could just replace." For the second time, I make eye contact with the man I thought I knew. His green eyes are intense. I place my napkin on the table. "If you'll excuse me." The screeching of my chair fills the silence that's settled over the table. Ignoring it, I walk away and head toward the bathroom with a racing heart. I don't want to ruin dinner, so removing myself before it becomes worse is the best plan of action.

I lean against the door once I'm inside, grateful the bathroom is empty, and close my eyes. Tears well behind my eyelids, but I refuse to let them fall. It's been a while since I've cried over him, and this moment isn't the most optimal one for me to have a breakdown over a broken heart.

"Whoa," I stumble forward when the door forcefully pushes against me. "What in the world?" I turn around, ready to face Hope. It'd be like her to leave her guests and make sure I'm okay.

"Hope—" My words freeze when I come face to face with a six-foot-one frame. "You're not Hope."

"Lex, I'm—"

I lift my hand to stop him. "Don't. We just need to get through this wedding for Hope and Toby. Then, we can go back to being strangers. Can you handle that?" I cross my arms and force myself to look him in the face, not willing to let him see the hurt seeping out of my pores.

After a few beats, he sighs and looks away. "Just know you weren't an investment."

"It sure felt like a cheap trade." I step around him and head back to the table. I pray the rest of the night passes quickly. If only this were our final interaction. The next few months are sure to test my patience and my heart.

2
LEX

I ROCK ON THE old swing set, the wood creaking with my slow movements. My house was owned by a family for many years, so their children had swings, and I love sitting out here when I need to think. It reminds me of childhood, of simpler times. Careful not to spill my coffee, I take a sip. The gray sky casts shadows over the mountains in the distance, dulling the reds and oranges that are predominant in fall.

It's my favorite time of year.

"Hey."

I turn my head to the left and find Hope walking my way through the side of the yard.

"Hi."

"I figured you were out here when you didn't answer the door." She takes a seat on the empty swing beside me. "How are you?" She gives me a meaningful look.

"I'm good. Did you have fun last night?" Despite my issues with Hudson, I want my friends' wedding to be amazing, and that begins with all the events before the big day.

"I did. Are you okay? I'm sorry I just dropped Hudson on you like that. I wasn't sure how to bring it up, but not warning you ahead of time was inconsiderate." Her lips press into a thin line.

I stop swinging, pressing my feet into the ground. "You don't need to apologize. I knew he'd have to be a part of it, considering he's Toby's best friend, but I guess a part of me was hoping they'd drifted apart and William would've taken the best man role," I say of another one of Toby's friends. I know that's not the case. Hudson and Toby have been best friends most of their lives.

"You know Hudson and Toby have an epic bromance. I don't think anyone would get between that."

"Even me..." I frown. "I mean, not that I'd want to. I don't want to be the cause for anyone to stop being friends, even you. I was okay until now, not needing to face Hudson," I spit out, trying to explain. I knew Hope and Toby would see him, even traveled to New York, where he now lives. I'm not going to interfere in anyone's friendship, but I'd rather not be thrown into the mix.

"I know you wouldn't, but you're *my* best friend." She squeezes the hand wrapped around the swing chain.

I turn on a smile and move past the topic. "It's only a few months, and then I won't see him again. Now, tell me about your ideas for the bachelorette party."

Hope furrows her eyebrows but doesn't push. "We want to go to Winford, like I told you. We'll have time to do girl things, so have no fear. The resorts have spas, so I think it'd be fun to pamper ourselves one day, then we'll all have dinner together."

As Hope tells me her ideas, I'm grateful she has a clear vision of what she wants. It'll make my planning easier and will *hopefully* limit my one-on-one time with Hudson. It'll be the best for all parties involved.

Nothing prepared me to face Hudson again. I knew it was only a matter of time, but I naïvely thought I could avoid him until the day of Hope's wedding. If some people don't meet their spouses until their wedding day, then surely I could wait to have a reunion with the man who broke my heart. Unfortunately, luck isn't on my side.

MEET AGAIN

A pang constricts my chest. Once upon a time, I would've been ecstatic about the opportunity to plan this with him. That was before my heartbreak.

"Anyway, tell me about Sarah's performance." Hope changes direction.

A wide smile fills my face, pride swelling inside of me. "I'm so excited for her. It's not Broadway, but it'll be a great addition to her resume and for college applications. She has the potential to make it big."

"You did, too." I roll my eyes are her comment. As if being a dance teacher is the worst choice.

"I never wanted that." I tilt my head, arching an eyebrow. "I love teaching and sharing my passion for dance, and that's okay," I defend.

After hearing so many people tell me I'm missing an opportunity by teaching instead of pursuing higher training and becoming a star, it gets old. Why can't people understand I don't need to be in the spotlight? I love what I do.

"I know, but I sometimes wonder if it's what you truly wanted or what you thought you were good enough for."

My eyebrows pull down as I stare at my best friend. Her words surprise me.

"Don't look at me like that. It's a question."

"I love teaching. It's what I'm passionate about. If I were fighting for a chance on stage amongst other amazing dancers, I'd miss the opportunity to share my love for dancing. It'd suck the fun out of it, and that's not because I don't think I'm good enough. Living the dance lifestyle is different... I don't think I'd love it as much." I sigh in exasperation.

Why can't people accept that running my own dance studio fulfills me?

"I know, sorry. Why don't we go have lunch? I need to run some errands and would love the company." She smiles her pearly whites, dimples showing.

"Let me change." Going out will help clear my mind and shake my mood. Seeing Hudson has stirred many emotions, some I buried so deep that they rattle me as they resurface. Nothing like an ex-boyfriend to make your insecurities reappear in your life.

I stand and walk into my house with Hope. After placing the coffee mug in the dishwasher, I go to my room to change.

"Ready?" Hope smiles when I step back into the kitchen.

"Let's go." I shimmy, and Hope giggles.

Looping her arm through mine, I lock up my house and head to her car.

"What errands do you need to run?" I ask once she's pulling out of my driveway.

"I need to drop off the deposit for our venue and meet with the caterer. We can have lunch at The Mill. I've been craving their food."

"Oh, yeah," I sigh, my mouth watering. "I'm always craving their food." The Mill is a lakeside restaurant that was a watermill back in the day. It has a beautiful view of the lake and town. This time of year, the fall leaves stand out, making the landscape magical.

"I knew you'd agree." Hope reaches for the volume and turns up the country song. She belts out the lyrics as she drives. Her singing is terrible, and I laugh as she squeaks a verse instead of actually singing it.

"I'm getting married!" she yells over the music, looking at me briefly with a blinding smile before turning her attention back to the road. I laugh at her outburst.

"Sometimes, I can't believe it. Toby and I have been waiting for this for so long, waiting for the right time."

"You deserve it," I grin. Toby and Hope are high school sweethearts. I've never met a pair that's a better fit than them.

"Do you have any ideas for the bridesmaids' dresses?" I shift my body toward her.

"I'm torn. I was hoping we could talk about it today. We can have coffee after lunch and brainstorm. I have a few ideas but can't settle on one." She grimaces.

"We'll figure it out," I promise.

We continue to talk about her different ideas as she drives out of town to the wedding venue. Mountains surround us as fall colors drown the green. It's a beautiful drive.

Ex-boyfriends or not, I'm going to enjoy this time and make memories. In the words of... I don't know who, but I don't need a man to have fun. Maybe it was Shania Twain?

"We're here!" Hope glows as she pulls into the long driveway to the historic estate they've chosen for the venue.

"It's breathtaking," I say as I step out.

"I know. It's always been part of my dream wedding. I was so excited when they had an opening, even if it's a shorter engagement."

"It'll be worth it. Besides, you have eight months, almost a pregnancy. If a woman can grow a child, we can plan a wedding," I assure her as we walk up the steps to the expansive porch before entering a grand entrance room with a huge chandelier. The back wall has floor-to-ceiling windows and glass doors that give a view to an outdoor area. In the distance, I can see a glimpse of mountains. It's a dream location for a wedding.

After the quick transaction, we're off to the caterer.

"I'll be quick with the caterer, too, and then we'll go have lunch. My stomach is about to yell at me to feed it." She pats her belly.

"Sounds good." I lean back in the seat, glad that Hope asked me to come with her.

Hope and I talk about the coming holidays, our Thanksgiving plans later in the month, and more ideas for the bachelorette party. In no time, we're at the caterer's location.

"Hey, what are you doing here?" Hope tilts her head and looks at Toby, who's walking out of the caterer's office.

"Uh, what do you mean? I told you I was coming to pay the deposit." He looks at his fiancée with raised eyebrows.

"No, you didn't. I told you I was coming." She points at herself.

"I sent you a message. I said we'd divide and conquer since you were driving to the venue."

Hope scrunches her nose. "I haven't checked it."

"Ah...so I'm not in the wrong." Toby winks.

"Hey..." My head snaps to the right, where Hudson appears from inside.

"Hi, Hudson," Hope smiles, looking at me out of the corner of her eye. "I guess we're done here, then, right?" She looks back at Toby.

I try to keep my attention on the loving couple, but same as last night, I can feel Hudson's stare burning into the side of my face. Soon I'll have his eyeballs seared into my face. When Toby wraps his arm around Hope and kisses her cheek, I look away, accidentally making contact with Hudson.

The look in his eyes is undecipherable, but it makes my heart skip and my skin prickle. Pain, sadness, and confusion flood me. I blink rapidly.

MEET AGAIN

"I'll wait in the car," I say before turning around and getting some much-needed distance between the man from my past and my current life.

I remember the days when I thought he and I would be where Hope and Toby are—planning our wedding, living a blissful life. But alas, we were destined for different paths than our friends. I've had a few years to accept that, but seeing him again since then still stings.

"Are you okay?" Hope whispers as she unlocks her car.

"Yeah," I wave her off.

She narrows her eyes and analyzes me, but I smile and slide into the car.

"Let's eat. I'm starving and craving the curly fries from The Mill."

"And their milkshakes," she drools.

"Definitely their milkshakes. Then, we'll discuss bridesmaids' dresses."

"I'm so excited," she exclaims, clapping her hands.

I focus on her energy and release the past.

Until my phone buzzes while we're getting seated at the restaurant.

Unknown number: Hey, it's Hudson. Toby gave me your number so we can discuss the bach party

I leave my phone in my purse. I'll respond later on.

3
HUDSON

"You already texted her?" Toby claps my back as we take a seat at a sports grill outside of town.

"Yeah, might as well start planning while I'm in town." It's not often that I visit Hartville, let alone for more than a day or two. My career keeps me busy since I work with clients all over the country.

"No other reason than that?" Toby smirks.

"Nope," I shake my head. "That ship has sailed."

"Ships tend to return to the dock," he lifts his eyebrow.

Right, ships that haven't been wrecked by a storm.

"You saw her reaction to seeing me." Lex looks beautiful, like always, but we have deep wounds that never healed properly.

"She was caught by surprise, which we both know she hates, and she's still hurt. We all expected it. It's why Hope didn't know how to tell her you'd be there." Toby shakes his head.

"Yeah," I nod and skim the menu.

"For what it's worth, I think it's time to move on from the past. Maybe having to plan this trip will give you the right time to talk about what happened." He clasps his hands and leans forward on the table.

"My focus is making this the best bachelor party for you." I smile. Toby has been my best friend since we were five. Living in a different state and having a demanding job wouldn't keep me away from celebrating this next chapter in his life.

"Okay," he leans back, relaxing his shoulders, and picking up the menu.

"It is going to be fun watching from the sidelines, though," he smirks, his eyes focused on the menu.

"Thanks for the support, buddy."

"Hey, I'm supporting you. Your number one cheerleader. I just won't be wearing a skirt and crop top." He laughs.

"Thank goodness. It's best for all of us that you don't," I smile and shake my head.

Thoughts of Lex swirl in my mind. Her reaction last night was exactly what I expected, but hearing her say aloud that she was a cheap investment surprised me. I never thought she'd voice it so publicly or that she considered herself that in my life.

Things were different when we were in college. Not only did the distance make it hard on our relationship while I was in school and she stayed in town, but we were already struggling with other issues.

I loved her, though. I never lied about that.

Seeing her after four years, a woman who accomplished her dreams, struck me with a sense of nostalgia and longing. She always talked about owning a dance studio, and she did it on her own. It's as if it made no difference if I was cheering her on or not. And that realization stings. Though, I can't blame her for it. What happened between us was on me. I see that now, although I was blind to it at twenty-one.

The waiter stops by, and we order. I focus on spending time with my best friend and leaving Lex in the past.

"What ideas do you have for this party slash trip?" I steeple my fingers.

"I'm not sure. We know we want to go to Winford in Vermont and ski. The rest is up to you, my friend. The girls will have a spa day one of the days, so we can either hang out or do something. Maybe you can check to see if they have something that'd interest us."

"Sounds good. I'll do some research. I'm sure I'll find something." As soon as Lex replies, we're going to have to start working out some details if we want Hope and Toby to have the best celebration.

♡♡♡

"Hello, son." My father greets me when I walk into their home.

"Father," I tip my head and sit on the couch across from him.

"How's Toby?" He places his tablet on the side table and leans back against the armchair.

"He's great. Excited about the wedding."

"Good, good. By the way, did you receive the e-mail I sent you about the LA mansion?" He raises his eyebrows.

"I received it but haven't opened it yet. I'll look it over tonight. Not much can be done until Monday, anyway."

"In our world, every day is a good day to close a deal." That's the Remington motto. Work like a dog, close deals, make more money. It's what's expected of me as well. Just throw a leash on me and hand it over to my father.

"*In our world*, but everyone else's world believes in unwinding. I'll look it over tonight," I say with finality.

I was always expected to be the person to take over the family business one day, especially after my brother broke family ties and went off to travel the world, which led to working with non-profit organizations. The same way my father did when his father retired. The Remington legacy. It wasn't always what I wanted, but no one says no to my father, let alone my grandfather.

"Oh, hello, dear. I didn't hear you come in." My mom walks into the living room holding a teacup. She's dressed to the nines even if she's been home all day.

"I just got here a few minutes ago." I stand and kiss her cheek.

"Were you with Tobias?" My mom sits on the armchair next to my dad's and places her teacup beside the tablet on the side table.

"I was. He's well and ready to marry Hope." Coldness is key in our family. Forget being laid-back and happy. The Remingtons don't believe in happiness.

"Wonderful. Be sure to tell us where they're registered so we can buy them a gift," my mother is the ever-present symbol of societal politeness. It's always irked me.

"I'll be sure to do so."

"When will you be back to New York?" My dad questions.

"I'm not sure yet. I have a few things to do in town. On Tuesday, I have a meeting in Portland, Maine, for a luxury home."

"Waterfront?" My dad sits forward, his interest piqued.

"Of course. They want two million for it."

"Get that deal," my dad demands. When his eyes are set on something, nothing will deter him from it. "It will be an easy sell."

"That's exactly what I plan to do. It seems another realtor in the area told them two million was too steep for the property, but they've done their research and know the price is competitive. They want to work with us, so it should be an easy deal to secure."

"I'll hold you to that." His face leaves no room for argument.

"I don't expect anything less," I say flatly.

"You two are always talking about work," my mother interrupts us as if it were a nuisance to her. She loves it, though. Our family business allows for her expensive lifestyle.

"Tell me about the engagement party."

"It was fine. Dinner, some drinks." I check my phone—still no message from Lex.

"Who is part of Hope's bridal party?" My mom takes a sip of her tea.

"Ellie, Lex, and I'm not sure who else."

"Oh…" Her face screws. "You saw *that* girl." I resist rolling my eyes.

"You know she's Hope's best friend. What did you expect? That you could completely remove her from every aspect of my life? Not even you have that power." I stand.

I wasn't blind to my parents' actions when I was eighteen and getting ready for college. There was no way that their oldest son wouldn't attend Columbia University like the rest of his family. It was perfect for their plan. My father decided to expand the business into the city, making sure I would be the one to manage that office under the pretense that it'd be preparation for taking over the realty agency one day.

Considering my father wasn't near retirement at that stage, I knew it was a ploy to create more distance between Lex and me. They never approved of her.

Anger filled me when Lex refused to move with me to New York after college graduation. I didn't want my parents to win, but it seems they did. She had other dreams, though, and I was too selfish back then to realize it. Now, as an adult, I know the sacrifice it would've been for her to move.

"Hudson," my father warns.

"I have to go."

MEET AGAIN

"Don't forget to look over that e-mail," my father adds, unbothered by the conversation. Why would he be? He won. They both got what they wanted—control of their son's life.

I don't know why I feel a loyalty to my family. It'd be so easy to break free and do what makes me happy, even if I have to surrender the money that comes along with the name.

The saddest part is that my parents are unfazed by my reaction. They don't care, so long as I'm living out the life they planned for me. They're happy even if it costs my own happiness.

I walk out of the door, almost crashing into their housekeeper on the way out. I run a hand through my hair and slide into my car. My knuckles turn white as I grip the leather steering wheel and take deep, even breaths. Maybe my brother was onto something when he skipped town and relinquished everything that came with the Remington name. I should give him a call. It's been too long since we've spoken.

By the time I get to Hart House, the inn where I'm staying, I've calmed down. My parents have space for me in their home, but I'd rather not stay with them while I visit.

Driving through the town I grew up in gives me an odd sense of belonging. Life in Hartville is slower and more wholesome. It's peaceful watching people walk around, talking with familiarity, and laughing. Hartville is home to ten thousand people, making it possible to feel like everyone is part of your family, yet it has enough population where you may not run into the same people every day.

As I change into sweatpants and a t-shirt, my phone pings with a message. Seeing Lex's name on the screen makes me smile. Who knew I'd have this reaction after four years of silence?

Lex: Bach party? Did you make that up?

Hudson: It's what they call a combined bachelor and bachelorette party

The bubbles on the screen appear and disappear a couple of times before her response comes in.

Lex: I knew that...

I chuckle at her reply.

Hudson: Sure you did...

Hudson: Anyway, we should talk about this event

Lex: I've already got a plan. I prepare our side of the trip and you prepare the guy's. If we need to check-in, then we can do so through here

She's clearly avoiding me. I shouldn't push. I should allow our distance to remain intact. But what's left of life if we don't throw caution to the wind?

Hudson: That's a flawed plan. There are things we'll have to discuss together. The last thing we want Hope and Toby to feel is disappointed because we couldn't put our differences aside

Hudson: We wouldn't be productive that way

Lex: Many people solve issues via text messages

Hudson: I'll be in town for a couple of weeks. We can get together and discuss details before I head back home

Lex: I don't think that's a good idea

Hudson: Like you said last night, we'll work together on this and after go back to being strangers once the wedding is over

That feels bitter as I type it. I hate that we ended up where we did after everything we shared. I didn't think that my parents would truly get between us, but I underestimated them.

ABI SABINA

When Lex doesn't reply right away, I grab my laptop and open my e-mail. Work will distract me. The mansion my father mentioned looks promising, and if we can secure it, we'd make a lofty commission. I write down some notes before I call the owners tomorrow morning. My father has a point about the housing market. Even Sundays are unforgiving when it comes to closing a deal. Another agent can sneak up on you and steal it if you're not careful or ambitious enough.

My stomach growls, and I close the laptop. I need to eat something before it's any later. Changing my sweatpants for jeans, I lock up and head out, walking to the diner nearby. What I love about the inn is that it's in the center of town. What I don't love is that everyone stares at me like I'm an alien. I'm a Hartville resident, purebred. It seems people have forgotten where I came from.

Have I?

As I walk in, I halt and smile. Lex's parents are standing up from a table.

"Hello, sweetheart, I heard you were in town. How are you?" Her mom, Bianca, smiles.

Her parents were always warm and welcoming. I was envious at times. Lex had a supportive and loving family nucleus while I had business talks from a young age, and parents too busy with their professional and social life to care about what I had going on. My parents never even attended one of my high school football games. It was pointless in their eyes.

"Hey, I'm good. How about you? It's good to see the both of you." Lex's dad is more closed-off, which I can understand. I hurt his little girl.

"We're great. Just had dinner. We need to get out of the house, or we'll age faster than we're meant to," Bianca jokes.

I chuckle and shake my head. "You look great."

MEET AGAIN

"Thank you. We have to get going, but I'm so glad I saw you." She smiles kindly.

"You, too. Mr. Leon," I nod.

"Hudson, nice seeing you," he says politely, shaking my hand.

As I take a seat at an empty booth, people around me stare and whisper. Ah, small-town living. The gossip never dies down. I can imagine what will spread next—Hudson's awkward interaction with his ex-girlfriend's parents. There will be rumors about what our conversation was about. Ignoring them, I open my messages and frown. Lex went radio silent after that last text I sent her.

> Hudson: I'm only suggesting what you already stated. If that's what you want, I'll be cordial and then head back to New York and you'll never hear from me again

> Lex: You're making a big deal about planning a bach party

> Hudson: You liked the word, huh?

> Lex: If that's what it's called, I'll use it

Hudson: Toby mentioned that you'll be having a spa day. I'll plan something for us to do that day, and then we can all have dinner that evening

Lex: That's fine. They want to ski, so I suppose most of the trip will be focused on that

Hudson: Are you skiing?

Lex: Of course not. I'll be on the ground more than standing on those stilts

Hudson: They're not stilts lol

Lex: They're horizontal stilts. I don't know. No, I'm not skiing. I'll stay at the resort and make sure the next event is planned and prepared, whatever that may be

Hudson: You're a dancer and don't have the grace to ski? I still can't believe it

Lex: It is what it is

Hudson: Let's meet this week to sort out details. I have a meeting on Tuesday, but I'll be free Wednesday morning

Lex: I have a job

Hudson: That doesn't open until the afternoon. We need to work through this, Lex. We're both adults now, we can handle it. Hope and Toby deserve it

Lex: Fine

I smile in triumph and lean back in the booth. That was easier than I thought, though selfishly, I used Hope and Toby's happiness to con her into meeting me. Did I manipulate the situation by guilting her? Yes. Do I feel bad about it? Only a little bit. It's for a good cause. At least, that is what I'm telling myself.

After all these years, I still feel excited about spending time with Lex. I haven't allowed myself the liberty to think much about her in the past, knowing it was for the best, but I'm an idiot for not realizing that she was and will always be the one who got away.

Wednesday can't get here soon enough.

4

LEX

My heart pounds as I sit in my car in front of The Bean, our town's coffee shop. I shouldn't be nervous. I should be indifferent about seeing Hudson. He's from my past, an ex-boyfriend. I can do this. I spent all of the last few days telling myself that Hudson is just Toby's friend. Interacting with him can be natural if I let go of what happened between us like he clearly has.

I can be Lorelai Gilmore meeting with Christopher. Cool, calm, and empowered. For the most part. She definitely had her moments of weakness, but I'll channel strong and determined Lorelai.

As confident as possible, I take a deep breath, reach for my purse, and step out of my car. Hudson stands from the small table he's sitting at when I reach him.

"Hey, I was waiting for you to order. Take a seat."

"Hi." My lips press together in a forced smile while my heart continues to race. *Deep breaths.*

"What do you want?"

"I got it." I pull my wallet out of my purse.

"Lex, just tell me what you want. It's on me." Hudson raises his eyebrows.

"No. I can pay for my own." I insist, pulling out a five-dollar bill and extending my hand toward him.

"Not taking it. I'm sure you can pay for your own, but it's my treat. Time's ticking. Give me your order, or I'll choose." He crosses his arms as his eyes widen. The white button-down shirt he's wearing stretches over his biceps. He's gotten more handsome with time, and I hate that I notice.

He was always good-looking—the most gorgeous guy in my eyes. I need to hamper that train of thought before I fall down the rabbit hole and get lost in Hudson-land. Map or no map, I'd get lost in him.

"A latte." I give in when I realize people are staring at us with a combination of confusion and surprised curiosity.

"That wasn't so hard now, was it?" He smiles triumphantly. It's a charming grin that screams danger. If he thinks he can storm back into my life, smile that dazzling smile, and I'll fall for him again, then I've got news for him. I'm not that easily affected by a grin, even if it was my favorite feature of his.

I roll my eyes and stare at him without a trace of humor, hoping that my face remains masked. I don't need Hudson Remington buying me a coffee. I can afford it on my own.

While he grabs coffee, I open my notebook with notes. I prepared for today so that we can make it as quick as possible.

"Hey, girl." I look up and see Diana, someone I went to high school with. "Are you and Hudson...a thing again?" Her eyes are saucers as she stares at me.

"No." I shake my head. I haven't spoken much to Diana since high school. We always share the cordial hello when we run into each other, but we're definitely not friendly enough for her to ask.

"What a shame." She looks at him talking to the barista. "He's sure gotten fine since high school. If I didn't have my husband, I'd stake my claim," she giggles.

Unimpressed, I look at her with narrowed eyes.

"Oh, I'm just joking." She waves her hand. "No need to get possessive."

"Possessive about what?" Hudson asks, now standing by his chair. "Hi, Diana."

She smiles like a fangirl. "Hi, Hudson. Oh, nothing, just girl talk." She winks at me as if we were best friends and walks away.

Hudson stares at me, tilting his head. "Possessive?" He smirks, likely coming up with his own conclusions. I'm not sure how much he heard. Diana wasn't exactly discreet about her comments.

"I don't know what she was talking about." Heat fills my cheeks. I'm not possessive about Hudson. He is free to be with who he wants. Preferably in New York, where I don't have to bear witness. I'm not a masochist.

"Okay... The barista will bring our coffees over so we won't have to be interrupted while we work."

"Right. Here's what I have so far." I push my notebook toward him.

He holds a corner of the page, twisting and turning it as he concentrates on what I've written.

"You've done a lot of research already," he lifts his gaze to me.

"We have a little less than three months to plan this with the holidays in between, and February is a huge skiing month in Winford. If we don't hurry, we may risk not finding rooms for Hope and Toby's preferred weekend."

"You have a point." He nods, skimming the information.

"I know," I grin.

"Always so modest," he chuckles. "I was thinking we could stay at the Astoria Resort. I know the manager and have been there a few times. The suites are spacious, and it has a penthouse, which would accommodate everyone."

"We're staying in separate rooms." I address that part of it first. "I was thinking two suites, but Astoria is one of the most expensive ones in the area. Not everyone has your budget." Namely me, but I know Ellie would also struggle to afford her share of a suite in a hotel like that one. And we'd be paying for Hope. I need to talk to the other girls going, but I know we all have a budget in mind.

"Compared to another hotel, it's not that big of a difference, and the manager will cut us a deal. It's a nicer resort, all the amenities are top-notch, and it has a renowned spa." He explains this so calmly.

"You don't get it. Some of us have to save up money starting three months ago for a trip like this."

"Don't say no before I have all the details. Let me get a price." He pulls out his phone without waiting for my response.

Annoyed, I bite my tongue and grab my notebook. The other hotels I found are great, and we'd fit comfortably in their suites within our budget.

"I messaged him. I'll let you know what he says when he gets back to me."

I shake my head, feeling inadequate. Once again, I'm not on his level. His parents always rubbed it in my face, and unintentionally, so did Hudson. He's doing it again. It's as if he's oblivious to the financial differences between him and most of the people in town. Only a small circle can reach Hudson's wealth. Our circle of friends is not it.

"What else do you have?" He leans forward on the small round table.

"Here you go." The barista smiles before I have a chance to speak.

"Thank you," I smile at her. Without another word, I take a drink of the hot latte, allowing it to comfort me.

Hudson is staring at me expectantly. "I'm waiting..." His voice holds a teasing ring to it.

"For? You already took control. Why don't you tell me what other ideas you have."

"Lex," he sighs.

"It's true. You come in, take over like you always do, and don't consider what other people may want or be able to afford." I lower my voice when I realize I'm drawing attention to us. It's part of the Cuban flare, or curse at times—talk loud and with my hands.

"I do consider it. We won't be paying full price. It doesn't hurt to find out all of our options. If it's the same as one of the other suites you found, which hotel would you choose?" He gives me a pointed look.

"Well, until we know, all my current research is null and void. I made plans revolving around the hotels I found as options. I called those hotels with questions."

"So let's look up this one and search what they have to offer, add it to the list." I've never in my life felt inadequate except around Hudson's family. Now, I feel that way around him, too.

Shaking my head, I say, "How about you find that information out, and then you let me know. I need to get going." It's too much, sitting here with him, memories and insecurities from the past resurfacing. I need space.

"Wait."

"I gotta go, Hudson. Let me know what your friend says. I don't want to do double the work, and you're set on staying at this place, no matter the cost." I stand, grabbing my latte and notebook.

I keep my head held high as I walk outside, the cold fall air burning my face. It's a relief, cooling me down and helping me see clearly. Maybe I was too harsh with Hudson, but our relationship was never easy, and today has been a reminder of it.

Maybe we were doomed from the start, but the teen in love was blind to the harsh reality of life.

***

"Hey," Hope says when I answer the call.

"Hi, what's up?" I cradle the phone between my ear and shoulder as I open the back door to the studio.

"How'd it go today with Hudson?"

"Ugh," I grunt, pushing the door open and carrying my bag into my office.

"That great, huh? Toby is gonna owe me dinner," she giggles.

"What?" I scrunch up my nose, settling in my chair and holding the phone.

"Nothing. Tell me what happened." She changes subjects.

"No, wait, did you and Toby bet on how it'd go?" When all I get is silence, I push. "Hope..."

"Fine. He swore you two would get along and work together without any issues, and I told him he was crazy if he thought that."

"Why would he think that?" My chair creaks as I lean back on it.

"Right? Has he been living in a different universe than us? Anyway, what happened?" Her question rushes out impatiently.

"It was okay at first, but then he brought up a resort that's out of our price range. I want the best party for you, I swear I do, but we have to consider all options and possibilities."

"I get it, trust me. We knew having a trip was a bit riskier because it's more expensive, but we've gone on a budget in the past, so it's possible to do so. What resort does Hudson want to stay at?" I'm so grateful she understands and isn't offended.

"Astoria Resort. He said he's friends with the manager, so he could probably get us a discount."

"That's a beautiful resort," Hope sighs. Hearing the way she says that, all dreamlike, I know I'm going to have to set my pride aside and let Hudson have this win if it's feasible for everyone.

"He also mentioned the penthouse, but I assumed we'd stay in separate rooms—guys and girls."

"Yeah, definitely. It'd be easier and less crowded. We can still have our girl time like that." I knew she'd agree.

"Did you discuss anything else?"

"Nope. I told him to let me know what his friend says. I had all these things lined out, but if we don't stay at any of the hotels I found, we'd have to start all over again." My thumb strokes the edges of a stack of papers on my desk.

"I mean, did anything about you guys come up?" I stare at my phone and place it back to my ear.

"Are you insane?" I raise my voice. "What would come up? We dated years ago and broke up. As simple as that."

"You and I both know it's not as simple as that. We all saw your reaction at the engagement party." Hope's voice softens.

"I was caught off-guard. Had I had time to plan, I could've been prepared to face him," I defend, though I know nothing would make seeing Hudson again easier.

"If you say so," Hope appeases.

"It's true," I argue, feeling defensive.

"I'm sure things will work out. I understand why you'd get upset about Hudson's suggestion. Let's see what his friend says. If not, we can go to dinner at the restaurant in the resort. Toby and I have gone, and it's great. Doesn't break the bank either."

"That's a great idea," I smile, jotting down a note on a post-it to look up the restaurant. "I'll do some research, and I promise I won't let my past with Hudson ruin this for you. I want you to have the best time. I can put my differences aside with him to make that happen." The last thing I want is for Hope to think that my personal issues will interfere with her wedding.

"I know that, Lex. I trust you, and I know you love me. We're best friends for life. Sisters through it all."

I smile, choking up at her words. "Forever," I add.

I'm so happy for Hope, though I know marriage will change our dynamic. It's expected, and I accept it. Seeing Hudson has just dug up a lot of feelings and memories I had pushed aside and ignored for far too long.

"I gotta go. I need to make sure everything is set for the first class."

"Of course, we'll talk later. Keep me posted."

"I will. Bye." I hang up and look around my office before standing and preparing for the first class. I'll be teaching the younger ballet group first, and they're some of my favorites. There's nothing like seeing the awe on little girls' faces when they learn a new dance step.

My phone buzzes, and I roll my eyes, thinking it's Hudson. I smile when I see my mom instead.

Mom: Hi sweetie how are you?

Lex: Hi mom, good and you? How's papi?

MEET AGAIN

> Mom: Good. Come over for dinner. I made rice and beans and picadillo
>
> Lex: Tostones too?

I smile. Despite living more than half of her life here, my mom still keeps true to her Cuban roots. And when she cooks Cuban dinner, I'm there.

> Mom: Of course
>
> Lex: I'll be there when I close the studio. You and papi can eat earlier if you want
>
> Mom: We'll wait for you
>
> Lex: Thanks mom

After setting my phone aside and checking that the music is ready to go, I turn on the lights in the waiting room and flip the lock on the front door, turning the Open sign.

Dancing and teaching have always been what I've wanted. Ever since I was a little girl, I'd stand on my toes and spin around, waving my hands softly while I admired ballerinas. I still remember the day my mom told me she'd enrolled me in dance class. I thought she was lying. From that day forward, I lived and breathed dance. And I never forgot the sacrifice my parents made to take me each week to a different town so I could attend classes.

It's part of the reason I dreamed of opening a studio in Hartville and giving children the chance to enjoy dance the way I did. Not every parent has the ability to travel somewhere else for their child to live their dream.

After my first class, I wave goodbye to the parents and greet the tap teacher who's starting class right after mine. As I'm turning away from the waiting room, the door opens. I turn to greet the student when I see Hudson standing there.

His eyes stare at me with a lopsided smile before gazing down my body. I cross my arms, shifting on my feet. Not that my arms will cover my black leotard and pink tights. Thank goodness I'm also wearing my pink chiffon wrap skirt.

"How can I help you?" I arch a brow.

"I was coming to give you an update on the resort." His hands slide into his pockets as his smile widens. "I like the look."

"I'm working. Couldn't you send me a text message?" I shake my head, ignoring his other comment.

"I wanted to see the studio." He glances around. His honesty surprises me.

"Well, I'm not open for a tour at the moment. What did your friend say?" I don't expect the price to be near our price range with the quick search I did on their website.

"He can give us a thirty percent discount for each suite."

My eyebrows fly up, and Hudson smirks arrogantly.

"I told you he'd make us a great deal. Have more faith."

"I'd still need to talk to the girls and make sure they're okay with it." Despite the discount, it's still a bit more expensive than the other options.

"I understand. I've already mentioned it to Toby."

"Okay. I need to get back to work."

"Text me later then." I lift my eyebrows and scrunch up my nose. "When you've talked to the girls and have an answer," he adds quickly.

"Right," I nod, turning away.

"Lex." I turn when he calls my name.

"I'm proud of you."

My heart skips a beat at the honesty reflecting in his eyes. I thought he'd think this was a joke after everything that happened and after I fought to stay in town when he demanded I move to New York with him. Maybe he can finally see that part of my dream of owning a dance studio had to do with Hartville, giving this town something that was all mine—not teaching just anywhere.

"Thank you, mami." I wipe my mouth after the most amazing meal. Spending time with my family has been exactly what I needed after my run-ins with Hudson.

"You're welcome." She smiles.

My grandma clears her throat at the table, and I smile at her. "Thank you, too, Abuela."

"That's better. I did teach your mother everything she knows." I laugh at her comment.

"You know, we ran into Hudson the other night," my mom's eyes widen slightly. My face drops, and I groan.

"Ooohhhh. Hudson? Your Hudson?" She points at me. "I heard he was in town."

"He's not my Hudson." I cross my arms.

"Good," my dad mumbles, but we all hear him.

"Manny," my mom chastises.

"Ay, es su niña," my grandmother says in Spanish, and I roll my eyes. I may be my dad's little girl, but this conversation doesn't need to happen. I'd rather avoid it altogether.

"I did love that boy," my grandma adds with a smile.

"Well, don't get any ideas." I point my finger at her.

"Ideas? Me?" Her hand lands on her chest, and she has the nerve to look offended. If anyone is a meddling woman, it's my abuela. She's also outspoken and owns no filter.

"Yes, you." I lift my eyebrows.

"I would never." She shakes her head with a mischievous smirk.

"Mami," my mom warns her.

"He does love my pastelitos and coffee. I should make him some."

"Please don't. That will only encourage him."

"Encourage him?" The three say at the same time, each with a different tone. My dad is appalled. My mom is curious, and my grandma looks like the Cheshire cat. *Great.*

"Nothing," I shake my head.

My grandmother begins speaking fast in Spanish, saying that Hudson was such an amazing young man who made me happy, and if he's back in town, then it must be destiny. I take a deep breath and clear the table, so I don't continue hearing her. I love my grandmother, but she's stubborn as a mule.

Hudson and I may have been good together at one point in time, but like many people, our relationship had an expiration date. The problem is that when something expires, it's not supposed to magically get more shelf life years later. Or maybe Hudson is like growing mold on that expiration. He did take over the planning like possessive mold.

MEET AGAIN

Ugh, get a life, Lex. You need sleep.

5
HUDSON

I'VE SPENT THE LAST four years questioning every choice I've made, beginning with pleasing my parents instead of fighting for the woman I loved. After some time, I had convinced myself it was for the best. I was angry Lex wasn't willing to fight as hard, but if I put myself in her place, I don't know if I'd have any more fight left in me.

My parents aren't easy, especially when they don't approve of someone. It was no secret that they thought Lex wasn't good enough. They never shied away from their feelings, even if she was present. Always turning their noses as if she was a nuisance. It's why I told her to move with me. We could start fresh away from my family's judgments.

She always pointed out that it wouldn't be a fresh start with me following my father's orders. She had a point.

Not seeing her through the years helped, but I never forgot about her. How could I? She was my lobster. I'm confident enough to appreciate a sappy *Friends* term.

Toby would also tell me about her dance studio and how she was succeeding. I haven't been happy since we broke up, but I can't blame it all on my failed relationship. The path my life's taken is far from ideal.

I grab my phone and search for my brother's contact. It's been a couple of months since we've spoken. Who knows where in the world he is right now.

"Hey, big bro. Long time no talk," Tristan answers the call. He sounds relaxed.

"Phone works both ways," I tease.

"Yeah, I know. I've been busy. How are you?"

"I'm good. I'm actually in Hartville." I lean back on the armchair in my room.

"Excuse me? Did we travel to an alternate universe?"

"Ha, ha," I say dryly. "I visit town. The same can't be said for you."

"You know I left it all behind for better pastures."

"Yeah, where are you now?" I don't know how he does it, but Tristan travels everywhere, finding temporary jobs on his way.

"I'm in Africa."

"What?" I check my phone. "What time is it over there?"

"Eleven at night."

"Sorry, were you sleeping?"

"Nah, I'm awake for a bit longer. Tell me about Hartville. Are Mom and Dad on your case?" He chuckles.

"About what?" I furrow my eyebrows.

"Anything and everything," his laughter grows louder.

"You know how it is." I cross my ankle over my knee.

"Yeah." We're both silent for a beat.

"Have you seen Lex?" His question doesn't surprise me. When everything happened in college, he tried to convince me it wasn't worth giving up on love. I'd never admit it to him, but he was right.

"Yeah," I snort. "It's gone as great as you can imagine, but she hasn't killed me yet. I'm actually in town because of Toby's engagement, and Lex is Hope's maid of honor."

"Ah, that'll be interesting." He is unsuccessful in hiding his amusement.

"It's already been. We need to plan a joint bachelor and bachelorette trip."

"So you've seen her more than once?" I can hear the surprise in his voice.

"Yup." I stand and grab a water bottle from the mini fridge.

"Anyway, what are you doing in Africa?" I'd rather hear about his life right now instead of talking about my failure to interact with Lex without it seeming like she wants to rip my head off.

"I'm volunteering at a non-profit to help a small village have essentials. It's amazing and such an eye-opening experience. These people have nothing, and they're so happy. I've never met a group of people who are the definition of pure and innocent joy." Passion drives his words.

"That sounds amazing."

"It's hard to put into words. I've been here for a few weeks already. It was a shock at first, not having certain things we're used to readily available, but it shifts your perspective about life. It's an experience I recommend to anyone." Hearing him talk flicks something inside of me.

I can't say the same for my own life, living and doing something I'm so passionate about. I settled into the family business because it was expected, and I was good at it. But I don't talk about my job the way Tristan does, or even the way Lex did years ago when she'd plan out her dream studio.

"I'm happy for you, Tristan." It's the truth, too, not just something older brothers tell their siblings. Tristan always knew what he wanted and didn't let anything stand in his way.

"Thanks. You know it's never too late to break away and do what makes you happy." His carefree mood turns serious.

MEET AGAIN

"Yeah." I leave it at that. I'm not even sure what I'd want to do. My whole life, I've been groomed to take over Remington Agency. Who am I without that?

"Just think about it. If you're happy with Dad, I support you. But if there's any bit of you that wants to do something else, make a change in your life, I have your back." I clear my throat upon hearing his words.

"Thanks. You know you can always count on me, even if you are saving the world and trotting the globe." I smile at the thought of my carefree brother working with villages in Africa. It sounds as if it's done him good.

"I know. And maybe things change with Lex," he suggests.

"I don't know. She hates me."

"She's hurt. It's expected. She probably uses hostility as a defense mechanism." His words of wisdom strike me with hope. I doubt this is the classic case of I like you, so I hate you.

"A lot's happened, and she's not leaving Hartville. She has her studio here. She's happy." *Without me.* I don't add that, not wanting to show more vulnerability than I already am.

"It's great she finally got her studio open. I know how much she wanted that. As for you, like I said, it's never too late to pursue a different path. I know you like working at the agency—though I suspect it's because you're good at it—but some things can change if you decide you still want that career." He yawns.

"Go to sleep. I bet you're bone-tired."

"Yeah, gotta be up early tomorrow. Glad you called."

"Me too. Bye, Tristan."

"Talk soon." The line goes dead, and I place my phone on my lap, staring at the screen.

I stand and stretch my arms over my head, needing to get out of this room. I guess it's another dinner at the diner. Maybe I'll walk around town later. Unlike New York, where people are out at all hours of the day and night, Hartville quiets down in the evenings, but a walk after dinner will still help clear my head.

I love the chill in the air that fall brings. I walk along Main Street, looking into the businesses closed for the night. The diner was quiet tonight, with no run-ins with the past or nosy residents to steer clear of.

After being used to the hustle and bustle of the city for so many years, it always shocks me when I visit my hometown. It's as if the part of me that lived here no longer exists. It's strange how that happens, how we transform and shift with time and experiences. The teen I was back then feels like someone else.

I peek through the big display windows of a clothes store. Not that I need anything, but there's nothing else to do walking down this sleepy street. Next, I look into the antique shop. It's been here for ages. Lex used to love going in when we were younger in hopes she'd find a treasure. I'd tease her about it, but she wouldn't care. She loved searching through the shelves and aisles, looking for a piece of history, as she'd call it.

I knew seeing her again would affect me, but I didn't realize how much. Guilt, nostalgia, and sadness all persist in filling me. Being away gave me the space and distraction I needed to not think about the past.

Work is busy, always traveling from one place to another. Wining and dining clients leave little space for reminiscing about ex-girlfriends—except when my friend Jameson subtly brings her up. All he knows is that I have an ex, but every so often, he likes to push.

I continue walking, seeing the barista in the coffee shop cleaning the floors. When I hear a noise a few feet away, I look up to see a silhouette. A smile lifts my lips as my feet propel me toward her.

"Hey."

"Oh!" Lex startles, dropping her bag. She turns around and sighs, closing her eyes.

"You scared me," she accuses.

I bend to grab her bag at the same time she does. Her breath catches. Lex steps back with wide eyes. I stare at her. Hair from her bun falls around her face, and her cheeks are pink.

"I didn't mean to. Here you go." I hand over her bag.

"Thanks." She turns to the door, locking it with the key in her hand.

"Did you just finish up now?"

"Yeah, the last class ended about fifteen minutes ago."

"Do you teach them all?" My hands sneak into my pockets as I take her in. She's wearing jeans and an oversized sweater. Her face is clean of any makeup, giving me a full view of her natural beauty.

"No, I have someone who teaches tap. I'm the ballet and jazz instructor."

"That's great." Silence stretches between us.

"Anyway, I gotta go." She breaks the awkwardness.

"Oh, yeah. Want me to walk you?"

Lex's eyebrows pull together.

"Just a friendly offer so you don't have to walk alone. These aren't the mean streets of a big city, but you can never be too careful." I lift my hands in mock surrender. I'm pushing my luck, but somehow I'm willing to see how far she'll let me go.

"No thanks, I drove." She points behind me, where I see a car parked on the street.

"Oh, great. I guess let me know when you've looked into the information about the resort. We should get that finalized so we can plan the rest of the trip." I'm stalling, not wanting her to leave yet.

Being in her presence makes me feel like Hercules, full of power and invincible. But even Hercules was defeated, ironically, as a consequence of love.

Lex sighs and shakes her head. "I'll look into it later tonight. I've taught four dance classes and dealt with parents. I'm tired and in need of a shower, Hudson. I doubt you're going to call your friend in the next two hours and tell him to book the suites." She steps around me. Her eyes reflect more than tiredness. I suspect I'm to blame for whatever emotion it is.

Maybe Tristan is right, and she's still hurt over everything that happened.

"Yeah, of course. I told him we'd give him a response one way or another by Friday. It shouldn't be too difficult of a decision. I personally think it's the best option, but everyone has to be on board."

"Exactly. I'll let you know tomorrow, then. Let me crunch some numbers and text the girls to get their input. It doesn't depend solely on me." She opens the passenger door and drops her bag on the seat.

"Sounds good. Talk to you then." I smirk.

Lex shakes her head and frowns. "Goodnight."

"Night, Lex." I watch her slide into her seat and drive away.

No matter how much time has passed, she's always owned a piece of my heart. Her beauty is part of it, but it's her, everything about her, that always captivated me. Despite the way my parents treated her, she was always by my side, cheering me on during football games, helping me study for exams, and sharing every piece of herself with me.

It should be us planning our wedding. Instead, she's barely tolerating me while I try to figure out what's going on between my head and heart.

I walk back to the inn to do some work. I may be in Hartville for some time, but I still need to close deals, or my father will get on my case. I can easily ignore him being six hours away. I can't do that when I'm staying in the same town. He's adamant I close that LA mansion, which means I'll have to travel to the West Coast soon.

Tristan's advice rings in my ears. Is this what I want? Am I fulfilled with the work I do? I don't have the same passion I heard him talk about, but I've never given thought to anything else. The money I've made could allow me to take some time to figure out what I want to do, but not with the living expense of New York City.

When I agreed to come to Hartville for Toby's engagement party, I didn't think I'd find myself questioning everything I've built for myself. The last few years have given me a chance to mature, though, and now I feel like I have the opportunity to rewrite the past. Starting with Lex.

Could we go back to what we had? I'm not sure we're the same people. We've hurt each other, grown up separately. We could very well not have anything in common anymore, too much time between us. However, a nagging continues to pull me in her direction, seeking her. I owe it to myself to see it through, even if she rejects me. Even if it's impossible to time travel to the past in order to change the present.

What I do know is that seeing her again has sparked light into my life. It's given me a different purpose and reminded me of who I was before fancy suits and business meetings.

ABI SABINA

6

LEX

After talking to Ellie and Jody, Hope's cousin, we agreed to stay at the Astoria. Their spa is top-notch, and pride aside, I know it would be Hope's first choice. I grab my phone, ready to text message Hudson. Running into him last night, seeing him around town, has brought about a swirl of sensations. I feel like that young girl who fell hard and fast for the football quarterback. Along with that comes the pain of knowing I wasn't considered good enough and the fear of being thrown to the side if Hudson realized it.

Regardless, we ended painfully.

With a deep breath, I pull my phone out and send him a message.

> Lex: Hey, spoke to the girls. We agreed on the Astoria.

I stretch and make coffee before I go over my choreography for my teen class this afternoon. They'll be performing at our town's Thanksgiving festival, and it has to be perfect by then. Showcasing what my students have learned is my favorite part of teaching. Seeing their evolution and later witnessing the town's joy and pride in watching them always makes me feel fulfilled.

After showering, I check my phone to see if Hudson's written back. Seeing his name on my screen makes my heart skip a beat. I shouldn't react this way.

> Hudson: Awesome, you won't regret it. Already told my friend, and he's got the suites saved for us

> Lex: Thanks

> Hudson: When should we meet again to discuss the rest of the trip now that we know where we're staying?

> Lex: Is it necessary? I think we can plan and just text. Don't you have to head back home?

I don't know why I ask. I don't like the way disappointment seeps in knowing he'll be leaving.

> Hudson: I'm in town for a bit longer. It'll make planning easier. Don't worry, I don't bite

MEET AGAIN

Lex: *eye-roll emoji*

I get dressed and throw my hair in a bun before leaving my house. I have some things to work on at the studio before opening, and it will distract me from the man who reappeared in my life—and is apparently set on actually seeing me.

Needing a break, I walk to the diner near the studio for lunch. I love dancing and teaching; I don't love crunching numbers and working on the business side of it. It's a necessary evil, though. I can grasp creativity and spin it into a dance routine. Math doesn't come as easily.

Looking down at my phone, I reach for the door and come up empty. I lift my gaze and trip over the lip at the entrance at the same time.

"Whoa." Arms wrap around me and keep me upright.

"Are you okay?" Hudson stares at me, his face inches from mine.

"Yeah," I breathe out.

"You sure? You've got a good grip on my arm," he chuckles.

I look at my nails that are digging into him and release my hold. "Sorry," I mumble, standing on my own. I just became a rom-com cliche by literally running into Hudson.

"No worries." His arm remains around my waist, a smile on his handsome face.

I swallow thickly and step back, forcing him to release me.

"Thanks," I nod and look around the diner. People stare, and heat flushes my cheeks. I'm not sure what's worse, falling on my butt or having people witness my ex-boyfriend coming to my rescue.

"Are you having lunch here?" Hudson asks, keeping his eyes on me.

"Yeah."

"Why don't we share a table? Like that, we can talk about the trip?"

I wrack my brain for an excuse. Would telling him I haven't showered in days and stink be an excuse to sit at separate tables? Far, far away. Not likely, seeing as he helped me up when I tripped and had his arm around my waist. Snug and comforting. I shouldn't think about that. When I remain silent for too long, he pushes.

"Just a bite to eat. No biggie, we need to plan anyway." His pearly whites brighten his face.

Sighing, I nod and walk to an empty booth. Hudson slides across from me with ease. How can he act so comfortable around me? He's probably moved on and sees me as someone from his past he can be friendly with.

"How have things been besides the studio?" He crosses his hands and leans back. His foot bumps against mine under the table, and I straighten in my seat, pulling them back.

"Good, great." I nod, unsure what to say. The past few years have revolved around the studio. It's not easy starting your own business, and it's required hours of work and attention.

"That's good." He nods.

"Yeah," I pick up the menu and read through the items to decide what I want today.

"I'm good, too."

I glance up at him. "I didn't ask." I hold back a smile.

"I know, but I figured you were wondering." He shrugs, resting his elbows on the table.

"You're so sure about that?" I tilt my head.

"Of course. Everyone is curious about other people."

"I couldn't care less," I shake my head. "No offense."

"None taken. You could say worse things, and I'd deserve it." Any trace of humor disappears, and he frowns.

"Yeah, but we're stuck planning this trip, so I have to decide if I want to be miserable or take it with stride." Fighting against him will only make this process more challenging. I can be polite.

"Makes sense." He looks over my head with a pensive gaze. When his eyes meet mine again, they're serious.

"You should know I hate what happened. I didn't want things to turn out the way they did between us."

"Hudson," I shift awkwardly in my seat. "Let's forget about it. No point." I shake my head, masking my emotions as indifference.

"We shouldn't, though. Don't you hate it, too?" His eyes bore into mine like mesmerizing mossy orbs. I can't look away, liking too much the regret I see reflected in them. I'm a masochist.

"You know I do, but it doesn't matter. Not everyone is meant to be in your life forever. Let's have lunch and plan the best bach party for our friends." I wave at the waitress.

Hudson sighs and leans back, his face masked in determination. He can be a real annoyance when he's persistent. We order lunch, and I pull out my phone to write notes.

"I need to call Astoria to check availability for their spa. We can have dinner as a group that night, like we mentioned. I'm guessing their restaurant is great. Hope mentioned they've eaten there before when they've gone on vacation." I shift into business mode, needing the emotional space from our previous conversation.

"Yeah, their restaurant is amazing. They also have a bar in the resort where we can have drinks. I think we should go into town one day, too. It'll be nice. Maybe for brunch."

"Great." I type in my notes app. "That'll give us a break from skiing one of the days."

"A break? We both know you won't need the break," he cracks a smile.

"I already told you I'll be in charge of making sure everything runs smoothly while you all ski."

"Yeah, I don't think it'll be good for anyone that you slide your feet into skis." He full-blown laughs now.

"Hey!" I kick him under the table.

"It's for your safety. You'll make stumbling into the diner today seem graceful," he continues to mock me.

"It's not my fault those things are out to get me." One time I tried skiing nearby when we were seniors in high school, and it ended up with a trip to the ER and a sprained ankle. Thankfully, I didn't break anything or get stabbed with those murder devices, but for a dancer, any injury is a prison sentence.

"They're inanimate objects. I would've thought that as a dancer, you'd have better stability and grace to ski. I was so disappointed," he shakes his head with his lips pressed into a firm line.

"Oh, shush!" I kick him again with my foot. "Dancing and skiing are not the same things."

"Clearly," he laughs.

"Whatever. What else?" I look at my phone screen. I've never been to Winford, and it seems Hudson has. He should have more ideas about what else we can do or where we can eat.

MEET AGAIN

"We could try another restaurant another night so that we don't eat at the same place every time," I suggest. Seeing the town would be fun. I'm all about visiting small towns and going into their local shops, especially if there's an antique store.

"Yeah. Since most of us will be skiing, lunch can be more laid-back at the resort. The rooms include breakfast, so that'll be covered."

"Okay, good," I nod. When the waitress appears with our plates, I move my phone to the side and inhale the delicious grilled chicken and mashed potatoes. Dancing all afternoon requires me to eat a big lunch.

"That looks good," Hudson eyes my plate.

"Your burger, too." It's surreal sitting across from him, sharing a meal as if we were friends. The pain still lingers in my chest, but it's also oddly comforting. It's dangerous to feel this way. Nothing has changed. Hudson still lives in New York. I'm still not good enough for him in his parents' eyes, and he still chose to follow their scripted path, ultimately giving them reason.

At the end of the day, Alexa Leon, daughter of Cuban immigrants, isn't the woman *the* Hudson Remington should get involved with.

I've always loved my background and ethnicity, proud of being Hispanic, which is why I could ignore Mr. and Mrs. Remington's snide remarks. It was when Hudson chose them over me that broke me.

After we finish eating, we stand outside of the diner.

"Thanks for sitting with me," Hudson smiles. "I'm traveling to LA for a few days, but I'll write to you when I'm back so we can continue planning."

"Okay. I'll work out some details in the meantime."

ABI SABINA

"Bye, Lex," he smiles. The way he says my name and the secret smile he shares make my heart skip a beat. Despite the five o'clock shadow and broader build, he's still got the same charms underneath his suit. I can only turn a blind eye for so long. Rabbit hole, rabbit hole, are you ready to catch me? I'm about to dive headfirst into Hudson-land.

I turn and walk toward the studio. An afternoon of classes is exactly what I need—an outlet for my creativity and to seek clarity on all these chaotic emotions.

7
LEX

"So you had to chase after the cow?" My body shakes with laughter.

"Yes, it was horrible. I slipped in the mud, and then the cow came toward me. The rascal," Ellie laughs along with me.

"Oh, boy. I would've paid money to see that," Hope chimes in.

We're sitting around her kitchen table for girls' night. We get together on Fridays a couple of times a month to catch up and hang out.

"Me too." I lift my wineglass.

"Laugh at my expense," Ellie shakes her head, but her smile is wide, contradicting her words.

"It's all in good fun," I tease her.

"Speaking of fun... Word around town is that you've been hanging out with Hudson?" Her eyebrows lift as her voice rings with question.

I roll my eyes and lean back in my seat, running my forefinger and thumb up and down the stem of my glass.

"I'm not hanging out with him. We had to get together once to talk about the bachelorette party." I narrow my eyes at Hope.

"Don't look at me that way. I need help. Between our jobs, house hunting, and planning a wedding, Toby and I are up to our necks with things to do. I know Hudson is a touchy subject, but I was hoping that after four years, it'd be tolerable." She scrunches up her nose.

"It is, right? Tolerable?" Ellie's eyes widen expectantly.

"It's something. I don't know if that's the right word." I take a sip of wine.

Ellie sighs beside me. "I thought after hearing the rumors that things were better between you two."

"Me too," Hope sags against her chair.

"You're both insane. I'm being polite, but that's the extent of it." My friends are insane. Do they think that Hudson and I planning this thing is going to get us back together? That's ridiculous. We still live in different states. We have the same issues that tore us apart. I don't care how handsome he looks or how familiar he feels or that deep down, it seems like he's the same person I fell for.

"Okay, but," Ellie leans forward on the table as if she's going to tell us a secret. "Fess up. You still get a little tingly when you see him."

I cough out an awkward laugh. "No." I shake my head, feeling heat rise up my neck.

"I think she's lying," Hope tells Ellie, smirking with mischief.

"I'm not," I object forcefully.

"She's getting all riled up, too. I believe she's even blushing," Ellie winks at Hope.

"You're both obnoxious." I shake my head, drinking the rest of my wine.

"And you're in denial," Hope says right as the doorbell rings. "That's our pizza." She stands and heads to the door.

"You really don't feel anything toward Hudson?" Ellie asks without a trace of humor now.

"What's there to feel? Anger, disappointment, hurt?" I shrug. "I'd rather not focus on it."

"What about hope, attraction, love?" She smiles softly.

"Love?" I scoff. "I can't love a man who didn't choose me or what we had. I can't be with a man whose family doesn't approve of me. What's the point in fighting for something that's already doomed?"

"The point is love. We all know Mr. and Mrs. Remington are a special breed. Even Tristan ran as far from them as possible when he graduated high school. Their own son. Maybe Hudson has a different handle on things now that he's older?"

"It doesn't matter, Ellie. I've got my dance studio, my friends," I smile at her, "and my family."

"I get it, but seeing Hope plan her wedding is making me wonder if I'll ever have what she and Toby found. Does that happen to you as well?" She frowns, her big eyes shining with sadness.

I don't tell her I thought I already had that with Hudson. It'd open a whole can of worms. Instead, I nod and sit straight when Hope returns with the pizza. Greasy, cheesy pizza always makes things better.

♡♡♡

Lex: I booked the spa day for Saturday when we're there

Hudson: Saturday was going to be brunch day

Lex: No

Hudson: Yeah…

Lex: You didn't tell me.

Hudson: I made reservations in town

Lex: Change them for Sunday. Saturday was the only day the spa had an opening. Apparently people book months in advance

Hudson: The restaurant didn't have a table for Sunday, hence brunch on Saturday

MEET AGAIN

I take a deep breath before I fling my phone across my living room. The spa is a must. It's what Hope asked for. Brunch can wait. I grab my phone again and begin typing at furious speed.

> Lex: Can you believe this guy? I swear, he has no consideration for my part of the planning. And you asked me if I felt anything? Heck to the N-O.

I send Ellie the message, letting out my frustration. I refuse to change the spa date or give that up, so Hudson is going to have to figure out another idea. He can go have brunch with the guys. My phone buzzes faster than I'd expect Ellie to respond.

> Hudson: I'm guessing that message wasn't supposed to be for me? Although, I'd love to hear more about these feelings...

"Argh!" I toss my head back. Rookie mistake.

> Lex: No feelings. That's what it says, spelled out. And no, it wasn't supposed to be for you

> Hudson: But you were talking about me, huh?

Lex: No

Hudson: It's ok, you can admit it. Your secret's safe with me *wink emoji*

Lex: You're infuriating

Hudson: You used to like that about me

Lex: A long time ago

Hudson: Some habits are hard to break

Lex: I'm done with this convo. Spa day stays on Saturday. It's our only girl time in the trip

Hudson: Don't run off now when the convos getting good

MEET AGAIN

Lex: Bye Hudson

I flip my phone over and close my eyes, mortification taking over. Hudson did not need to know that we were talking about him. Embarrassment fills me. If the earth could swallow me up right now, that'd be great. Knowing Hudson—if he hasn't changed—he'll bring up that text message the next time I'm forced to see him and make it a bigger deal than it is.

I stand and slip on my shoes. I need to take advantage of the weekend and grab groceries before laziness takes over, and I end up ordering takeout. Actually, I wonder if my mom or grandma cooked today. That beats takeout. I'll call after running errands.

Fresh air will do me good, too. Thanksgiving is right around the corner, and our town's decorated to the brim. I love seeing all the stores adding to the holiday feel and sensing the magical energy that surrounds us this time of year.

Bundling up, I head out of my house and embrace the cold as I race to my car. The drive to the center of town is quick, and it seems people are tired of being cooped up. The town is bustling despite the colder temperatures we're seeing this week.

Spying The Bean up ahead, I decide on some coffee before shopping. I'm craving their cinnamon twist latte, and it's only available this time of year.

"Fancy seeing you here." A deep voice washes over me as I'm making my way to the coffee shop.

I look to my left to see Hudson's bright smile. It's too soon to face him after that text message disaster. I put on a mask of annoyance and avoid looking directly at him.

"Are you following me?" I narrow my eyes.

"Of course not. I'm staying at the inn, and the room gets suffocating after a while."

"You're staying at the inn?" I scrunch up my nose.

"Yup." He walks beside me.

"Why don't you stay at your house?"

"Correction, my parents' house." He lifts a hand as if making a point or objecting in court.

"Same thing."

"Nope, it's not. Anyway, I canceled the brunch reservations."

"Really?" I stop, tilting my head and looking directly at him now.

"Yeah, you were right. I know you ladies want to have an uninterrupted spa day, so brunch can wait."

"Just like that?" I cross my arms.

"Yes," he chuckles awkwardly, running a hand through his hair.

"Huh..." I nod.

"What?" He lifts his eyebrows.

"Nothing. I thought you'd put up a bigger fight."

"It's not in my best interest." One side of his mouth lifts. "After all, I need to see how to change those non-feelings into the real thing." He winks, and my mouth drops. I freeze in place.

"Don't get any ideas." My heart pounds as I try to play it cool and catch up to him.

"I've got quite a few ideas," he leans down and whispers. His breath tickles the side of my neck, causing me to shiver.

Confusion slams into me. Why is he saying those things? Hudson clears his throat and straightens, adjusting the sleeves on his coat.

"I'm gonna go." I give him a tight smile as I walk away from him.

MEET AGAIN

When I reach the storefront, I slip into the coffee shop with a million thoughts racing through my head.

His actions and words don't make sense with our history. Why did I like it? I shouldn't. Hudson broke my heart. Our split was cold turkey. We went from speaking every day to having a huge fight and never seeing or talking to each other again after being together for years. It just ended as if it was all a dream.

I blink away the tears filling my eyes and step forward, ordering the cinnamon twist latte.

I spent weeks crying over him, questioning everything, but my pride didn't let me write or call him. Maybe I wanted him to be the one to take the first step in hopes that he wouldn't choose New York over me. I knew it was a losing game. His family business was always his end goal, despite complaining about it.

I wish things would've turned out differently. If he worked locally, maybe they would have, but I suspect his parents wanted him away from me. It wasn't the first time they had tried to break us apart. Eventually, we weren't a strong enough front to fight against their manipulations. To this day, I can't face Mr. and Mrs. Remington. There aren't many people I despise, but those two are top on my list.

I shake away the memories and sit on an armchair, letting the soft and worn cushion hug me in a comforting embrace.

The same way he disappeared from my life, Hudson slammed right back in—unannounced and striking. I look up when the coffee shop door opens and notice him step inside. I frown. If he wants to continue that conversation from earlier, I'm not up for it. I thought I had overcome our relationship, or the end of it actually, but it seems I only suppressed it so I could survive.

He stands tall and confident while he waits for his turn to order at the counter. I'm not sure if he knows I'm here, but it gives me a moment to watch him. His hands are in his pockets, a trait he's always had. His hair is messy, and his square jaw is tight and peppered with facial hair. My heart remembers what it was like to be loved by Hudson, and it's betraying my brain's plan to not think about him.

He was always caring and considerate. He knew how to turn my mood around and when to give me space if I was upset. He respected my dance schedule and never used it against me when I had a recital to practice for. Instead, he'd show up with flowers and a proud smile.

I thought we were unbreakable. It still breaks my heart to think that we no longer have a tie to each other or have the confidence and freedom to...just be there.

My chest aches, and my throat clogs with emotions. I bite my lower lip to prevent people from seeing it tremble as tears cloud my vision. I close my eyes, trapping the tears, and take a deep breath hoping the suffocating sensation eases. When I finally feel okay, Hudson is nowhere to be found. He must've left. *Poof.* In the blink of an eye. Just like four years ago.

I subtly wipe under my eyes and take a drink of the warm, cozy latte. My head presses against the back of the chair while I will my emotions to get under control. My heart and mind are confused. Working alongside Hudson on this bach party crosses my wires. I'm used to being normal around him, carefree, but then I remember we're not together anymore, and it's like a whole new wave of pain. While he's away, out of sight, it's easier to cope. I've done well in the four years since we broke up.

But having him in town, running into him, and receiving messages from him, feels like I never got the closure my heart desired and needed in order to move on. The scariest part is that I'm not sure if I want that closure.

MEET AGAIN

All the good memories flood at once, overshadowing the painful ones. At twenty-five, I still have time to get over my ex and meet a great guy, but Hudson was always my ideal guy. How do I move on from that without feeling like I'm just replacing him?

Maybe I need to buy ingredients to bake cookies and spend my evening drowning all these questions and uncertainties in flour, sugar, and chocolate. And my Girl Power playlist.

8
HUDSON

"Good work, son," my dad nods, lifting his glass of whiskey.

We closed out the Los Angeles deal with the owners' asking price and a good chunk of commission for us. The buyer basically ripped it from our hands.

"Thanks." I take a drink of the strong amber liquid.

"When will you be heading back to New York? I assume after Thanksgiving seeing as it's already next week." He eyes me over the rim of his glass.

"Yeah, probably." I've liked getting reacquainted with my hometown. I hadn't realized how much I missed it until now. I keep pushing back my trip to the city. Reality is that Lex probably has something to do with it. Not probably, *does* have something to do with it.

"Probably?" He arches a brow and places his glass on the side table next to his armchair. He suddenly looks like the head honcho for a mafia. His eyes are scrutinizing and unimpressed.

"Yeah, I'll likely head back for a few weeks, then return for Christmas." I have no idea if my parents are spending Christmas here or not. They tend to travel for the holidays.

My dad tilts his head and studies me with a narrow gaze.

"Does this have anything to do with that girl?"

"What?" I stare at him with furrowed brows.

"Listen, son. I know you liked her. She's pretty, I'll give you that, but she's the kind of woman you have fun with. She's not

MEET AGAIN

the marrying type. Alexa doesn't have anything to offer. She sure doesn't fit into our circle. What would she talk to clients about? Her little dance classes? She's a teacher, and not even an educational one. Imagine taking her to an event. She'd feel amazing on your arm, but she's not on our level. Never has been." He shakes his head.

Anger pulses through me. Heat fills me as I listen to the unbelievable garbage he's saying. I've put up with a lot from my parents, but this is crossing a line. I won't allow him to disrespect Lex like this.

"She's not someone you just have fun with." It disgusts me to know he'd even say something like that.

"She's successful, runs her own business. She accomplished that by herself by working hard. You know how hard it is to manage a business, but you never started anything from scratch. You took over what was already established. It takes work to keep it successful, but neither of us had to take a risk like Lex did." I stand, shaking my head as my hands curl into fists.

"If you stopped looking down at people, then you'd see the world for what it is. Not everyone lives in the bubble you and Mom are in. There's more to life than socialite parties and one-upping your so-called friends by bragging. Everything in your circle is despicable and unfulfilling."

I turn and walk out of the house before my anger gets the best of me. Hearing him talk that way about Lex, as if she's disposable, brings out the worst in me. It's not the first time we have had a conversation like this. My mother is even more ruthless than my father when it comes to Lex. They think treating people this way is acceptable, as if they were gods. Tristan had the right idea of breaking away from them and finding his own path.

As the older brother, I thought I was supposed to be the wiser one, but it seems he had clarity and guts that I lack.

I peel out of their driveway and onto the road. I drive aimlessly, breathing deeply to keep my anger in check, but every time I replay his words, it amplifies my irritation. I become enraged all over again. Part of the reason it's been so easy to stay in New York is because I don't have direct contact with my family. I only talk to my dad for business and leave it at that. It's easy from a distance. Being in Hartville forces me to see them more often.

I slow down when I notice flakes falling. I didn't think it'd snow yet. A smile forms as I think about Lex. She loves the snow. We haven't spoken in a week, not since I ran into her on the way to The Bean. I saw her sitting there when I walked in, but I decided I had pushed too far when we were on the sidewalk. Work has helped me stay focused and fight my temptation to send her any messages.

Today may be the day I break that. I can admit defeat, even if it's against my own willpower. When it comes to Lex, I don't think I ever had much power. It seems some things don't change.

Pulling into town, I park near the inn and wander, watching the snow fall harder now. The few people walking around town laugh and stare in wonder. Snow isn't a foreign concept in this area, and yet people always act like it's magic.

I see the dance studio a few doors down. The lights are still on, and it seems like people are inside. That means Lex will see the snow. I smile at that. All I ever wanted was for her to be happy, and I thought getting away from the town where my parents lived would grant us that. Seeing her studio, the people that walk in and out of it, the students she has, it all makes sense why she wouldn't want to give this up. I knew it then, but desperation blinded me.

My feet push me toward the studio and halt. What am I doing? I can't just walk in there. I check the time on my watch and hang back. She has about fifteen minutes left of class. I'll never admit to anyone that I searched her schedule online. Being this close to her, having another opportunity to talk to her and see her, makes me do crazy things.

I walk closer as the minutes pass and look in through the big windows. I can barely see the class through the waiting room, but Lex is smiling as she teaches some steps to her older students. Knowing she accomplished her dream makes me proud of her. I also hate that I didn't get a chance to stand by her side, cheer her on and support her like I always imagined I would.

I was so in love with her, but my selfishness stood in our way. She didn't deserve that. She deserved a man who would honor her wishes and give her what she wanted. I failed her, and I failed myself. No one has compared to her. I can't even say I've given anyone a real chance since Lex walked out of my life.

I lean against the edge of her building with a side view into the window. When the students walk out of the dance room, I straighten and wait for them to leave. A few of their moms smile at me as they go home. I should worry about their knowing grins, but I don't back down. Squeals of joy ring when some of the girls notice it's snowing, and I chuckle at their enthusiasm.

When the last student is gone, I enter the studio. Lex comes out to the waiting room and freezes.

"What are you doing here?"

I smile and shrug, taking her in. Her bun has a few strands that have fallen, and her face has a sheen of sweat from dancing. She's wearing leggings and a long-sleeve fitted shirt that opens in a wide V toward the edge of her shoulders. Her outfit shows off her body without being provocative, and I clear my throat to gain some self-control.

"It's snowing," I blurt out, looking at her eyes and hoping she didn't notice me checking her out. She's gorgeous.

"Really?" Her chocolate eyes light up.

"Yeah. It started a little bit ago." She rushes to the big window and stares outside. That's when I notice the same wide V from the front of her shirt is on the back, leaving her shoulder blades exposed. It's tempting to reach out and feel her skin, kiss her shoulder.

"It is," she exclaims, turning around to face me.

"Come on." I grab her hand, but she pulls back.

"You love the snow," I stare in confusion at her hesitation.

"I need shoes." I look down and find hot pink toes.

"Right." I nod and watch her slip back into the dance room.

Lex is back in no time and out the door without waiting for me. She stares up into the sky, arms spread wide. Watching her squeezes my heart. She's perfect.

"I thought you'd want to know." I step closer to her.

Her head tilts back so she can look at me. "I love snow," she sighs. "Thanks." Big flakes land on her hair.

"Anytime."

When she spins around, I chuckle. Then she begins to dance, and I can't help it. I reach out for her hand and grab it, whirling her around. Lex stops and looks at me, her lips parted, her nose and cheeks red from the cold. My thumb brushes across the top of her hand. The silence is full of emotions as we look at one another with intensity.

Breaking the spell, I step back and extend our arms before I spin her around again. Her free hand reaches out, palm up, catching snowflakes. I tug her back to me, and she crashes into my chest. With no distance between us, I look down into her eyes and find a myriad of emotions staring back at me.

I comb my other hand into the side of her head. When she leans into my touch, I close my eyes. I've wanted to feel this again since the day we broke up, but I didn't have a right to.

"Hudson." The way she whispers my name, a cross between sadness and longing, tells me she isn't unaffected.

"Yeah?" My voice is gruff.

Lex blinks her eyes open, focusing on me. When she steps back, I feel her absence immediately.

"I should get back inside and clean up." Melancholy vibrates off her. Her voice is low, and her words devoid of emotions.

"Do you need help?" I don't want her to walk away like this.

She looks at me for a beat in silence, then shakes her head. "I've got it. Nothing new I haven't done before." She steps around me and walks toward the door. Before opening, she looks at me over her shoulder.

"Thanks for telling me about the snow." A small smile lifts her lips, and I feel like so many unspoken things hang between us.

"You're welcome. Glad you could enjoy it."

She nods and slips inside while I stand out here, trying to get my head on straight. My feelings for Lex are still there, but our situation is the same. Unless I'm willing to make a change in my life and career, there's no point in pursuing it. We'll end up hurt again, and I won't be able to forgive myself.

I'm not making the same mistake twice and telling her to give up her dream. I'm the one not fully living mine, and I need to reevaluate where my life is going and if it's what I truly want. I refuse to end up like my parents, married to someone who only cares about money, social status, and impressing others. I want a real marriage one day. I want children who will be proud to call me Dad. I want a wife who loves me for me, not for the size of my bank account or the events we'll attend as if we were models on display for others to pick apart while we pretend to tolerate one another.

I want honesty and love, and I had that with Lex and let it slip away. Regret once again consumes me. She was the best thing in my life. She was the only person besides Toby I could count on and confide in. Now, we're strangers sharing snippets of moments based on memories we made.

I want what we had again. Determination drives me, and I walk into the studio, pulling the door open with force.

"Lex," I call out. When I see her wiping under her eyes with a broom resting against her shoulder, my heart stops.

"Hey," I reach her and crouch down so I can look at her face. "What's wrong?" I whisper, pulling her hands away.

"Nothing," she shakes her head, but I see the red in her eyes.

"Why are you crying?"

"I'm not." Her stubbornness makes an appearance.

I tilt my head and lift my brows. "Don't lie to me."

"I'm not lying. They're allergies. From the snow." She lifts her chin in defiance.

"Allergies?" I bite back my smile. "Since when?"

"It's a new reaction."

"Does it only appear when your ex-boyfriend is holding you and not man enough to speak up?"

She ignores me, turning around and sweeping the floor. I pull the broom from her grip.

"Hey," she argues.

"Talk to me, and I'll return it."

"Hudson, I'm tired and hungry. Give me the broom so I can clean up and go home." She holds her hand out, but I shake my head.

MEET AGAIN

"Tell me what's wrong. I'm sorry, I got caught up in the moment."

"That's just it. We shouldn't be getting caught up in any moment. We're not together anymore. We broke up four years ago, and now you're in town after not visiting for how long? You think you can waltz right in and act as if you didn't hurt me, as if you didn't break me." Her head slings back with her words as tears fill her eyes.

"I don't think that," I run a hand through my hair. "Of course not. Don't you think I was also hurt?" I lift a hand in exasperation.

"It broke me, too." My finger roughly presses into my chest, but Lex scoffs.

"It did. I couldn't sleep or eat. I could barely work. I wanted to call so many times, show up here, but I didn't have the guts to. At first, I was angry that you wouldn't accept my plan. We could've had it all. Then, I realized my mistake, but it was too late. Too much time had passed for me to come crawling back and begging for forgiveness." I take a deep breath, needing her to hear this.

"I loved you with every fiber of my being. You know that. Do you think I could let that go so easily?"

Lex stares at me motionless other than the heaving of her chest.

"You were everything I wanted," I continue when she remains silent. "But when I realized you deserved better, I stayed away. No one should endure the crap treatment my parents put you through, nor a guy who was too blind to realize that you were telling me exactly what you wanted and needed but refused to listen."

ABI SABINA

I pace back and forth, dropping the broom to the floor with a loud clank. This is what we didn't get to do, hash things out. If I'm being honest, this confrontation is long overdue.

"Tell me what you want. I'll give it to you." I stare at her, standing a foot apart.

Lex shakes her head. "I don't know. I need space."

Her words stab me, and I nod. Before I walk away, I look at her and say, "Just believe that it wasn't easy for me either. I loved you."

9
LEX

Between preparing for the recital for the Thanksgiving festival and planning Thanksgiving dinner with my parents, I haven't had time to think about my last encounter with Hudson. It was intense. The days that followed it were draining, but I soon had to get into recital mode, which has always helped me escape the real world. I've become a pro at avoiding reality and embracing anything that gives me the opportunity to do so.

The things Hudson said were all words I wished he would've spoken years ago. They don't change what happened, and they don't replace the fear I felt when I thought about what it'd be like to lose him a second time.

The situation with his parents hasn't changed, and I am worth more than put-downs and subtle jabs about who I am, what I do, and where I come from. It was never flat-out said, but I know that part of the Remingtons' problem with me is that my parents are Hispanic on top of being a part of the working class. The Remingtons have a certain idea about who they associate with, and my family and I don't meet those standards. Even they aren't ignorant enough to voice that publicly, though.

Besides, my background doesn't define or limit me. I believe there's more to people than where they come from, and I always treated them with respect despite knowing their feelings toward me. I refuse to fall to their level, but a girl can only take so much. Would marrying into that family be what was best for me?

Hudson may have told them to drop it and stood up for me, but he was in the middle between continuing the family business and his girlfriend. Sometimes I wonder if our breakup was a blessing in disguise. Things would only have gotten harder as he started working at the agency.

It doesn't take away the pain, though, or the fact that I loved him regardless. Or that hearing him say I was all he wanted with his broken-up words didn't affect me. Of course, it did. I believed in us. I wanted the same things he did. Life had other plans.

"Are you ready?" I turn around and see my mom smiling at me.

"Almost." I swipe my lips with the red color and smile at her through the mirror. *Deep breaths, Lex. You've got this. Ignore Hudson. Focus on the girls' performance.*

After my pep talk, I ask, "Do I look okay?"

"You look beautiful." She hugs me when I stand. "It's going to be amazing."

"Thanks." I take another deep breath, nerves ricocheting all around me. It's the third year my students have performed at the festival, and I still get nervous each time. They've worked so hard preparing for this, and I'm proud of my girls.

My mom and I walk out of the studio toward the stage where the performance will take place. The weather is holding out, so I hope it continues to do so until the performance is finished.

"Good luck, mi amor." My mom kisses my cheek when we reach the side of the stage.

"Thank you. I'll see you and Dad after the show."

Excitement buzzes around the girls as they wait behind the stage, checking each other's make-up and hair.

"How are you? Are you ready?" I smile at the teen girls.

"Yes, we can't wait." Clara squeals.

MEET AGAIN

"And Rachel's boyfriend has front row seats," Mel teases a blushing Rachel.

"He's sitting with Luke," Clara sighs. "He's so cute."

I laugh at them and shake my head. To be young again. I check the music and make sure everything is set for their performance. After the mayor speaks and welcomes everyone, he'll introduce the girls. Then, we can all enjoy the rest of the festival.

It's an all-day event with booths around the center of town, cornucopia competitions to see who can create the most beautiful one, and games for children. There will also be a pumpkin pie contest, and I'm looking forward to tasting the different ones.

It's the best way to kick off Thanksgiving tomorrow.

"Oooooohhh..." a chorus rings around me. I look at the girls with confusion. They're giggling and pointing somewhere past the stage toward the audience.

"Lex, look who's here," Mel giggles.

"Her BF," Clara adds.

I follow their pointed fingers and see Hudson in the audience. Arching a brow and giving them my best teacher glare, I cross my arms.

"Girls." They lift their eyebrows at my tone. "He isn't my boyfriend, and you shouldn't be gossiping."

"My mom says they dated," Mel whispers to Clara.

My glare hardens, and they zip their lips. Thankfully, the mayor walks on stage. Being the center of my students' gossip is something I'd like to avoid a million times over.

We're all quiet as the mayor speaks. When he introduces the girls, I give them a thumbs up and move to the side of the stage to watch them. I smile when I see how many people have gathered to see their performance and the way they look on with amazement.

Everyone gives them a standing ovation when they bow, and I clap along with them, wearing a proud smile as I walk up on stage.

"Thank you so much for being here for our girls and cheering them on. I'm so proud of you all," I say when I'm handed a microphone.

"You've worked hard and continue to astound me with your talent. I'd also like to take this special moment to share some exciting news we received a few weeks ago. Sarah," I reach my hand out to her.

"She's a hard worker, dedicated, and determined. After lots of work, she was invited to participate in a musical in our local city. I'm proud of her and proud to see our youth striving. Congratulations." I smile at her and then hug her tightly while everyone claps and cheers for her.

"Thank you," she whispers.

After I've greeted the parents and other people from town who have stopped me to share their congratulations, I meet my friends.

"They were great," Hope gushes. "I wish I could dance like that."

"You're not terrible, babe," Toby teases her, his arm wrapped around her waist. She slaps his chest and rolls her eyes playfully.

"Congrats, Lex. It was a great performance," he tells me.

"Thank you. It's all on the girls."

"No way, you're their instructor." Ellie gives me a side hug.

"Yeah, but they do the work. I can't do it for them, only teach them," I shrug. I've been in my students' shoes, and I know how much it takes to get where they are. I had to give up some things in order to keep my commitment. I did it because I loved it.

"Hey," Hudson walks up to us. "Congrats, Lex, that was amazing."

"She won't accept it. For some reason, she's crazy and thinks she has nothing to do with how her students perform," Ellie laughs.

I roll my eyes. "Anyway, I'm going to take this stuff to the studio. I'll see you guys in a bit." I carry the heavy tote bag filled to the brim with props. It's the perfect exit to avoid Hudson.

Once I've put them away, I check my makeup in the mirror and take a deep breath. I haven't seen Hudson since last week, and I haven't had the courage to process how I felt.

"You look beautiful. You don't need any more of that stuff." My gaze lifts, and I catch Hudson's eyes through the mirror.

"You really need to stop sneaking up on me here." I cap my lipstick and slip it into my purse.

"Habit, I guess." He shrugs, staring at me intently.

"I'm really proud of all this," he waves a hand. "I know I said it when we first saw each other, but seeing your students perform was amazing. You're doing great things, Lex."

"Thank you." I smile genuinely.

"You're welcome. Are you coming back out?"

"Yeah."

"You don't mind that I'm around, right?" His gaze pierces me.

"Why would I mind?" I cross my arms.

"Well, the other night was a bit intense, and you asked for space. I don't want you to feel uncomfortable." He shifts on his feet, scratching his stubbled jaw.

"I'm okay," I assure him. "Besides, I can keep you at a distance." It's a big fat lie, but I'm still channeling Lorelai Gilmore. *And failing*.

I shoulder my purse and walk toward the door. He's right beside me. His heat envelops me, and when the back of his fingers brush against mine in featherlight touches, I shiver. Such a small thing, but it gets a big reaction from me.

"Are you sure about that?" He smirks when I look up at him with wide eyes.

The reason I need space from him is because I know how easily I can fall for him. I also know how painful losing him is.

Hope, Ellie, and Toby are a few feet away. When they see us walking together, all three raise their eyebrows, not hiding their curiosity.

"Well..." Ellie looks between us. "Who wants pie?" She smartly changes the subject.

"Me," I drool. "And coffee. It's freezing."

"Oh, yeah. I could go for a latte from The Bean. I need to take advantage when I come into town," Ellie nods, looping her arm in mine and leading me toward the coffee shop.

She leans in and whispers, "Don't deny it. You and Hudson are scorching. I don't know how you're freezing. I can feel the heat from a distance." She fans herself.

I laugh at her and shake my head. "Definitely not."

"Right," she gives me an incredulous look.

"I mean it," I defend.

"Uh, huh. I know you do." She placates me like a child.

"Whatever," I shake my head. "Just take me to coffee and pie."

"That's exactly what I'm doing. And if you're good, you might even get a side of hunk." She winks, and I let out a loud laugh.

"What's so funny?" Hope pushes between us, standing in the middle.

"Nothing," Ellie shakes her head.

"Yeah, right. Not nice leaving me out."

"Well, you were with the topic of conversation," Ellie lifts her eyebrows. "Not our fault."

MEET AGAIN

"What? You were talking about Hudson? I knew something was going on," she whispers. "Tell me everything." Her wide eyes swing to me.

"Nothing to tell," I shake my head. "I promise."

"I think she's holding out on us," Ellie tells Hope conspiratorially.

"I agree." Hope looks over her shoulder to where Toby and Hudson are.

"Stop," I hiss.

"Yeah, definitely something going on by that reaction," Hope nods as if she's proved a theory.

"There isn't. Things have just been..."

"Complicated?" Ellie offers when I pause, unable to find the right word.

"Exactly. I blame you," I point to Hope.

"Me, why?"

"Because you're marrying his best friend, and you had the bright idea of making us plan this party together." I cross my arms.

"I can hear you talking about me," Hudson calls out.

"Ugh," I drop my face into my hands and feel a blush creep up my cheeks.

Hope and Ellie laugh beside me. Everyone is getting the wrong idea, and all I want is coffee and pie. I want to not think about Hudson, the things he's said, or the way I feel around him.

"I expect a full update on Friday at our girls' night," Hope whispers.

"Whatever," I walk up to the counter when it's our turn and order a latte. Hope and Ellie order as well, and thankfully they drop the subject.

Once we're back outside, roaming the festival on the way to the pie contest, Hudson has moved to my side.

"Are you having dinner with your parents tomorrow?"

"Yeah," I nod.

"That's good. Is your mom making that pumpkin flan she used to make?"

"She makes it every year. You know that."

"It's so good. To this day, I still crave it on Thanksgiving," he confesses.

"Really?" I look up at him, my nose scrunched up.

"Yeah, it's delicious." He rubs his hand over his mouth.

"It is pretty good, but I love pumpkin pie."

"I know," he chuckles. "You'd let me have your slice of flan if I gave you my pumpkin pie."

I shake my head, unable to hold back my smile. "It was a good trade-off." I nod, remembering that. I had forgotten about it.

"It was. We made a pretty good team," he smiles down at me with such a bright and open smile I want to fall into him.

"Hudson." My head snaps toward the voice, and my mood drops.

"Dad, Mom," he nods at them as if they were business partners and not family.

Mrs. Remington stares at me with disgust, and I duck my head, stepping away from Hudson. I'm not in the mood to deal with her. I never am, but less so on a day like today. I catch up with Hope, Ellie, and Toby. I hadn't realized how much further behind them we were.

"Are you okay?" Hope asks.

"Of course," I nod with a smile.

"Can't stand them," she rolls her eyes.

That makes two of us, but I keep that to myself. They aren't worth draining my energy over. My mood gets a little better when we reach the pie contest booth and get samples of each person's pie. We cast our votes once we're done and satisfied. Although, I don't think I'll ever have enough pie.

At some point, Hudson walks toward us. His frown is directed at me.

"I'm sorry about that."

I wave him off. "No need to apologize."

"I do, and you know it. They won't bother us anymore."

"They're your parents. They don't bother you." I don't add myself into that because it'd be a lie. His parents don't need to speak to me in order to bother or offend me. Silence speaks louder than words in their case—or should I say, a stink-eye speaks volumes.

Hudson reaches for my hand and pulls me back away from our friends. "Lex, they may be my parents, but I don't agree with the way they treat you. I never have, and I've been vocal about that."

"You may have been vocal, but your actions contradict that. I get it, though. I'd never ask you to choose between your family business or me." My words come out harsher than I intend.

Hudson tilts his head and looks at me with pleading eyes.

"It's fine. I have thick skin, and they don't affect me anymore." I pinch my forearm as if proving my point.

"They affect me, though," he says with conviction.

I shrug with pursed lips. "That's on you, Hudson. I don't mean that in a rude way, but you need to figure out how to deal with that part of your life while maintaining a relationship with them." I can't solve that for him. I know he never had a strong relationship with his parents, and it's part of the reason he got along so well with mine. However, it's on him to make a choice.

"Yeah," he nods. When he turns toward someone who greets him, a piece of me crushes. The truth that divided us all those years ago is still a wedge between us.

Sometimes love isn't enough to make a relationship survive. I learned that the hard way.

10
LEX

"The festival was great yesterday," my mom says as we sit around the table, eating.

"We're so proud of you," my dad adds.

Smiling at them, I nod. "It was fun. The girls did such a great job. I can't wait to watch Sarah perform in the musical next year."

"She must be so happy," my mom smiles. "It was nice to see Hudson, too. Did we tell you we ran into him a couple of weeks ago at the diner?" My mom's eyes gleam.

My dad scoffs beside her.

"Yup," I glare at my mom.

"You two play nice. I invited him to come for dessert."

"What?" I shriek, my eyes widening.

"Bianca," my dad warns.

"He was spending Thanksgiving alone. I insisted. No one should spend this holiday without loved ones. When he asked me for my pumpkin flan recipe, I gave him a better option—come eat it with us."

My heart races with nerves. Why in the world would my mother invite him for dessert? She always loved Hudson, but she knows how hurt I was when we broke up. She could've just sent him a slice of dessert. But that's not how she works. My mom has a big heart, the biggest I know, and her home is always open to anyone and everyone.

Why wouldn't Hudson spend Thanksgiving with his parents? I figured he would since he's in town.

"You're right. No one should spend Thanksgiving alone, but..." My dad presses his lips together, glancing at me.

"No, it's okay." I shake my head.

"Since I saw you walking together at the festival, I assumed you'd be okay with it," my mom frowns.

"It's fine." I plaster on a smile so that she doesn't feel guilty. She has the best of intentions and maybe a dash of mischief. She always did love seeing Hudson and me together.

I try to focus on the conversation throughout the rest of dinner, but my mind is focused on the front door, anticipating a knock announcing Hudson's arrival. Despite what it might look like from the outside, having him at this table doesn't mean anything. We aren't back in time when we were in a relationship.

"How are the wedding plans coming along?" My mom smiles.

"Good. I forgot to tell you that I went with Hope to pay the deposit for the venue. It's beautiful."

"The wedding is at the Malcolm Manor, right?" my dad asks.

"Yes. It's her dream venue. I had only seen pictures, but seeing it in person makes a huge difference."

"I can imagine," my mom sighs.

A knock at the door startles me, and my mom's smile widens. She's definitely up to no good.

"I'll get it." She pushes her chair back and stands.

When she's out of earshot, my dad leans in. "Are you okay with this? You know your mom gets excited and makes impulsive decisions at times."

"It's fine, Dad. I've had to see more of him, so it's okay." I assure him with a small smile.

MEET AGAIN

"Come in, come in," I hear my mom's excited voice from the foyer.

I take a deep breath in hopes that it slows the pounding in my chest. I don't even know why I'm nervous. It's not like it's the first time I see him. We've had to talk and see each other. I saw him yesterday. But things went south after running into his parents. Not to mention his not-so-subtle hints about how he feels seeing me again.

I wish I could shake it off like Taylor Swift.

Hudson walks into the dining room with a smile. "Hello." His eyes collide with mine immediately.

"Hi, Hudson." My dad stands to shake his hand.

"Hello, Mr. Leon. I brought some sweet wine to drink with dessert." Hudson lifts the bottle in his other hand.

"Sounds great. Why don't you take a seat." My dad motions to the empty chair next to me.

"Yes, please sit. We'll clear the table and be ready for dessert in no time." My mom smiles.

"Thank you, and no rush. Please finish eating." Hudson smiles my way. "Hi, Lex."

"Hey."

"We're already done. We were just talking about Hope and Toby's wedding." My mom grabs her plate and my dad's.

"I got it." I push back my chair and reach for the plates in her hand, stacking them with mine. "I'll bring out dessert, too."

"I can help," Hudson offers. "It's the least I can do for inviting me over."

"I've got it." I nod.

Memories flood me seeing him sitting at the table. All the holidays where he chose to stay in Hartville to celebrate with my family instead of traveling with his to whatever fancy resort they were heading to. Those were the times he put me first.

I place the plates in the sink and turn on the faucet so they can rinse before putting them in the dishwasher. Steps echo behind me.

"I've got it, Mom. I'll grab the platters in a second."

"I brought them in already." Hudson's deep voice washes over me, and I turn from the sink to see him placing the platters on the counter.

"I hope it's okay that I'm here. I thought you knew, which is why I didn't tell you myself." He keeps his eyes on mine, holding me captive with those green orbs.

"She mentioned it while we were eating. I also suspect you not mentioning it was purposeful," I arch an eyebrow. "You weren't going to set yourself up to be uninvited."

"Ah..." he nods, failing to find the right words.

"Thought so," I pat his chest and open the dishwasher.

"Let me help you, and we'll finish faster." He moves to the dishwasher and reaches for the plate in my hand, sliding it into its spot.

"Thanks," I smile. My chest constricts. Something as silly as filling the dishwasher together shouldn't get a reaction out of me.

We're done in no time, and I take the desserts out while Hudson carries the plates and spoons. Seated at the table, my mom cuts the flan while I slice the pumpkin pie, serving everyone a slice.

"No offense, Lex, but I'm here for the flan," Hudson says as I'm about to plate a slice of pumpkin pie for him. I pause mid-serve and stare at him.

"Okay." I nod, and apparently, gravity had other plans at that moment to make the slice of pie fall off the spatula.

"Oh, no!" I try to catch it, but it's no use. It slips through my failed attempt and lands in Hudson's lap.

MEET AGAIN

"Oh my goodness, I'm so sorry." I go to reach the slice and stop myself. That would just make this entire situation more awkward.

"It's okay," he laughs and picks up the pie. "I guess the pie wanted me even if I didn't."

My parents laugh across the table while I blush.

"It's really okay, Lex." Hudson stands. "Sorry to the pie police, but I should throw this out." He eyes me with a smirk.

"Yeah." I nod, mortified, and sit down. "That's so embarrassing," I cover my face as my parents continue to chuckle.

"And what a waste of good pie, too," I add, causing their quiet laughter to ring louder.

"It's not a big deal. You're making it more than it was in your head." My mom attempts to ease my embarrassment.

Hudson returns, and I notice a wet spot on his thigh.

"I ran a wet rag on the spot so it wouldn't stain," he explains.

"Of course," I nod. "I really am sorry."

"It *really* is okay," he smiles, teasing me.

"Here, sweetie," my mom lifts a slice of pie and slides it onto my plate.

"Thanks." I stare at the plate for a beat before eating a slice.

Thankfully, the rest of dessert goes by without any other mishaps. My parents ask Hudson about his job and his life in New York. I listen intently, getting as much information about the man I once loved.

"I've had some great opportunities with work," Hudson says. "However, sometimes it feels like I'm on the go twenty-four seven. It'd be nice to slow down a bit. I'm still young and have the energy to travel and meet with clients, but eventually, I'll want a slower pace."

"That makes sense. All work and no play isn't the right way to live," my dad tells him.

"You have a point. Real estate is just a demanding career, especially when you have nationwide clients." Hudson glances at me. I've been quiet, listening and assessing my feelings.

"Bianca, this is better than I remembered. Thank you for inviting me." Hudson smiles at my mom as he finishes off his last bite.

"Have more, please."

"I think two slices are my limit." He taps his stomach.

"I'll wrap some up for you when you leave."

"I won't say no to that." His smile is dazzling.

"And this sweet wine is great. Did you buy it in town?" My mom lifts the glass, taking a sip.

"I saw it at a market in Dornby, actually. I was on my way back from Portland meeting a client when I stopped to grab a few things."

"Well, it was a great buy." My mom nods, smiling. "Don't you agree, Lex?" She tilts her head and lifts her brows.

"It is really good," I agree. The wine is smooth and compliments our desserts. However, sitting beside Hudson provides a different lightheaded feeling that the wine can't.

"I'm glad you like it. I was hoping you would." The way he looks at me is full of meaning, as if he was thinking about me when he bought it, even if it was before my mom invited him over.

"If we're all done, I'm going to clear the table and put away leftovers. Manny, will you help me?" I roll my eyes at my mom's obvious plan.

"Yes, cariño." My dad shakes his head. I'm sure he's also onto her.

MEET AGAIN

Alone in the dining room, Hudson turns to me. "Do you think she wanted to leave us alone?

I snort. "Nope, not at all." I pull my eyebrows together and shake my head as I chuckle.

Hudson laughs along with me. "It was nice to come over. I know things are weird between us, and I get it, but thank you."

"How come you didn't go to your parents' house?" I can't help but ask.

"Wasn't feeling it. To be honest, we hadn't really talked about eating together. We mentioned it once, but it wasn't exactly my ideal plan."

I frown, tilting my head and taking in the disappointment in his eyes.

"I'm sorry to hear that."

"It shouldn't surprise you. It's not like I loved spending time with them before."

I shrug, frowning. "It doesn't matter. They're still your family, and I guess I thought—"

"That since I decided to work in the family business, I was all cushy with them? No, Lex. I can't tell you why I decided to work for the family business. Guilt maybe? Not steering from the expectations set for me. Because I'm an idiot."

"Hudson..."

"Just because I work with my dad doesn't mean we're friends. It doesn't mean that I condone the way they treat you." He reaches for my hand, squeezing it.

My skin prickles and heats. His touch sears me, flooding me with emotions I've tried to push aside. I clear my throat and nod.

"Anyway," he pulls his hand away. "I'm sure it doesn't seem that way to you."

"It's more complicated than that."

"I guess throwing pie at me was part of your revenge?" He cracks a smile.

I sag into my chair and cover my face. "I didn't mean to. Honestly, I'm so sorry."

His deep chuckle envelops me. "I'm only teasing you. You can't even tell." He shifts, looking at his pants.

I follow his gaze, too, checking if they're stained. The way his pants stretch across his strong thigh makes my pulse race. Hudson is all man, and he's grown since we were together. I will my eyes to stop checking him out and fail.

"Let's go." He scoots back and tugs my hand.

"Where?" I look at him as if he's crazy.

When he points to the window in the dining room, I see it's snowing. A huge smile splits my mouth, and I head for the back door without waiting for him.

"I'm two for two," he says behind me. I spin around to face him with my arms spread wide.

"You are," I nod.

I wonder if he can be two for two with my heart as well. It seems as if the more time I spend with him, the more my guard drops. Staring at him now, seeing the way he's looking at me, fills me with hope.

When he stalks toward me, my breath hitches. He stops inches from me, his hand moving to my hair and running his fingers through it.

"You've got snowflakes all over you." His voice is low and rough.

"It's the point. Dancing in the snow is much more fun than in the rain." I step back and move around freely, inhaling the cold air and letting it fill my lungs and cool my heated skin.

When I turn around to look at Hudson, he smiles in such a way that it takes my breath away. When he extends his hand, I take it. We begin to slow dance, and every fiber of my being feels as if it's put back together. I rest my cheek on his shoulder and close my eyes.

"Could it be that we have a chance to make things right now?" His question is a low whisper that's almost drowned by the pounding in my ears.

I lean back and stare at him.

"Is it even possible?" Neither of our situations has changed.

"I want it to be," he confesses.

Tears blur my vision, and I wish that things were different. My heart fears opening up to him again, only to end up broken once more.

I remain silent, soaking up this moment. I don't want anything to ruin it if it disappears just as fast as it came. When Hudson returns to New York, I'll be left here, and this will just have been a reunion to add to the list of memories.

11
HUDSON

Having Lex in my arms makes me feel complete. I never want to let go, but I hate seeing the tears filling her eyes. My hand squeezes hers as I tighten my hold around her waist. I want her to know what seeing her again is like for me. I'm not hiding my feelings.

"Say something," I whisper.

"I don't know what to say." She shakes her head softly and looks over my shoulder.

"Do you still think about me?" If she's not sure where to begin, I'll ask questions.

She tilts her head to the side as her eyes meet mine again and purses her lips.

"Yes." She breathes out her response as if she's been trapping it for too long and needs to finally exhale.

"I think about you all the time." My fingers caress her back where I'm holding her. Lex shivers and leans into my touch, making me smile.

"I've never stopped thinking about you, actually. It's not once in a while that I remember you exist. It's every day. It's when I accomplish something and want to share it with you or when I get home after a long day and need to talk to someone." I shake my head. I miss her. It's been four years since I've been able to hold her, but no matter the amount of time, she'll always be the one who got away.

MEET AGAIN

"My friends in New York make fun of me, always asking if I've talked to you or if I'm too much of a chicken to do so. I am."

Lex smiles sadly, a tear slipping down her cheek. Keeping our hands joined, I reach and swipe away the tear. Then, I kiss her cheek. She draws a sharp intake of breath, eyes wide.

"I wish we could talk like normal people, that you wouldn't hesitate around me. I get it, though. I hurt you. I broke us."

"You did." Her words hold no blame or resentment, just stating a fact. "It killed me. I always thought we were stronger than your parents' judgments and disapproval, but at the end of the day, they won." She shrugs, defeat sagging her shoulders.

"It was more complicated than that. I never stopped loving you, but we were stuck on two different paths."

"And we still are."

My gaze burns into her as I shake my head.

"We are, Hudson. You live in New York and work for your father. My dance studio is here. I'm not giving that up. I'm sorry. I loved you, too, but you knew my dream. Working for your father wasn't yours when we were together. I just thought..." She throws one of her hands in the air, exasperation pulsing from her.

"I know." I keep my grip on her tight, needing her warmth. "I didn't have the courage to step away back then. I did what was expected of me and what I'm good at."

"Is it enough? Does it fulfill you? Or are you just good at it? Because I'm good at checking people out at the grocery store, but it doesn't fulfill me. What about the dreams you had? What happened to those?" Passion and determination fuel her words and light a fire in her eyes.

Shaking my head, I look away. She's right. I pushed aside my dreams to not deal with my father. It was easier to give in than live constantly fighting. Tristan left after his graduation. That was always his plan, but I wanted to stay in Hartville with Lex. I'd have to see my parents, and the drama wasn't worth it, in my opinion, back then. It ended up being worse than I could've imagined.

"Hudson, you deserved to follow your dreams. When you started making plans, disregarding my ideas and dreams... I don't know. You took control and focused on what worked for you, and that hurt. The guy I knew wouldn't have taken such little consideration for my future plans. Not to mention, we had *our* future plans we had made."

"You're right." I have nothing else to say. Everything she's expressing is exactly how things were back then, and I ruined it.

"I'm sorry. All I can say is I regret it and repeat it until you believe it." The snow has stopped falling, yet I'm still holding her as if we were dancing.

"I believe that it was hard for you, but that doesn't mean things are easier now. If anything, I'd say they're more complicated."

Unless I quit my job, I know she's right. And doing so will have great repercussions that I'm not sure I'm ready to face. As easy of a solution as it sounds, it's an intricate web that could lead to more challenges.

"How about for right now you dance with me?" I smile at her.

When she nods, I hum her favorite song and begin to move around the yard. Everything feels right in this moment. It's as if I'm back in time, Lex is mine, and I have no worries. How much longer can I live without her? No one has filled that void, not that I've tried very hard to meet someone.

I've focused on my career and becoming someone clients trust, proving myself despite my age. At twenty-five, some clients prefer my father since he has more years of experience. Others will have no choice but to give me a chance, and I've strived to prove to them my worth and knowledge, getting my name around in the real estate market. If I had to lose the love of my life, then I was going to be the best at my job. I thought that would make it worth it. It hasn't, though, and having Lex here in this moment has proven that.

♡♡♡

"You're heading back to the big city on Tuesday, huh?" Toby lifts a brow.

"Yeah, duty calls." I shrug. "But no worries, your bachelor party will still be top-notch. I won't slack on planning just because I'm away." I lift my beer and take a drink. When he called and asked if I wanted to grab a bite to eat while Hope had her girls' night, I quickly agreed.

I was tired of being in my room and replaying last night with Lex.

"I'm not worried about that. Lex won't let you slack," he laughs. "But I guess I thought you'd stay longer."

"You know I can't." I shake my head.

"Well...you can."

"If I quit my job, divorce my family, and move in with you," I joke about the last part.

"You'll get a pretty penny for that apartment in New York. You can afford a house here," he chuckles.

"And what would I do?"

"Remember that sports app you started to create in college and then forgot about because you thought you needed to follow in daddy's footsteps?" He gives me a pointed look. Toby may respect my parents, but he never agreed with my decisions. He knew me well enough to know it wasn't what I wanted.

"That was just for fun. I didn't have a future creating sports apps, especially with all the competition nowadays."

"Imagine if you would've launched it back then."

"I didn't, so there's no point in driving myself crazy with that." I grab a wing from the basket.

"No," he shakes his head, "but you have the skills, and you loved that. Remember when we were in school and trying to brainstorm ideas on how to be better at certain plays? Create an app where athletes can type in the skill they're struggling with, and it generates tips and ideas for their practice." Toby's smiling as if he came up with a genius idea.

"That's what coaches are for."

"Sure, but a coach has a ton of players to deal with. This app is something people can use on the side. You can even team up with professional athletes and have them be guests on the app, provide their professional advice." He's talking a mile a minute, throwing different ideas my way.

It's true I used to think about creating my own app, combining my love of sports with the ever-growing technology market, but I never saw it through. Listening to Toby talk spikes that excitement I used to feel. I should've studied computer science instead of business and real estate.

"You can do that job from anywhere, too." He arches a brow. "I know you've been spending more time with Lex than just planning the trip. If you still feel for her, maybe this is your chance to make things right. Not just for her, but for you. How happy will you be in ten years working at the agency, wondering what if?"

"I thought we were coming out to relax and talk about sports or something." I deflect.

"I'm relaxed." He leans back in his seat, his arm draped across the chair beside him.

"Yeah, because you're putting all your attention on me," I laugh.

"Hey, whatever works," he shrugs with a smile.

"I'll admit that app idea is cool, but I'm not sure how effective it is with search engines at people's fingertips."

"I could say the same for all those e-reader apps, and yet there are a ton of them. Or how many social media platforms exist nowadays? It's all about market research and creating something specialized to that audience."

"Are you an accountant or business guru?" I tease.

"I could be both." He smiles triumphantly.

"I don't know. I'll admit being in town has forced me to face some things I haven't wanted to address, but it's not that easy."

"I understand. Just want you to know that if you want a change in your life, it's possible."

"Thanks, Toby. I'll drink to that." I lift my glass.

"Cheers."

Throughout the rest of the night, I think about Toby's suggestions and ideas. The technology geek in me starts to calculate and turn ideas to see if it's a winning possibility to create a sports app with that angle. It'd be amazing, especially if I could get professionals to give advice. That would set it apart from just searching for ideas on a browser. Personal experience from someone who plays professionally would be a huge selling point, even from college athletes.

When I was a kid, I would've given anything to hear one of my favorite players give me pointers, even if it was through an app or an interview.

More than excited about the prospect of working on something I love is the idea that I could do it from anywhere, including Hartville. The fallout could be great, though, and I'd need to take my time. I can't make a rash decision. If I cut ties with the family business, I'm cutting ties with my family. I need to be ready to face that and confident in my plan. However, Toby may have given me the push and inspiration I needed.

After dinner, I clap Toby's back and smile.

"Thanks for coming to town and helping with the bachelor party," he smiles. "I appreciate it more than you know."

"No need to thank me. It's why I'm your best friend."

"I'll see you before you go on Tuesday. We can have dinner with Hope."

"Sounds great. I'll still be here the weekend. No need to get sad and miss me yet," I joke.

"I don't miss you." He shoves me. "But I am glad you were here for a few weeks."

"Aw, you do miss me." I ruffle his hair since I know he hates that.

"You're a jerk. Think about what I said." His expression turns serious. "I have a feeling you were already thinking of a plan to stay here. If you want to get the girl, go for it but do it right this time."

"Yeah," I nod.

"Lex has been through a lot. I never told you this, and I promised Hope I wouldn't..." He looks around the sidewalk.

"What?" I furrow my eyebrows.

"Man, you know I respect your family because I respect you. When Lex was opening the dance studio, your parents made

MEET AGAIN

it difficult for her. I don't know what their deal is with her, especially since you two had broken up already. She wanted to rent the building, but your dad bid higher, trying to steal the contract from her. Lex ended up having to buy it instead, at a higher price than she'd likely have paid if it weren't for your dad jumping in. He said he had plans for an office there, but we both know that's probably not true."

I freeze, listening to Toby speak. I want to say that it can't be true, but my parents are Class A jerks like that. Why would they continue to torture her after we'd broken up?

"I-" I shake my head and clear my thoughts. "Are you sure?"

"I'm positive. It wasn't fun to witness, and Lex almost gave up. Buying the building was out of her budget plan, but she found a way. She was thrown into the gossip mill, people talking about an ongoing rivalry with your parents."

"I'm glad she did." I slide my hands into my pockets, my mind reeling. "But I hate she had to endure that. Thanks for telling me."

"I thought you should know." He claps my shoulder. "I'll see you tomorrow."

"For sure." I nod, shake his hand, and walk away from the restaurant with a million thoughts. My parents never know when to stop pushing. That attitude will ruin them eventually.

12
LEX

> Hudson: Hey, how are you? Any updates I should know about for the bach party?

I STARE AT HUDSON's message with a racing heart. He's been back in New York for a week, but the night of Thanksgiving has been etched in my mind. I didn't see him again, but Hope made it a point to tell me she saw him before he left, and he asked about me.

I'm starting to think my best friend is a traitor.

I've been so confused since he waltzed back into my life. He's crossed my mind plenty of times, but I thought I was over him. He was a memory of the past, a boyfriend who broke my heart. In reality, he's the only boyfriend I've had. I guess four years doesn't erase a six-year relationship. Not when I thought he was the one I'd marry someday.

And just when I was getting used to seeing him around town, he returned to New York, reminding me that we lost our chance long ago. Or maybe we lived the length of the relationship we were supposed to.

I rub my chest and take a deep breath. The conversation we had on Thanksgiving has been weighing heavy on my mind. From the outside, it might seem like Hudson and I have an opportunity to make things right, but I already know what heartbreak by Hudson feels like. I don't want a re-do of that feeling. Although, hearing him say that we could have a second chance made me feel hopeful.

Confusion times a million. I throw myself back on the sofa and clutch my phone to my chest before replying to his text message.

> Lex: Hi, no main updates. I'm meeting with Hope this week to get some more details. Spa day does have to stay for that Saturday

> Hudson: I know. I canceled brunch, remember? The guys will hang out while you girls get pampered

> Lex: That's right. Sounds good

> Hudson: How are you?

> Lex: I'm good. You?

Hudson: Good, long week at work with the holidays

Lex: I can imagine

Hudson: Have you thought more about what I said?

Lex: Honestly?

Hudson: Of course

Lex: Seeing you is confusing. Hearing you say you think about me...I don't know

Hudson: It's the truth

Hudson: I miss you. Maybe this message is four years too late

MEET AGAIN

> Lex: Yeah, it kinda is

> Hudson: But you miss me too? *wink emoji*

> Lex: Lol...I miss what we had

I take a deep breath. I didn't expect this conversation to take the turn it did. Do I miss Hudson? I do. More than my pride cares to admit. It could be time that I set my pride aside.

> Lex: Yes, I miss you. You were someone important in my life. It's difficult to move on from that

> Hudson: It is.

> Lex: That doesn't change our reality though

> Hudson: Maybe our realities change

Lex: Vague much?

Hudson: I've got you talking to me, acknowledging me as more than a nuisance. We've made great progress since you threw daggers at me at the engagement party. I'm not going to give that up now

Lex: Why now?

Hudson: I don't know

I can understand that. Why couldn't we have this conversation four years ago? Maybe we weren't at that place yet. We weren't mature enough. So many uncertainties tie me to Hudson. All I know is that as much as I may hate to admit it, seeing him again has sparked something inside of me. I was happy with my life, but I remember what having him in it felt like. It's this immense joy and peace, and I long for that feeling.

Hudson: I'll be in Hartville for Christmas. Maybe we can have dinner when I'm there?

MEET AGAIN

Lex: Maybe

Hudson: Phew. At least it's not a big fat no

Lex: Lol

Hudson: I need to go. I'll talk to you later

Lex: Bye

I remain on the couch and close my eyes. I'm not sure I signed up for a blast from the past. However, my heart is jumping at the possibility. It's also a traitor, but it's time I let go of past resentment and hurt.

After seeing the honesty in Hudson's eyes, I can't deny we both felt pain from losing one another. His family is still an issue, though. He works for them, and they don't approve of me. Can our relationship truly strive and evolve if that ugly ghost is always haunting us?

Knowing he didn't have Thanksgiving with his parents is also an indication of their current relationship. I wouldn't blame him nor be surprised if he faults them for the end of our relationship, but he still chose to stay working in the company.

I take a deep breath. Career choices are influenced by a lot of things. Hudson always felt responsible, like he had a loyalty to keep, especially since his younger brother always made a point to remind his family he wouldn't stay.

My thoughts are a mess. My heart's a bigger mess. It's like a giant junk drawer. Behind my eyelids, I can fantasize about a relationship with Hudson now. It'd be amazing, but when I return to reality, he'll leave home, and I'd stay here. Long-distance relationships are difficult, and with his parents living in Hartville, I can only imagine how much more difficult they'd make my life. I've already had to deal with them more than I'd like.

I stand, stretch my muscles, and walk to the window in my living room. A smile replaces my pursed lips as I see it's once again snowing. I love this time of year.

Without a second thought, I grab my coat and slip on my boots. When I make it out to my patio, I hold out my arms and spin around. Snowflakes land on my palms and melt. It's starting to stick on the ground, creating the beginning of a white carpet that I'll admire for days.

Visions of dancing in the snow with Hudson hit me, and I sigh. I've been stuck on that memory since it happened.

I shake my head and clear my mind. I need to stop thinking about him. It's like he's invaded my brain. If he had that power, I bet he'd do it on purpose to wear me down. Whatever this is, it's working. Everything lately reminds me of Hudson, and it's because he was back in town, living a life parallel to me. He was right there, so close within reach. Many times I wondered what would've happened if he wouldn't have stayed in New York after graduation.

MEET AGAIN

And all of these questions and what-if scenarios are the ones that hold me back from moving on. I can't seem to let go of him. I loved him too much to just forget, even years later.

"Breaking news, old flames are burning again." Ellie storms into my house.

"What?" I turn to look at her when she walks into the kitchen. She's wearing a bright smile, and it reminds me of the Cheshire cat. I should be worried.

"That's the word around town."

"What are you talking about?" I'm afraid to ask.

"Oh, nothing," she says slowly and drawn out. Her smile is still wide.

"Clearly, it's something." I cross my arms.

"People are talking about how you and Hudson have been spending time together again. There are rumors and bets about whether you will get back together and how soon it will take for that to happen."

"Say what now?" My eyes bug.

Ellie shimmies around my peninsula counter to stand in front of me.

"You heard me. People think you two are getting back together, and I have to admit that I ship it."

"We're not getting back together," I shake my head. "There's nothing to *ship*. Unless it's those rumors all the way to the moon."

"But there's some truth to those rumors because you were spending more time together while he was here."

"Yeah, to plan this party, trip, whatever. You know, the reason you came over today?" My heart's starting to race. I can only imagine Mr. and Mrs. Remington's reaction when they hear this. If they haven't already.

"But there's more, right? There has to be some truth to this." Ellie looks at me with doe eyes full of hope.

I shake my head, unsure of what to say. "I don't know," I finally let out on a sigh.

"I knew it!" She dances around my kitchen. "They're in love," she sings out.

I can't help but laugh at her ridiculousness.

"We're not." I grab the pitcher of lemonade I made earlier from the fridge. "Now, let's talk about Hope's bachelorette party." I asked for her help so we could work together to sort out the details.

"I'll let it go for now." She waggles her eyebrows.

I shake my head, serving two glasses, and head to the round kitchen table where I have my notebook and laptop.

I haven't spoken to Hudson except for that short text message conversation on Thursday evening. He continues to steal my thoughts, though.

"What do you have so far?" Ellie gets into planning mode.

"We have the spa reserved for Saturday. The idea right now is to drive out Thursday morning and return Tuesday. We'll arrive Thursday afternoon, so we'll either relax when we arrive, or people can ski before dinner."

"I think it depends on how tired we are Thursday. I'd love to be able to decorate the suite before Hope walks in."

"I was thinking that as well. How can we stall her?"

"I can drag her around the resort, gushing about it. We can say the guys are taking our suitcases up to our room, and you can go with them. Maybe Hudson can help you decorate." She waggles her eyebrows again.

Laughing, I shake my head. "You're ridiculous. That's a good idea, though. It won't take long to decorate. I was searching for some ideas online. Look at these." I open my laptop and show Ellie the decorations I've found so far.

"So no eggplants?" She winks.

A loud cackle escapes me, and I throw my head back. "I don't think Hope would appreciate that."

"I love the rose gold balloons. That banner is pretty, too." She points to a gold glitter banner that says, Miss to Mrs.

"I love that one and this one." I point to the banner with the modern calligraphy script that reads, "Pop the champagne, she's changing her last name."

"Oh, yes," Ellie exclaims. "I love that even more. And those balloons. It should be easy to find the letters to spell out bride."

"Definitely." I nod my head. "We should get her a veil, too, right?"

"And a sash that says Bride to Be."

"What should we get for us?"

"We could do sashes, too. A different one for each of us. It's us three and Hope, right?"

"Yeah," I nod. Jody, Hope's cousin, will also be celebrating with us.

"What about a bridal shower? I know it's off-topic." Ellie leans back in her seat and takes a sip of lemonade.

"Her mom is planning it. We're doing things backward since they want to ski for the bach party. I think she's planning it for early March."

"Awesome. I'm so excited about this. It's not every day I can dress up and go to a fancy event." Working at the farm keeps Ellie in jeans and shirts with her cowboy boots. The few times she can dress up, she takes advantage, but she's a country girl at heart.

"Amen to that. It'll be fun to wear a long dress and have our hair and makeup done."

"Yes. I'm most excited about a spa day, though. Are we getting massages? Please tell me yes," she begs.

I laugh at her desperation. "Massages are a must. We're also getting facials and going to the steam room. Oh, and they have a jacuzzi with an amazing view we can take advantage of."

"That sounds divine. I can't wait." She drops back on her chair as if her muscles have already fully relaxed.

"Same. It'll be nice to take a vacation." Even if it involves my ex-boyfriend, who apparently wants to try again.

"For sure. I'm exhausted with trying to keep the farm running at maximum."

"What's going on?" I furrow my eyebrows.

"It's just been stressful. It's normal to have ups and downs like this, but that doesn't take away the worries and financial stress." She leans her elbows on the table.

"I can imagine. Every business has its highs and lows."

"Yup. Anyway, back to planning. What else are we doing? Knowing you, we aren't skiing every day," she teases.

I stick my tongue out and look at my notebook.

"Hudson and I had said Friday can be ski day since it's our first full day there, and we can have dinner at the resort or go into town and have an early dinner after everyone's done skiing if they're not too tired since we'll likely eat at the resort on Saturday since we'll be at the spa."

"How long is our spa treatment?"

MEET AGAIN

"Three to four hours, I believe." It's our day to relax, so I don't want to rush it. We have unlimited time to use the steam room and jacuzzi since those are open to clients at any time.

"In the morning?" She tilts her head.

"It's at noon. I figured we could have a big breakfast before."

"So why don't we do this. If everyone is skiing on Friday, they'll probably be tired. We can have dinner at the resort on Friday and go into town for an early dinner Saturday since we'll be relaxed and rested."

"That works. I'll run it by Hudson to make sure it fits in their plans. They were going to ski while we're at the spa." I jot down the note, so I don't forget.

"Yeah, let him know."

"Great, thanks, Ellie. Although I'm planning the trip with Hudson, I want to make sure we make it memorable for Hope when it comes to a bachelorette party."

"She's going to love it." Ellie squeezes my arm. "How about we go grab a bite to eat. This lemonade is great, but I'm hungry."

"Oh, snap. I had snacks and forgot about them." I slap my forehead.

"Your mind's preoccupied with a certain hottie. It's understandable, and you're forgiven," she winks.

"No," I shake my head and roll my eyes. "More like you storming in here with rumors clouded my mind and threw me off."

"Still, it's about a certain hottie." She points at me and winks.

"Let's go eat." I close my laptop. "If you have any other ideas, let me know."

"Sounds great, Lex. This is going to be amazing." She links her arm in mine.

Once we make it to Da Nonna, the Italian restaurant in town, I look at Ellie and debate telling her about my text message conversation with Hudson. She could help put things into perspective.

"You're good with pizza, right?" Ellie looks at me.

"Yes." I love the pizza here.

"Good." She goes back to looking through the menu.

I do the same, attempting to focus on dinner.

"Pineapple and pepperoni?" She glances up at me with a hopeful smile.

I scrunch up my nose and shake my head. "Nice try, but pineapple doesn't belong on pizza."

"Does so," she argues.

"Nuh-uh." I shake my head again, proving a point.

"If it didn't, people wouldn't like it, and places wouldn't serve it." Ellie raises her eyebrows in a challenge. She has a point there, but that doesn't mean I like it.

"Half and half?"

"I don't know why we argue each time if we always end up doing the same thing," she giggles. I laugh along with her because it's true. She tries to push pineapple on me, I refuse it, and we always share the same pie with pineapple on half of it. I'm a pepperoni lover, so that's all I need to be happy.

After ordering, I take a sip of water and look at Ellie.

"What?" She asks, looking down at herself and back at me.

"Nothing," I shake my head.

"We haven't started eating yet, so I can't be dirty yet."

"You're not dirty." I laugh and lean back. "You promise not to say anything? I just need a sounding board."

"I knew you were holding out on me," she exclaims loudly.

"Shhh…" I widen my eyes.

"Sorry," she whispers. "Anyway, spill your dirty little secrets to me."

"No dirty little secrets to spill. Hudson asked me if I wanted to have dinner with him when he was in town for Christmas."

"And? Tell me you said yes. I knew there had to be truth to these rumors."

"I don't know what to do." I hide my face in my hands. "On one hand, he's Hudson." I lift my gaze to hers.

"I get it. He's that guy for you, the one." She smiles wistfully.

"But our same issues are still an issue." I frown, slumping in my seat.

"What if that changed?"

"Do you think he'd quit his job?" I give her a pointed look.

"Crazier things have happened," Ellie shrugs. "I don't know."

"I want to be hopeful, but..."

"You don't want to get hurt again," she finishes off for me.

"Exactly, and we both know I'm not the Remingtons' favorite."

"They're so...argh," she presses her lips together. "Infuriating. After what they did to you when you were going to rent the studio." Ellie shakes her head, her jaw set tight.

"I know. I don't think Hudson knows about that either. It's like his parents are out to ruin me, and I don't know why if Hudson and I had already broken up." I never understood their motives. They had already gotten what they wanted. Why would they sabotage me? Everyone knew Mr. Remington didn't need a storefront in town.

"They're the kind of people that are just mean. Plain and simple." She has a point there.

"Amen to that." I lift my water glass. Ellie clinks her glass to mine and giggles.

"I think you should go to dinner. Maybe this time you have a better chance. Hudson isn't dependent on his parents. I mean, he is because he works for the agency, but you know what I mean. He isn't fresh out of college with only his family business flashing bright lights at him. He could have other opportunities."

I know she's right, but the question is if he'll take those or continue pleasing his parents. The only way to find out is by giving him a chance to prove himself. If I'm being honest, the idea of going to dinner with him without the pretense of planning the party makes me giddy. My heart skips a beat at the thought.

13

HUDSON

"Hello?" I answer my phone on the way to the office after a meeting with a client.

"Hey, big bro. Why aren't you at work? Are you playing hooky? You make me proud." Tristan laughs.

"How do you know I'm not working? Just finished up with a client. Not everyone can travel the globe," I mock.

"That's where you're wrong. Everyone can if they do it right. Where are you?"

"Why are you so curious about my location?" I turn the corner.

"Just wondering if you're near that bagel shop I love. I'm kinda hungry." Humor laces his voice.

"Wha—" I stop walking, causing the person behind me to crash into me.

"Watch it," the guy yells, throwing his hand in the air.

"Are you in town?" I look around, watching the lunch rush pass me by.

"Yup, your office chair is comfy. It's the perfect height for me to rest my feet on your desk."

"You better not dirty any of my papers."

"Impossible. They're stacked neatly, and your desk is impeccable. It's clear you're the oldest child," he laughs.

I begin walking again. "What are you doing here? Why didn't you tell me you were coming?"

"It was a spur-of-the-moment decision. About that bagel?"

"I'll do you one better. Meet me at that burger joint we went to for your birthday three years ago." I make a left, switching routes.

"Ah, now you're talking. See you there in a bit." Tristan hangs up.

I haven't seen my brother in over a year while he's been busy living the nomad life. Looking forward to spending time with him, I pick up my pace and hope the restaurant isn't packed. I could use some time with someone who isn't involved in my job. My friend, Jameson, is usually around to talk, but he's blissfully enjoying his new relationship, and I don't want to be the Debbie downer in his life.

After returning from Hartville, something's been missing, and I know it's Lex. My conversation with Toby has also been on repeat in my mind, slowly chipping away at my resolve to put my dream of creating a sports app to rest.

I grab one of the few empty tables at the restaurant and check my phone while I wait for Tristan to arrive. The office is a few blocks away, so he shouldn't be too long.

I read through my recent text message conversations with Lex. They've been straightforward about how our days have been. I put myself out there, but I need to prove to her that things could be different this time. I'm not sure how to do that. I can't just quit my job without having something else lined up.

"Hey." Tristan slaps the table, causing me to jolt and look up at him.

I stand and hug him, clapping his back. "It's good to see you."

"Same, big bro." He grips my shoulder and smiles at me.

His hair is longer and messy. His skin is tanned despite it being December. He looks as if he hasn't aged, with the same boyish style he always had.

MEET AGAIN

"How are you?" He asks when he takes a seat.

"All good here. Working before taking a few days off for Christmas. You know how this time of year can be unpredictable." People either stop searching for properties or rush to buy something before Christmas so they can celebrate in their new home. It's crazy, in my opinion, but I'll never turn down the chance for a sale.

"Yeah," he nods. "You sure you're okay?" He narrows his eyes.

"Of course. Why wouldn't I be?" I laugh.

"Because when we spoke a few weeks ago, you didn't sound completely okay. How did things with Lex finish up?"

I shrug, flicking the corner of the menu with my thumb.

"Complicated," I finally say.

"Ah, I expected that. Tell me what's going on. I can help." He leans back with his hands behind his head.

I scrub a hand down my face, collecting my thoughts.

"I told her I missed her, that I think about her every day. Things are complicated, though."

"As you already said." He smirks. "You know what I think?" He leans forward on his elbows and stares at me.

"You gotta stop caring what Mom and Dad think. Forget it, man. I've learned that if they don't support us, it's a sign of their character, not ours. Live your life. Trust me, it'll make you a lot happier."

"I know you have a point, but it's my career we're talking about."

"And you can separate your career from your personal life like everyone else." He shrugs as if it were common sense. Maybe to most people, it is.

"Did you know that Mom and Dad tried to interfere in Lex renting the dance studio? Toby told me recently. Apparently, they tried to buy it from the owner, attempting to make Lex lose the opportunity. Instead of renting, she was forced to buy at a higher price so Mom and Dad couldn't steal it from her."

I still can't believe that. Toby wouldn't lie to me, but I can't comprehend why my parents would go through that trouble.

"Why in the world would they do that?" His eyebrows dip, confusion written all over his face.

"I have no idea. To be jerks because they know they can be?" There's no other reason. We were already broken up.

"Sometimes, I wonder how we came from those two. It seems that the older they get, the less they care about others. Or maybe they never did, and we're just old enough now to know the difference."

I frown, nodding. He's right. I knew my parents were a piece of work, but the more I witnessed their actions, the more I realized that they were coldhearted. It's almost like they have fun making others miserable.

"Does Lex know that you know?"

"Nope. Toby told me in confidence." I scratch my jaw.

"It's good to know. Living away from Hartville makes it impossible to know what's going on."

"What can I get you?" A waiter walks up to our tables.

We place our orders, and I relax into my seat, looking around the packed space.

"Are you heading to Hartville for Christmas then?" Tristan lifts his eyebrows.

"Yeah. I kinda miss the town."

"You miss the woman, but I'll accept your excuse," he chuckles.

"I miss her, too. I don't know how to explain it. I hadn't spent a lot of time in Hartville since college, and it reminded me of everything I love about our hometown."

"I get it. Any chance you've got the passenger seat empty and some space in your trunk?" Tristan smirks.

"What?"

"You've become dense, brother. I'm headed to Hartville for Christmas, too. Do you think Mom and Dad will be happy to see me?" His eyes gleam with mischief.

"Not a chance," I laugh. "But I'm glad you'll be there. How did this miracle happen?"

Tristan hasn't been around for Christmas in two years, choosing to stay wherever he is that time of year.

He shrugs, leaning back on his seat and extending his long legs to the side. "It was time for a Christmas miracle?" He gives me his best smile.

"Nice try." I arch a brow.

"The work I was doing ended for now, so I thought I'd come see you and see how Lex acts around you." I still don't buy his excuse, but I drop it. I'm glad he'll be around for a couple of weeks.

"Whatever the real reason, I'm glad you're here."

"Me, too. Are you having dinner with Mom and Dad on Christmas?"

"I honestly have no idea. For all I know, they have plans to travel to Paris." I shrug. I haven't put much thought into it, nor do I care much. My reason for heading to Hartville has nothing to do with a family dinner and everything to do with the woman from my past.

As if reading my mind, Tristan laughs and shakes his head. "You're in deep," he points at me.

I was always in deep with Lex. Now, I only need a plan to make her see we can have a future instead of shredded memories.

We get back to my office, and I see Tristan's bag in a corner. "Where are you staying?"

"Your house," he shakes his head at the absurd question.

"What if I don't have space?"

Tristan laughs and claps my shoulder. "Good one. You've got a huge apartment, and you live alone. From my understanding, you don't have anyone in your life. That wouldn't help your case with Lex." He shakes his head in amusement.

I shove him playfully and round my desk. Pulling out a spare key I leave in a drawer, I toss it to him.

"I'll be home around seven. We can grab dinner or something."

"Sounds good. I'm going to take a nap." He rubs his eyes, a yawn widening his mouth right on cue.

"We can order dinner and stay in, too. I'll probably be tired by the time I get home."

"That's a better plan. If I'm asleep when you get there, wake me up, or I'll be up all night." He grabs his bag and slings it over his shoulder.

"Will do."

Tristan leaves my office with a quick wave. I have no idea what brought him home, but I'm glad to see him. It's been too long since we've spent time together. Despite the different paths we took in life, Tristan is my best friend. He, Toby, and I were inseparable, being only a year apart.

Grabbing my phone, I open my messages app.

MEET AGAIN

> Hudson: Have you put more thought into dinner when I'm in town?

I set my phone to the side and get back to work. Eating a big lunch wasn't ideal. I could go for a nap. What I used to love about real estate is what lately has been bothering me. No workday is ever the same. I work with different clients and properties. It keeps things exciting. Although, recently, I've been tired of running around and meeting with different people, competing to get the best deal. It takes a lot of energy, which means I need time to refuel.

My phone buzzes on my desk, and I instantly grab it.

> Lex: I've put thought into it but haven't decided if it's a good idea

> Hudson: Spending time with me is always a good idea

> Lex: Hmmm...Idk about that

> Hudson: What can I do to convince you?

Lex: Promise you won't break my heart...

Lex: And we both know that's not a promise you can make

Hudson: I never meant to

Lex: I can understand that but it happened anyway

Lex: And that scares me

Hudson: One chance. One dinner without using the bach party as an excuse

Lex: In town where your parents will find out?

MEET AGAIN

Hudson: I don't care about that

I'm so tired of my parents controlling my decisions, even subconsciously. I've come to realize that I allow their presence in my life to gear my path without me even wanting them to.

Lex: Maybe I do. You get to go back to NY and ignore them. I'm stuck living in the same town as them

Hudson: They won't bother you

Lex: Right... *eye-roll emoji*

Hudson: I'll make sure of it, promise

Hudson: One dinner. You can choose the restaurant

Hudson: I'll be the perfect gentleman

Lex: Why do you insist?

Hudson: Is it working?

Lex: Ugh

Hudson: It is! It's me, Lex. I'm the same guy despite what you might think. Give me a chance to prove it to you and make up for the past

Lex: Fine

Hudson: You won't regret it

Lex: I hope so

MEET AGAIN

Hudson: I never should've let you walk away and I'll always regret that

Lex: It was the wrong timing

Hudson: It didn't have to be. We made it through high school and part of college. I just wanted us to be able to live our life without my parents shadowing us

Lex: They did anyway

Hudson: I know that now. I thought living away would give me the space I needed but realized that wasn't the case

Lex: Well, yea you're still working for your dad

Hudson: I know, I know. I was naive and hopeful

Lex: I can understand that

Hudson: So dinner when I arrive. I'll let you know the exact day I get into town when I'm sure. Tristan showed up unexpectedly, so he'll be heading to Hartville for Christmas too

Lex: Wow, I don't think I've seen him since he graduated high school

Hudson: I know. It's good to have him home for a bit

Lex: I bet. Enjoy your time with him

Hudson: Thanks Lex. I'll talk to you soon

Smiling, I set my phone down again and work to a different tune. Knowing I'll see Lex in a couple of weeks makes things look brighter. I plan to make this an unforgettable date and

MEET AGAIN

prove myself to her. I also have two weeks to figure out my next steps if I want a future with her. Hopefully, Tristan can provide some perspective.

14
LEX

I HANG UP THE phone and stare at the screen full of apps. I can't believe what just happened. I stand and dance around, still in shock but full of excitement. When I saw a call from a random number, I hesitated to answer because who wants to get stuck rejecting a telemarketer? It's always awkward, and then I feel bad if I have to hang up on them.

But with the dance studio, I've learned to answer any call that comes in. It had been a while since I had spoken to Michelle, a girl I danced with growing up, though we always kept each other updated in our careers. She went on to dance professionally and later switched paths to teaching at a prestigious school.

It turns out that she's organizing a big dance conference for dance students, and she asked if I'd want to teach one of the classes. They expanded the conference last minute, adding some extra classes.

She also mentioned that there would be workshops for dance teachers with new choreography trends that I'm more than welcome to participate in if I'm interested. As if I'd turn that chance down. SIGN. ME. UP.

This will be an amazing opportunity for my growth as a dancer and teacher and for the studio. It will expand our name and prestige and hopefully give my girls a chance to make it to one of these schools if they aim for that. I know Sarah would die for a chance to attend a school of the arts that will open doors for her to perform professionally.

An e-mail notification pops up on my phone from Michelle, and I read its contents before opening the conference program. Michelle originally thought of me to teach about small business dance studios and how to combine a passion for dancing with teaching and running a business. I'll also have a chance to teach a ballet choreography to the group.

I have a month to prepare before I travel to New York. The irony isn't lost on me. Hudson would get a kick out of hearing this, but this conference is one weekend. My life and career are in Hartville. I can't lie, though. Being in New York with the possibility of seeing him and his life in the city makes my curiosity spike.

First, I need to get through dinner with him when he's here for Christmas. My stomach flutters. I've been secretly giddy about seeing him since he mentioned he'd be back for the holidays. Hudson makes me feel that way, no matter how much I may try to avoid it. I think I'm past the point of hiding it, but I have to tread carefully. Our path has been covered in a land mine, and I don't want this chance to explode in our faces.

Checking the time, I jump in the shower and get ready to head to the studio. If I need to come up with a full choreography in a month, I need to get to work right away. This choreography needs to blow their minds. It's my chance to prove myself outside of my hometown.

A small piece of me feels as if I need to do this to show others I didn't settle with teaching. I got asked many questions when I was younger. There were rumors that I decided to teach because I wasn't accepted to any school. People like to stir drama, and I normally stay in my lane because I know the truth in my heart.

But I won't lie... It'd be great to prove to them my worth, especially the Remingtons, who tried to ruin my chances.

Once I'm in the studio, I turn on the music and just feel the beats, allowing my body to guide me as I relax and clear my mind.

Dancing has always been my safe place to land, the thing I do when I need to gain perspective, feel free, or escape from the real world. It's my haven.

As I dance, different steps come to me, and I jot them down in my notebook. Repeating them, I get a feel for the choreography, changing things around.

I feel like I'm on top of the world. I squeal and turn in circles. My cheeks hurt from smiling so much. Alexa Leon has her groove back—professionally and, dare I say, romantically.

Changing back into my jeans and sweater, I head out for lunch before opening the studio. My steps are light as I walk through town toward the diner. Happiness pulses through me as I smile and wave at people I pass on the sidewalk.

"Hey!"

I smile and look at Hope. "Hi, are you on lunch break?"

"Yup, are you? Want to grab lunch together?"

"Diner?" I smile.

"That's where I'm headed. I thought you'd be home." We walk side by side.

"I was at the studio, actually."

MEET AGAIN

"In the morning? You're normally there in the morning later on in the month. Well, I guess it is December, so the end of the month is holiday season." She's rambling with her face scrunched up as if trying to figure out my schedule.

"Oh..." I turn and find a disgusted expression staring at me.

"Hello, Mrs. Remington," Hope says to divert her attention.

"Hope, so lovely to see you." She gives her one of her infamous polite smiles. "You must tell me where you're registered. I asked Hudson, but you know how men are. He hasn't told me yet." Her eyes slide to mine.

"Or he's been too busy with the wrong people."

I clench my teeth and take a deep breath. *Ignore her. Ignore her. She's not worth it.*

"Mrs. Remington, I appreciate you asking, but as you can see, I'm busy right now with my *best friend*. Once we're registered, you'll hear from us the same as everyone else." I gawk at Hope's response and stare in awe at her courage to speak up.

Why do the Remingtons always mute me?

"Of course," her smile is now fake as she walks away.

"I can't stand her," I say.

"I know. Ignore her. Tell me what you were up to." Hope thankfully changes topics.

"Let's sit, and I'll tell you." I open the door to the diner, and we grab an empty table.

"So mysterious. Spill." Hope raises her eyebrows.

"I got a call from someone I danced with. She asked if I'd be interested in teaching a class at a huge dance conference she's organizing next month."

"No way," Hope exclaims with wide eyes. "That's amazing, Lex. Congrats." She reaches over the table and hugs me.

I laugh and lean back. "I know. I'm so excited. I can also take a class if I want, which will be amazing. I'm teaching about opening your own dance studio and balancing business and teaching. Then, I'll teach them a choreographed routine, so I went into the studio to start working on it. I want it to be amazing." I clutch my hands together.

"It will be," Hope says with conviction.

"I'm so excited. It's a weekend conference with amazing classes and workshops." My face is bright with a smile.

"I'm so proud of you." Hope shakes her head in awe. "Where is it? In Dobson?" She asks about the closest city to us.

I shake my head and press my lips together. When I scrunch up my nose but remain quiet, Hope furrows her eyebrows and asks, "Well?"

"New York."

"No way." She slaps the table, laughing boastfully. "This is hilarious."

"Shush," I slap her arm.

"I'm sorry, I'm sorry." She waves her hand, drying under her eyes. "It's just...wait 'til Hudson finds out."

"Hope!" I chastise in a whisper-hiss. The couple at the table next to us look at me with raised eyebrows and a knowing smile.

"Can you not be so loud?" I glare at her.

"Sorry," she looks at me with amusement.

"I think it's great, though. Maybe you could stay at his place." She waggles her eyebrows.

"I am not staying at his place. I'll book a room at the hotel closest to the school where the conference is taking place."

"Things can change by then. I hear you're having dinner with him when he comes to town." She crosses her arms and arches a brow. "I can't believe you didn't tell me," her voice is accusing.

"How did you find out? Also, I agreed to it the other day and hadn't seen you."

MEET AGAIN

"Is your phone broken?" She shakes her head. "Toby told me because, unlike you, Hudson told his best friend."

"Ugh," I toss my head back.

"Are you ready to order?" A waitress comes by and drops two glasses of water.

"Yes, please." I thank the universe for the interruption. "I'll have the grilled chicken with mashed potatoes."

"I'll have the roast turkey sandwich," Hope orders.

When the waitress walks away, she looks at me.

"Dinner then, huh?"

"Yeah," I sigh. "I don't know what I'm doing or why I agreed to it, but..." I pause, trying to collect my thoughts.

"You still care about him and want to spend time with him," Hope finishes for me.

I nod in silence.

"You have nothing to lose. It was clear something still lingers between you two. I will say, if things work out, you owe Toby and me since we practically brought you back together." She waves her hand with an air of superiority. She could fit in with royalty with that move.

"You forced him on me," I deadpan.

"Force, brought...potato, potahto." She shrugs, taking a sip of water from her straw.

I roll my eyes and chuckle.

"I'm only teasing you," Hope smiles.

"I know. I'm confused, to be honest, but I want to see him," I confess.

"I'm glad you're listening to yourself." Her eyes soften, making me feel more confident in my decision.

"Yeah, figured I'd know best." I shrug.

"I agree."

"How's the house-hunting going?" I switch topics, wanting to catch up on her life as well.

Hope screws her face and shakes her head. "Not good. Hudson is supposed to have some properties lined up for us to see when he comes into town."

"Hopefully, you'll find something you love soon." I know how stressful house buying can be. It took me a bit to find the house I loved, and I moved heaven and earth to get it—with a little sprinkle from my Fairy Godmother, AKA my parents, who helped me a bit.

"From your mouth to God's ears," Hope sighs.

Our food arrives, and we talk about the wedding, my ideas for the workshop, and Christmas plans. Every year my friends and I get together before Christmas to celebrate. I have no doubt that Hudson will join us this year since he'll be in town, and I hope it's smooth sailing.

It's as if he's suddenly full-blown back in my life. The scary thing is how effortlessly it's been. Our first encounter was rocky, and the following few times, too, but after that, things changed. And Thanksgiving was definitely a turning point.

So much for channeling Lorelai Gilmore. Here I am, opening up to my ex. Actually, maybe I channeled her too well. I just hope Hudson and I end up better than she and Christopher did.

"I'm glad we had lunch together," Hope says as we stand outside of the diner.

"Me too. You're getting married soon and won't have time for your best friend." I pout exaggeratedly.

"Oh, please," Hope rolls her eyes.

"I'm only kidding." I hug her tightly. "It's going to be the best new chapter of your life," I whisper before pushing back.

"I know, but I'll always have time for my best friends."

MEET AGAIN

"How jealous will Ellie be that she missed out on lunch?" I tease.

"So jealous. Let's take a selfie and send it to her." Hope laughs, holding her phone up. The photo is blurry since we're both laughing, but she types out a message and sends it to Ellie in our group chat.

"Can't wait to see her response. Gotta go before my boss comes searching for me," Hope jokes.

I blow her a kiss and walk back to the studio while she heads back to work at Town Hall. Our lives are changing, but one thing that is certain is that our friendship is rock solid. I'm glad I have such amazing friends to live these experiences with.

If it weren't for Hope and Ellie, I don't know how I would've overcome my break-up with Hudson or the drama I went through with his parents when I was acquiring the studio. We've always been there for each other, and that's priceless.

As I'm getting ready to open the studio, my phone pings with a message. Smiling at what Ellie's response will be, my heart skips a beat when I see Hudson's name instead of hers. Goodness, I'm reacting like a teen in love.

Hudson: Hey, how are you?

Lex: Good and you?

Hudson: Good, good. I'll be in town next week

Lex: Wow already?

Hudson: Lol don't sound so surprised. Besides you already agreed to dinner so no backing out

Lex: Just thought you'd be here the following week closer to Christmas

Hudson: I have some work to do in the area and some showings for Toby and Hope

Lex: I heard

Hudson: You talking about me?

Lex: No. Hope brought it up at lunch today

MEET AGAIN

Hudson: You wound me

Lex: I try

Hudson: Lol you still have the same sarcastic humor

Lex: You bring it out

Hudson: I'll take that as a compliment

Lex: Whatever you want

Hudson: So dinner when I get back. You and me, no excuses. I arrive on Wed. Are you free Thurs?

Lex: I close the studio at eight. Why don't we do Saturday?

Hudson: Because I don't want to wait to see you

I stare at his message while my heart thunders. Is he serious? Could it be that Hudson never got over me either? All this time, I was sure he had moved on, found someone else who would fit his lifestyle, and be accepted by his parents.

Hudson: Hello? Did I lose you?

Lex: Sorry no. I'm here. Thursday works

Hudson: Good. I can't wait to see you, Lex

Lex: Yea...

Hudson: "I can't wait to see you either, Hudson"

MEET AGAIN

Hudson: Wow thanks. I'm so glad you're also excited

Lex: Ha-ha

Hudson: Don't ruin my fantasy

Lex: Never

Hudson: I'll see you Wed

Lex: Thursday

Hudson: Sure, whatever you think *wink emoji*

I roll my eyes, but a huge smile has conquered my face. He's definitely making it a point to show me he's thinking about me, and I love every second of it. It doesn't erase the pain of the past, but holding resentment only makes me miserable. I now have no doubt he'll show up at the studio on Wednesday. The idea of seeing him sooner than I thought makes my entire body buzz, and butterflies fly rampant in my belly.

I was naïve if I thought I could see Hudson again and not feel an ounce of emotions. If I thought I could look at him in the eyes and feel indifference. I've always been weak when it comes to him, and I don't hate it. He gets me. At least, he used to get me. If he's back in my life, I owe it to myself to see if there's something deep that still sits between us.

Lex, you're in deep trouble. If I feel this way after a few text message conversations and a dance in the snow, once he brings out his charms, I'll be putty in his hands.

"Alexa, turn off these feelings," I call out in the studio and drop my head against the wooden barre in the dance room.

"I can't find a device under the name These Feelings," Alexa responds like the trained AI she is, but even she can't find a solution to the mess in my head. Considering we have the same name, it's like I'm talking to myself. I laugh at her response and shake my head.

I scramble when I hear a knock on the door and move toward it to unlock it.

"Sorry, I was working in the back and lost track of time," I lie as my first student walks in. Switching mindsets, I go into teacher mode and get to work.

My students were already gossiping about Hudson and me at Thanksgiving. No need to fuel them and their parents' ideas by daydreaming. Small-town charm equals small-town gossip.

15
HUDSON

I'VE BEEN WAITING THREE weeks to see Lex again. I plan to spend the next few weeks making up for lost time and showing her I'm serious about us. I stayed away for a long time because I thought it was for the best. After seeing her again and reconnecting, I realized how foolish it was.

"Are you going to see her tonight?" Tristan asks when we get to the inn. The drive up here felt eternal, but I'm glad my brother kept me company.

"Yeah." I carry my bag up the stairs beside him.

"I thought you were having dinner tomorrow." He smirks knowingly.

"We are, but I want to see her today." I've never been one to hide my feelings, always opting to express myself than care what others will think.

"Good luck," he chuckles.

"I don't need luck." I shake my head.

"Cocky much?"

"Nah, just confident enough. I know she feels this." I unlock my room door and look at my brother before walking in.

"Are you going to see Mom and Dad tonight?" He's avoided my questions about them.

"Nope. I'll wait until tomorrow. I'll walk around town tonight and grab a bite to eat. It feels good to be home."

I lift my brows, surprised by his words. Tristan prefers to travel the world than spend time in Hartville. He chuckles and shrugs.

"What? It's nice to come home every once in a while. It grounds me to my roots."

"It does." I nod. "If you need anything, call me. Not sure I'll eat with Lex, so maybe we can grab dinner if not."

"Sounds good." He opens his door. "Good luck, bro." He winks and walks into his room.

Luck. I don't think I need luck. If Lex knows me like I think she does, she wouldn't be surprised to see me at the studio tonight. I hinted as much in our messages. I may have asked her to dinner tomorrow, but I won't pass up a chance to see her sooner.

I set my bag on the bed and unpack to kill some time before heading over to the studio. As I walk, the cold air slices through my cheeks, and my breath puffs like smoke. I'd walk in freezing temperatures without the proper clothing if it meant I'd see Lex at the end.

I stop outside of the studio. Moms sit inside the waiting area looking through the glass where the last class is finishing up. I smile as I see glimpses of Lex through the window. She's talking to the girls with a wide smile. To think that I wanted her to give this up so she could live with me in New York. It would've been a terrible mistake.

My eyes scan down the length of her body. Her leotard and leggings show off her curves, and I want to run my hands down them, re-memorizing every inch. She's stunning.

Her eyes collide with mine, and I'm taken aback. The chocolate brown orbs stare into me as if they could see my soul. I smile and wink, watching her attempt to refocus on her students.

Thankfully, she finishes soon after because my patience is wearing. As people start to walk out of the studio, I watch Lex's movements through the window. People look at me with raised eyebrows. I guess the rumors are still turning.

I sneak in after the last person has left and smile as I walk past the waiting room into the dance room. Lex looks over at me with an arched eyebrow.

"What are you doing here?" She cocks her hip and tilts her head.

"What?" I ask with innocence. "Didn't we make plans to see each other today?"

"Nope." Lex shakes her head, her attempt to hide her smile futile.

"Darn, I must've gotten confused." I scratch the side of my head where my hat ends.

"Likely." She nods.

"Hmm…nope, I don't think so. It's coming back to me now. We spoke. I told you I'd see you on Wednesday. You tried to correct me by saying Thursday, but I assured you it wasn't a mistake. So, here I am on Wednesday," I open my arms wide.

Lex giggles, shaking her head. When her teeth bite down on her bottom lip as she smiles, I walk closer to her.

"I wanted to see you."

Her eyes round, her breath hitching. I reach for her hand and stroke my fingers against her knuckles. Lex shivers. I turn her hand over, caressing her palm before linking our fingers together. It's like my pieces have snapped back into place.

"Hey."

"Hi," she whispers.

"How are you?" I stand closer.

"Good. How was your trip?"

"Never-ending. I thought I'd never make it back and see you."

"You exaggerate." She rolls her eyes.

"It felt eternal. I kept thinking about you, and it made the trip seem slower. Thankfully Tristan kept me distracted." My free hand smooths up the side of her neck and rounds the back of her head. I tug her to me, kissing her forehead.

My eyes close as I breathe her in, risking her rejection. Instead, Lex leans into me and sighs. When I lean back, I stare into her eyes and bring my hand to cup her face, stroking her cheek with my thumb. I want to take her lips in mine and remind her how good we are together.

Instead, her stomach growls, causing me to laugh.

"Oh, my goodness." Lex steps back, breaking the contact and hugging her stomach. Her cheeks burn with embarrassment.

"It's okay." I continue to laugh.

It growls again, and she widens her eyes before looking away.

"Goodness," she mumbles.

"I've got a great idea. Let's grab something to eat and fill that belly." It's the perfect opportunity, and I plan to grab it by the horns.

"How'd I know you'd say that?" She laughs.

"Because you know me well," I smirk.

She takes a deep breath, her smile dropping.

"I did know you well. Do I still? I don't know." She shakes her head, moving around the dance room.

"Have dinner with me and make your own judgment. I'll behave and won't try to sway your opinion." I keep my face straight.

"Right, since when have you never pushed the envelope a bit?" She raises an eyebrow.

"You see," I clap and smile. "You *do* still know me. I'm the same guy, Lex." I open my arms.

"Well, that's not true. I have gotten more handsome and a bit stronger," I flex my muscles. "The scruff is new, too." I run a hand along my jaw.

"I've noticed," she mumbles and snaps her wide eyes to mine.

I guffaw, closing the gap between us. "I heard that."

"I didn't mean to say it out loud." She shakes her head, crimson once again flushing her face.

"Want to know a secret?" I whisper, standing toe-to-toe.

"What?" Her question is quiet.

"I've also noticed your changes, and I like them all." I wrap my arm around her waist, tugging her to me. She rolls her eyes up to look at me. "All of them," I emphasize, my voice deeper than usual. When our bodies become flush, she gasps in surprise at my bold move.

Taking the chance, I capture her warm lips with mine in a soft kiss. Lex sighs, bringing one of her arms around my back. It's chaste at first—a simple reconnection—then, it deepens. I thought I'd never have her in my arms again. When I'm with her, everything feels right. I forget about my family, my job, the pressure I'm under. Peace surrounds me in her presence.

"Whoa..."

The female voice that just said that hits me like a bucket of ice water. I step back, and Lex freezes, staring over my shoulder.

"I'm sorry. I seem to have walked into the past. Like, four years ago. Who knew I could time travel?"

I turn and see Ellie smiling at us.

"Although, I will say I approve." She points at us.

"Hey," Lex says, her lips pressed into a straight line. "What are you doing here?" Her voice is tight.

"Not meaning to interrupt this moment. I saw the light on and thought I'd say hi, but you were already greeted in a much better way." She shimmies her shoulders, and a deep laugh escapes me.

"Goodness..." Lex tosses her head back and stares at the ceiling.

"No worries, I'll let you get back to whatever this is." Her finger wiggles between us. "Maybe lock the door, though."

"I'm going to get changed." Lex turns around but stops and looks at me. It seems as if she wants to say something but instead shakes her head and disappears into the back room.

"So..." Ellie waggles her eyebrows. "Working your magic?"

"Uh..."

"Don't get shy on me now, Hudson. Just know, if you hurt my girl again, I've got a collection of shotguns that I'm not afraid to use. I could get some target practice in, now that I think about it." She turns her head, staring off as if thinking about it.

"No need," I say quickly.

"Good, good." She nods, staring at me. "She had it rough when you two broke up. Be sure that you won't leave her again before you drag her along."

"I'm not dragging her along, Ellie." I cross my arms and turn to look at her straight on.

"I hope not."

"I hurt, too. She wasn't the only one," I defend.

"Sure, I believe that, but you went on to experience a new chapter of your life while she stayed here questioning her worth."

"What?" I furrow my eyebrows.

"You didn't hear it from me," Ellie sighs and looks over my shoulder, likely making sure Lex isn't within earshot.

"She thought she wasn't good enough. She couldn't compete against your family, no matter your differences with them, and that affected her. Your actions went against everything you told her."

I scrub a hand down my face. "I know," I confess. "I never meant for it to happen that way."

"I believe that, but it doesn't take away that it did." Ellie squeezes my arm. "Just be sure you can keep your promises this time around."

"I'm working on it." I nod, feeling all the happiness from earlier deflate like a saggy balloon.

"Good. I'm gonna go. Tell Lex I'll call her later."

"Okay, see you, Ellie."

"Bye." She waves and walks out of the studio, leaving me with bombarding thoughts and guilt.

I need to right the past before Lex and I can move forward. No more impulse kisses until she knows how much I care about her. I don't want what happened to linger as resentment between us. It's easy to get caught up in her, but I need to make it a point to work through it.

"Did Ellie leave?" Lex returns in jeans and a sweater. She shoulders a bag.

"Yeah, she said she'd call you later."

"Oh, okay." She shifts on her feet, looking everywhere but at me.

"You okay?"

"Yeah, great." Her smile is forced, but I drop it. I don't want to push her too forcefully. Spending quality time with her will allow me to bring up the past without being abrupt about it.

"Let's grab some dinner and feed that monster in your stomach," I tease with a wink.

"Ugh," she huffs out. "I've been dancing for hours. My lunch is long gone. No need to insult the monster." She pats her belly.

I chuckle and guide her out of the studio with my hand on the small of her back. We pause while Lex locks the door, and then we head to the diner. Ellie's words continue to run through my mind. The last thing I want is for Lex to think she isn't good enough for me. She was always too good for me, but I told myself I deserved her. If it weren't for my parents, who knew where we'd be today. We could be happy in love, never having experienced the pain of losing each other.

Unfortunately, that's not the case, and I can't throw all the blame on my parents. I was a player in the downfall of our relationship, but it hurts to hear that Lex questioned how amazing she is.

We sit at a table, and I look at her, reaching for her hand. Her eyes look between our hands and my eyes, her eyebrows lifted, and an amused smirk across her lips.

"People are whispering," she says.

"I don't care." I shrug and squeeze her hand, making a point that I'm not letting her go. Let the town talk.

"I want you to know that you were everything I ever wanted. I never doubted that and what happened between us had nothing to do with you and everything to do with me being an inconsiderate jerk."

Lex stares at me in silence.

16
LEX

"Say something." Hudson squeezes my hand as I continue to look at him, trying to gather my words.

"I…" I shake my head. "I wanted to be enough for you to stay, but I shouldn't have interfered in your career, either." We both are at fault in some way.

"A career I always told you I didn't want. I felt responsible for following in my family's footsteps, but I shouldn't have." He shakes his head.

"I just despise that you let go of your dreams for theirs when they don't really care. I know they're your parents, but I watched the disappointment on your face time and again as we grew up when they wouldn't show up for you or support you. You deserved better."

"I had better—you—and I threw it away." Hudson casts his eyes downward.

"Hey—Whoa…this seems intense."

What is it tonight with all the interruptions? First Ellie when Hudson and I were sharing our first kiss after all this time, and now…

I look up and jump to my feet.

"Tristan!" I hug him.

He laughs heartily and returns the hug. "Didn't expect you to be so happy to see me. I bet this is twisting the envy knife into Hudson's stomach right now. Let's make him a little more jealous."

I laugh and shove him playfully, looking at Hudson to find him with furrowed eyebrows. I sit back down and smile at Tristan.

"How are you?"

"I'm great. Came to make sure this guy behaves." He juts his thumb toward Hudson.

I chuckle and shake my head. "Always the same, Tristan."

"I refuse to change," he announces. "Can I sit? Are you guys on a date? I thought it wasn't until tomorrow."

"Told you I didn't need luck," Hudson tells him and winks at me.

I roll my eyes and look between them as Tristan takes the liberty to sit next to his brother.

"We were busy," Hudson says.

"Well, now you're busy with me." Tristan gives him a boyish grin. He may have grown up since the last time I saw him, but his personality is the same.

Hudson grumbles something under his breath and looks at me.

"Is it okay if he stays?"

"Of course," I smile.

"Great." Hudson sounds less enthusiastic.

"Don't worry, big bro," Tristan slaps Hudson's shoulder. "You won't have to compete for her attention. I'll let you have the spotlight."

I giggle at his jabs and look at Hudson. He lifts a brow and tilts his head, giving me an, *Oh, really,* look. I shrug and bite down my smile. That kiss from earlier still makes my body buzz. Having him in town again, knowing he came to see me when he arrived, makes me feel special. It's how Hudson always made me feel when we were younger, as if I were his entire universe. He was also mine.

Maybe it shouldn't have happened. It's a risk to my fractured heart, but Hudson has a way of wrapping me up in his charm, something I've fought against recently.

"How have you been?" I ask Tristan. I can't remember the last time I sat at a table with the Remington brothers. It's been years.

"I've been great, traveling and learning about life." He leans back in his seat. His hands clutch together and rest on the table.

"How about you? Finally opened the studio. It's great, Lex."

"Thanks. It's been…an experience." I nod slowly. There's no need to let them know the struggles I faced when acquiring the space. Hudson narrows his eyes and looks at me. I ignore his expression and smile.

"I'm glad you did." Tristan smiles. "So what are we gonna eat? I'm starving."

"Lex is starving, too," Hudson's eyes dance with amusement.

"Shush." I kick him under the table.

"I missed it…" Tristan looks between us.

"Nothing. Let's order, yeah?" I look at the menu. What I could really go for is a greasy, cheesy burger. My lunch was minimal, and I taught most of the classes today.

After the waitress takes our orders, I listen to Tristan tell us about his recent trip to Africa. It's fascinating to hear about different cultures and the way other people are helping less fortunate communities around the world.

"Are you returning to Africa after the holidays?"

"I'm not sure yet. I have a spot available if I decide to."

"Where will you go then?" Hudson turns to his brother, clear this is news to him.

Tristan shrugs and smiles. "Wherever the wind blows."

"You always were an adventurer." I smile at him.

"Someone needs to be the fun one in the family," he elbows Hudson and laughs.

"I'm fun, just don't have a need to pick up and leave every few weeks or months."

"You do have other things holding you in place." Tristan winks at me. Heat creeps up my cheeks, and I look down, clearing my throat.

"I do." Hudson's voice is serious.

I look up at him and find him staring intently at me. The heat in his gaze makes me freeze. The seriousness with which he looks at me penetrates my soul.

Thankfully, the waitress interrupts the intense moment to bring our food, and the mood shifts to something lighter. I tell them about the studio, my students, and my favorite classes to teach.

"Do you want my pickles?" I look at Hudson and then freeze.

His smile is wide and meaningful. That was a blast from the past. I used to always give him my pickles, and it just came out.

"You know I do."

"This is weird." Tristan looks at us, his eyebrows pulled together.

Hudson ignores him and pinches the round slices with his fork. I guess some things are engraved in our memories and difficult to break.

"Oh, is the rumor true?" Tristan's smile curves with mischief. He isn't as affected by our past quirks.

"What rumor?" I ask slowly, heart picking up pace at what it is he's going to bring up.

"That you're teaching at a huge conference next month?"

I glance at Hudson, then back at Tristan. "Yeah."

MEET AGAIN

"Wow, that's fantastic." He smirks. "How long will you be in New York?"

I knew it was coming. Leave it to him to stir things up. Hudson sits up straighter and looks at me.

"New York?" His eyebrows lift.

I was hoping to see how things went between us before I brought it up—not that I expect anything to happen just because we're in the same city. Honestly, I've been a mess thinking about it.

"Yeah," I nod awkwardly. "I got a call from a friend last week, and she invited me to teach a workshop, so I said yes. It'll be a great opportunity for the studio and hopefully my girls."

"When is it?" Hudson shifts in his seat, his attention captive.

"In a month." I glance at Tristan, who is smiling triumphantly. I glare at him, but he shrugs and continues to eat his burger.

"We'll talk more about it later," Hudson says with confidence.

"I'm so glad I got to witness this moment," Tristan chuckles, and I kick him under the table.

"Hey, now." He lifts his hands. "No need for aggression."

"That was hardly aggression," I roll my eyes.

"He was going to find out eventually. Who better than me to tell him?" He smiles, keeping his eyes on mine and ignoring Hudson.

"Me." I lift my brows.

"Ohhh...maybe, but it wouldn't have been this fun." Pride fills his face.

I shake my head at his meddling and risk a look at Hudson. He's still staring at me with an expression I can't quite pinpoint, but it makes my skin prickle.

ABI SABINA

The rest of dinner passes without any more meddling and some conversation. I know Hudson wanted to have dinner alone, but I'm glad Tristan joined us, even if he spilled the beans about the conference. It's been so long, and seeing the two of them interact makes me smile. They joke with each other and still act like best friends despite the way their lives have taken different paths.

"I'm sure I'll see you around." Tristan hugs me when we stand outside of the diner.

"It was good to see you." I smile at him.

Hudson grabs my hand and tugs me toward him, leading us away from the door.

"Were you going to tell me about this conference?" He arches a brow.

"Yes."

"Really?" He steps closer. "Because I recall you had time to do so earlier."

"I was distracted." Hudson's lips quirk, and I can't help but stare at them for a beat too long. I lift my chin and gaze into his eyes. My heart pounds, but I keep my confidence in check.

"By?" He tilts his head.

"You," I challenge.

His hand goes to my hip, squeezing me. I shiver and take a deep breath, chest shaking.

"Tell me about this conference. I want exact dates, your schedule, and where you're staying. I plan to take up every bit of free time you'll have." His breath tickles my ear.

My body fills with chills. This is what I knew would happen when he found out.

"It's three days. January thirteenth to the fifteenth. I'm driving down the twelfth since the conference begins early on the thirteenth." I love the way his body encases mine, keeping me warm from the cold night.

"We'll talk more about it tomorrow night. I'll pick you up for dinner."

"I'll have to go home and shower before. It'll be late." Every inch of my body is fluttering.

"I don't care the time. I'll be there." He bends his head and kisses my cheek.

My breath hitches, overwhelmed by this man and his closeness.

"Let me walk you to your car."

I nod and walk beside him, thankful there aren't many people out at this time in our town. Hudson's fingers tangle with mine. I never thought we'd be here again. Some things still confuse me and make me hesitate, but I am enjoying his company too much to put thought into it. I need to know if our situation was *the right guy at the wrong time* or just *the wrong guy*.

"Is eight-thirty okay to pick you up for dinner?" We stop by my car.

"It should be. I'll do my best to be ready by then." If I do my hair tomorrow morning, I can go home, take a quick shower, and change.

"Great." He reaches for the car door but keeps my other hand in his.

"I'll see you tomorrow." His lips gently brush my cheek, and I swoon like cartoons with hearts floating over their heads.

"Goodnight." I slide into my car and look at him before closing the door. Hudson stands on the sidewalk, watching me drive away.

Tomorrow is going to be interesting, especially after our kiss and neither of us denying our feelings. I can blame Alexa's lack of help on that one.

17

HUDSON

I'VE BEEN IN SUCH a good mood about my date with Lex that not even my father's constant badgering about work could ruin it. Being in the same place as him creates a different dynamic at work that I can ignore when I'm in New York. It's the same when he travels to New York to do some work. Things run smoother when he's not around trying to control everyone.

It doesn't help that he caught wind of the gossip floating around and tried to question me about Lex. I put a stop to it before he could give his opinion.

I knock on Lex's door with a wide smile. Excitement moves through me. I wanted tonight to be special, but due to the time, a restaurant in Hartville was the best choice.

Hartville isn't a tiny town, having a lot more options than other small towns I've visited, but it's not like New York, where restaurants are open late, and you can find something to eat at any hour of the night.

We're going back to Monroe's, where I first saw her at Toby's engagement party. I hope to make up for that reunion.

"Hey," Lex says when she opens the door.

I stare at her in silence, my eyes sweeping up and down her body. She's wearing a black and white floral long-sleeved short dress and thigh-high black boots.

"Aren't you going to be cold?" *Not the best opening, Hudson.*

MEET AGAIN

"I've got tights on and a coat." She smiles and reaches behind the door and pulls out a long black wool coat and scarf.

"Okay, good." I nod. Nerves cast a spell on me, muting me as if it were our first date ever. All my confidence has slipped away upon seeing her like a traveler in the desert when he reaches an oasis only to realize it's a mirage. Yeah, my confidence right now is as real as that mirage.

"Are you okay?" Her eyebrows pull together as she looks at me.

"Yup." I nod. "You just look stunning, and I forgot words."

Lex lets out a throaty laugh. She shakes her head and steps out the door, locking it.

"Come on, smooth operator."

I reach for her hand, kissing the top of it. "You do look beautiful. I was so confident here, and then I saw you, and I don't know…" I shake my head. "You took my breath away."

"You look handsome, too." Her smile is flirty.

"Thanks." I open the car door for her, starting to regain my composure. Once I'm in the car and pulling out of her driveway, I feel like myself again.

"How was your day?"

"It was good. I'm working double with planning my workshop for the conference, but it's all worth it."

I glance over at her quickly and see her smile is wider.

"That's exciting. You're talking about running your own studio, right?" I turn left and head toward Monroe's.

"Yeah." Lex shifts in her seat. "I'm also teaching a choreographed routine. It has to be something simple enough to teach in three days, but that leaves an impression. I hope this opportunity expands my business and helps my students get their name out there for their future."

"I'm sure it will. You've always been talented."

"Thank you." She bends her head, her long hair falling from behind her ear and covering part of her face. Blindly, I reach and put it behind her ear. I may be driving, but I still want to see glimpses of her gorgeous face.

"How was your day?" Lex doesn't comment on my move, but I felt her shiver.

"It was good. Same ole, same ole, to be honest. Although, I did take Hope and Toby to look at some houses."

"How did that go?" The leather in my car creaks when she shifts.

"It was okay. They haven't found something they love yet, but I'm hopeful that we'll find something after the holidays. The Hartville housing market is tricky." I stop at a red light and look at Lex. Her face glows from the street lights shining in through the car window.

"I'm sure they will." Her eyes scan my face, and I wonder what thoughts are crossing her mind.

"The light's green," Lex says, breaking our contact. "Where are we going, by the way?"

"Monroe's," I smirk at her.

"Risky," her voice holds a hint of amusement.

"Wanted to make up for our first re-encounter." I reach for her hand and squeeze it.

"I do love that place."

"I know, so I figured we'd switch out that sour experience for a memorable one." I open her fingers and link mine with hers.

"Memorable, huh?"

"Yup."

"You're too confident about that."

"Now that I've composed myself after seeing you, I am," I nod firmly. "We have history, Lex. Good and bad, but I hope

MEET AGAIN

that the good outweighs the bad and allows us to begin this new chapter on a positive note."

"Me too," she whispers.

We arrive, and I park, walking over to open the door for her. I hold my hand out, and Lex takes it without hesitation as I help her out of the car. As soon as I give the hostess my name, we're seated at a table. The restaurant is dim, and some tables are taken, but it isn't full, so we have privacy.

"I know you'll be busy while in New York, but I'd love to see you. I want to show you around and give you a glimpse of my life there." I hold my breath, knowing this is a touchy subject for us.

"I'll have to double-check the schedule."

"I doubt you'll be at the conference around the clock." I raise my eyebrows.

"No, but I can't tell you an exact time." She cocks her head and leans back on her chair.

"Fair enough." I nod and look at the menu. "Would you like some wine?"

"Yeah, that'd be great."

"What do you like?" I look up at her. She's scanning the menu.

"Do you like Merlot?" Her warm eyes meet mine.

"Perfect," I nod and lift my hand to signal the waiter.

"This feels a little weird, right?" Lex giggles.

"I think it feels right. I've missed you, as I've said before. I know I have a lot to prove to you, and our living situation hasn't changed, but I'm looking at all aspects of my life and figuring out what I want." I confess and reach for her hand across the table.

"What does that mean?" Her voice trembles.

"I'm not sure yet, but what I'm certain about is that I regret leaving you. I let my anger push me away from my parents so I could distance myself from their control, and it ultimately broke us." I shake my head, frowning.

Lex nods in silence, eyes looking down at the table. The waiter brings our bottle of wine, serving us each a glass. I thank him and smile.

"Let's talk about the present." She finally looks at me after the waiter's left.

"Good idea," I smirk. "Cheers." I lift my glass. When she does the same, I tap mine to hers and take a sip. My eyes train on the slope of Lex's neck as she tilts her head back to drink her wine. Smooth skin I dream of kissing.

"Are you enjoying having Tristan here? I hadn't seen him in so long, but it doesn't seem as if he's changed much." Lex chuckles. She's oblivious to my daydreaming, and I clear my throat.

"I am. I think it had been about a year and a half since I saw him."

"That long?" Her eyes widen.

"I know, it's crazy. He's been traveling and moving around so much that he barely comes this way. I can't say I blame him. I'd rather not have to deal with our parents after picking up and leaving against their wishes." Tristan took a huge risk knowing he wouldn't return to my parents' house.

"Wow. I bet you are happy to see him, then, especially for the holidays."

I nod. I'm not very forthcoming with my emotions at times, but that doesn't take away from the fact that I miss having my brother around and am glad we're spending time together—even when I get annoyed that he interrupts an impromptu date like last night.

MEET AGAIN

"Are you ready to order?" The waiter stops by our table.

"Oh." Lex's eyes widen.

"Can you give us a minute? We got distracted talking." I wink over at Lex.

"Of course," he nods and turns away, unimpressed yet polite.

"I should know what I want since I love this restaurant, but I always get torn between a few dishes." I watch her scan the menu with her nose scrunched up. This woman is perfect in my eyes. I can't help but continue to imagine what our life would have been like had we stayed together.

Days of making memories and nights spent loving her. We could have been married by now.

"I'm going to have the barbecue pork ribeye." I rest my menu on the table and grab my wineglass.

"That's so good here. I'm going to have the bourbon maple chicken breast. I haven't had that in a while." She practically drools.

"It's like you're more excited about the food than me," I tease.

"I kinda am," she shrugs apologetically. "Don't take it personally, but I need to feed the monster." She pats her stomach.

"I've heard the complains it makes," I chuckle. "No offense taken."

"Hey!" She taps my leg under the table much like she did last night. I like this playful side of her that isn't guarded or measured. It reminds me of how we were in the past, and it gives me hope that we can regain that part of ourselves.

"Everyone's stomach growls," she defends.

"I agree. Yours just likes to protest a bit louder." I wink and chuckle when the toe of her boot collides with my shin.

"Ouch." I reach down and grab her ankle.

My fingers hold her foot in place before smoothing up her leg just below her calf. I stroke my thumb along the backside of her leg. Her boot hides her skin from me, but her eyes burn into mine. The look on her face tells me my touch affects her despite the layers of material.

I slide my hand back down, giving her ankle a squeeze before releasing it. Lex's lips are parted, her chest rising unevenly. I want to kiss her again, soak up all that she has to offer. She's my fuel, my energy, my everything. How did I let her go so easily? How did I let my anger interfere with what we had? Why did it take me so long to see her again?

I'm kicking myself for not going back to her on my knees and begging for forgiveness sooner, but I didn't see a solution to our problems back then. I won't make the same mistake twice.

Lex clears her throat and takes a drink of wine. Her chest is flushed.

"Anyway, I bet your stomach is also a loud monster when you're hungry."

"Wouldn't you like to find out." I waggle my eyebrows.

A boisterous laugh moves through her. Lex's hand lands on her chest as her body shakes with humor.

"That makes zero sense," she shakes her head while still laughing.

"I don't know. It sounded better in my head," I defend.

"Jokes were never your strong suit." She continues to laugh.

"I did have other strong suits." I lift my brows.

"You did," she nods, all trace of humor leaving her.

"One of my strongest suits was..." I take a drink of wine, prolonging the anticipation of what I'll say, making her squirm.

"Loving you," I finally add. The look on Lex's face turns serious, her eyes sad.

"I can't argue with you on that. I always did feel loved with you."

I tangle our fingers again and stare into her eyes. "You were easy to love." Seeing her again, spending time together, I realize that she's still easy to love. She's still the same person. I hope she still sees the same in me despite the choices I made.

"What are you doing for Christmas?"

I don't comment on her abrupt change of subjects and smile. "I'm not sure. Tristan and I will have dinner."

"With your parents," she adds.

"Not sure," I shrug. "I don't think a Remington family reunion should happen on Christmas. I'd like to still enjoy this holiday in the future, and that would likely ruin it for me."

"Hudson." Lex tilts her head.

"It's true." I'm not blind to my family's dynamic. "In all honesty, I wouldn't be surprised if my parents have a trip planned they didn't tell us about."

"Well... You could come have dinner with us. The both of you." I caress the soft skin on her hand with my thumb. Her invitation fills me with a gentle emotion I haven't felt in a long time.

"I don't know. I don't want to impose."

"My parents would love it." Her lips twist to the side.

"They did invite me over for flan on Thanksgiving," I wink. "But would you? Love it?"

"The idea is growing on me." She turns my hand over and traces the lines on my palm. The tickling sensation fills me with want. Desire to have her be mine again, to share our lives together, to spend quiet evenings in our own home. All things I always thought we'd experience.

"I'll talk to Tristan," I nod.

"Let me know what you decide so I can tell my parents and make sure my mom makes enough flan to satisfy your sweet tooth."

"I will, but please make sure it's okay with them first." I close my fist around her fingers.

"Okay," she breathes out.

"Are you ready to order?" The waiter returns. He must've noticed our interaction and given us more time than necessary before interrupting our date. I'm grateful for his intuitive nature.

"Yes," I nod.

We each place our orders, and he takes the menus, leaving us once again alone. I refill our wine glasses and grin at Lex. I've got the most beautiful date.

"Is there something specific you want to see while in New York? It'll be your first time visiting the city."

"I don't know. I spent so much time resenting the place that I need to take a step back and look at it through different eyes."

"Do you trust me?"

Her face screws, and I clutch my chest in pain.

"You wound me." I fall back in my seat and dramatize my reaction.

"Let me plan an evening," I say after she's finished giggling.

"Okay," she nods, giving me the green light. I plan to make her trip unforgettable, but first, I need to win her over during the holidays.

18

LEX

My date with Hudson on Thursday was great. More than great. Fantastic, amazing, dreamlike. It was so easy to fall back into how we were with each other. We've had two months to slide into this since I saw him at the engagement party, and he's been persistent in getting together. That's one quality he definitely hasn't lost. Hudson and persistence go together like Oreos and peanut butter (don't judge—it's an amazing combo).

I never thought my heart would stop hurting enough to give him another chance, yet he makes my heart beat to a different tune.

I turn on the lights in the studio and lock the door behind me. Although it's Saturday, I need to work on my workshop presentation and choreography. Tonight I have a Christmas gathering with my friends, and Hudson will be there. It'll be like our re-debut because I know he's going to make it a point to show everyone that there's something brewing between us.

Fingers crossed, I'm not awkward about it, especially since we haven't discussed our relationship status, which is totally fine since we're still getting reacquainted without the whole resentment issue creating a barrier.

Clearing my mind, I look at my notes and practice what I have choreographed so far. I get lost in the steps and movements until I'm sweaty and breathless. Once I turn off the music, I notice a knocking sound. My steps guide me to the front of the studio. Hudson stands on the other side of the glass door, trembling and holding coffee. My heart skips a beat.

"Hey, sorry." I step aside for him to enter after unlocking the door.

"Hey, it's okay. I should've known you wouldn't hear me." He stomps his boots on the rug at the entrance. The snow is all dirty already, what I hate about it, but I'll take any type of snow.

"It's nice and warm in here. I brought you some coffee and a snack since I know you get sucked into dancing and lose track of time." His smile is dazzling and brightens his eyes.

"Thank you." I reach for the cup he hands me. "Come on." I lead him to the dance room and smile when he toes off his boots before stepping inside.

"I don't have chairs here. Think you can handle sitting on the floor?" I smirk.

"I may not be the most flexible person, but I was an athlete. I see your challenge." He removes his coat and drops to the floor ungracefully.

"Smooth," I giggle. "Were you outside for a long time?"

"Just a couple of minutes, so I guess it was good timing." He takes a drink of coffee. "Good, it's still hot."

I do the same, inhaling the comforting aroma. The caffeine bursts in my mouth, warming me from the inside.

"I brought you a blueberry muffin." He opens the paper bag.

"Yummy. Thanks for this." I lift the cup and reach into the bag for the muffin.

"Don't thank me. It was purely for selfish reasons."

"How so?" I tilt my head, stretching one of my legs out to the side. His eyes track my movement before lifting to my face.

MEET AGAIN

"Because I wanted to see you, especially after you turned down my dinner invitation last night." He arches a brow and gives me an intense stare.

"I was exhausted," I tell him the same thing I said yesterday. After a later-than-usual night on Thursday that ended with another amazing kiss at my doorstep and the extra work I've been doing for the workshop, I crashed hard yesterday when I got home.

"I know." He winks. "I'm only teasing you because I want to see you and want you to believe that I'm invested. I've learned from my mistakes." He leans forward a bit. It's almost a subconscious move.

"Well, I'll see you tonight."

"About that. Can I pick you up?" He takes a bite of his own muffin while he waits for my response.

"So we're going *together*?" I widen my eyes in meaning and fail at hiding my grin. I had a feeling he'd ask.

"You better believe it. I'm making a statement." A proud smile widens his mouth.

"And what statement is that?"

"That you're mine."

Butterflies swarm my belly upon hearing his words, and I can't help the warmth that fills me. It's definitely not from the coffee.

"What do you say?"

"I want to say yes," I admit, my heart thundering.

"Then say yes," he whispers, leaning forward again.

My body moves of its own accord until we're inches apart. His gaze flickers from my eyes to my lips, and I can smell his woodsy cologne from here.

"Argh!" He yells and jumps to his feet. "Sorry."

I look up in a daze, confused, until I find a wet coffee spot on the floor and on his jeans.

"How did that happen?" I shake my head.

"I don't know. The cup slipped from my hands, apparently."

I guffaw, falling back on the floor.

"Not funny," he grumbles.

I stand and grab napkins from the cupboard and hand them to him. I don't think wiping the wet spot on his thigh would be a good idea—just like it wasn't when the pie landed on him on Thanksgiving. My laughter continues to resonate around the space, especially after seeing how uncomfortable Hudson is.

"Thanks." He shakes his head.

"I'll clean the floor." I head into the bathroom, where I have the cleaning supplies stored as well. Most of the coffee landed on him, so the floor is a quick wipe.

Hudson's attempt at cleaning his jeans is not as successful.

"I should go change. Hopefully, this wet spot doesn't freeze on the way to the inn."

I laugh again, unable to hold it back. The brown spot is impossible to miss.

"Thankfully, I have a long coat." He looks down at it and back at me.

"I'm sorry, but it's hilarious."

"It would've been worth it if I had kissed you like I wanted to."

"Well, now, you would've dirtied my clothes, and I still need to finish working." I cross my arms and arch my eyebrow. I was also hoping for a kiss when we inched toward each other.

"How about a kiss now to make me feel better?" He pouts.

"You're ridiculous, trying to con me into a kiss." I roll my eyes.

"Will you at least be my date tonight? Even if I smell like a giant coffee?" He waves a hand down the front of his body.

"Hmm...I am a coffee lover." I step toward him, holding on to his biceps. His muscles flex as his eyes stare into mine.

"Yeah," he nods quietly.

Getting on my tip-toes, I press my lips to his cheek. "I'll see you tonight, Hudson." I step back and smile. The way he's looking at me gives me chills.

"Tonight, Lex. I'll pick you up at seven."

"I'll be ready," I wink.

"Are you nervous?" Hudson beams before knocking on Toby's door. His smile brightens his face. Joy radiates off him, and I suspect it's because of the statement we're about to make. Although, with the rumors going around town, our friends shouldn't be surprised. I mean, they're all my friends. It's not like I'm meeting Hudson's for the first time.

I wouldn't say I'm nervous, except I've got wild butterflies banging against my stomach. I'm excited to see my friends and unwind after some crazy couple of weeks. I'm happy to see Hudson. Combining those two things just makes for unknown expectations that give me a bit of the jitters. Of course, I won't admit that to Hudson.

"Absolutely not." I shoulder the canvas bag that's holding the baked brie I made.

He arches a brow and tilts his head incredulously.

"Fine," I sigh and drop my arms dramatically. "I'm not *nervous*. I'm...anxious." I scrunch up my face.

"Not helping the matter." He turns to look at me. Holding both of my hands, Hudson's eyes search mine.

"Is it because of us? Of course it is." He shakes his head. "You wouldn't be nervous to come to your friend's house otherwise."

"Yes. No. Uh...this isn't coming out right. What I mean is that I don't want to make a big deal about this." I signal between us with my chin since my hands are warm in his, and I don't want to break that contact.

"It is a big deal," he states matter-of-factly.

"Yeah, but I don't want everyone to make a big deal about it and put us in the spotlight. I want to have fun, spend time with my friends, and eat good food."

"And meet me under the mistletoe?" His eyes gleam.

I chuckle and turn my face to the side, biting my lip. Hudson holds my chin and angles my face back to his. "I love your smile. Don't hide it."

My breath hitches and I blink up at him.

"Don't stress about tonight. Ellie already caught us kissing. Tristan interrupted our date. Toby and Hope already questioned me when I took them house hunting. I'm pretty sure we won't give them a shock factor."

"I'm being ridiculous."

"A little, but I like it." He kisses the tip of my nose. "You're freezing." He knocks on the door with two firm taps, and it instantly opens with a smiling Hope standing on the other side. If I didn't know any better, I'd guess she was spying on us. Who am I kidding? Of course she was. It's Hope.

"Welcome, welcome." She winks at me.

"Hi, Hope." Hudson smiles at her.

MEET AGAIN

"Hey." I look at my best friend, who's staring at me with a crazed smile.

"So glad you're here...together." She waggles her eyebrows. Her squeal matches the crazed look.

Hudson chuckles, keeping his hand in mine.

"We are, too," Hudson says as we enter the house.

"We?" Hope's eyebrows shoot up as she stares at me. If it's possible, she's narrowing her eyes at the same time. She looks like she got a bad botox injection.

I'll be getting an interrogation soon. Hope will make it a point to sneak away with me tonight and ask me all the questions about information I haven't shared. I'll also get some smack for not running to her right away.

"Go on into the living room, Hudson. Lex, I need your help in the kitchen."

Darn, that was faster than I predicted.

"Sounds good." Hudson winks knowingly. He grabs the canvas bag from me and moves toward the living room.

"What in the world. Why haven't you called me and updated me on this?" Hope's voice is a shrill whisper, her eyes wide.

"I knew something was going on, obviously, but to show up together, holding hands, having him kiss your nose."

"I knew it! You were spying on us." I point at her.

"Of course I was. His lights showed through the window five minutes ago. I wanted to know what was taking so long."

"I don't want this to be the topic of conversation tonight. I want to have fun like we always do and allow things to flow."

"Okay, but I want details another day." She points at me and arches an eyebrow.

"I will give you that." I smile and squeeze her arm.

"I think it's great." She loops her arm in mine and leads us to the living room, not even bothering to go into the kitchen to keep up with her pretense. We all knew it was a coverup to get me alone.

"Hey! Where were you?" Ellie looks between Hope and me with crossed arms.

"I needed her help in the kitchen," Hope lies.

"Mmhmm... I could've helped, too." Ellie arches a brow and tilts her head unamused.

"You can help me next time," Hope nods with excitement and sits beside Toby on the sofa.

I roll my eyes and smile at Toby and Tristan. Everyone is sitting in the living room with appetizers spread around the coffee table.

The small house is decked out in Christmas decorations. Hope loves the holidays, so it doesn't surprise me one bit. Ever since we were kids, she's loved decorating. If she could keep her Christmas tree up year-round and decorate it according to the different holidays, she would.

"I grabbed you a glass of cider," Hudson grins.

"Thanks." I move around the living room to sit on the chair next to him.

"What a gentleman, that brother of mine," Tristan smirks.

"Where were you today?" Hudson asks him.

"I had to run some errands." Tristan's response is vague, but I shrug it off and look at Ellie.

"How's the ranch?"

"Ugh." She tosses her head back.

"What's wrong?" Toby asks.

Ellie scoops up a gooey piece of brie onto a cracker and shoves it in her mouth before responding. I look at Hope, who is equally confused. Running a dairy farm isn't easy work, but Ellie's family knows the business well.

After she's finished chewing, she looks at all the expectant eyes. "It's nothing major. Dairy farming isn't what it used to be, and the competition is stiff. But let's talk about something else, like you two arriving together." Ellie waves between us.

"We were coming to the same place, so I picked her up." Hudson keeps a straight face, but I can see the tips of his lips twitching.

"I was coming, too, and you told me to find my own ride." Tristan smiles crookedly.

"I told you if you were running late, to get another ride. You were off who knows where since you're vague-responding each time I ask you."

"And yet I arrived before you. Oh, the irony." Tristan smiles at me and winks. I can't help but laugh.

"How's the house hunt going?" I ask Hope and Toby. Apparently, we're all playing musical chairs with our topics of conversation to avoid what we don't want to talk about.

"Horrible." Hope shakes her head. "I love this house. It's cute and cozy," she smiles at Toby. "But it's small." Their two-bedroom house has one bathroom that isn't attached to the master bedroom, and it is tiny. I can understand why they'd want to upgrade to something bigger.

"We'll find the right place for us," Toby reaches for her hand.

"I know," Hope sighs, leaning into him. They have such a loving relationship.

A slow stroke tickles the back of my neck, right where the collar of my sweater stops. I peek toward Hudson and see him smile. His arm is draped behind my chair in a relaxing pose, but what no one can see is the way he's touching me. It's a featherlight caress that makes my skin tingle.

Without his coat on, I can see the way his beige sweater fits. It isn't tight, but the fabric stretches across his broad chest and biceps. His strong thighs are parted in that way men sit that takes up more space than necessary, and yet I'm not annoyed. His dark jeans frame his legs in a way that makes me sizzle.

He's so handsome. The last four years have helped him mature from a college guy to a man. I suspect a lot of that maturity also comes with practically running a real estate empire. Hudson doesn't have time to play around.

My friends talk around me, but I'm too focused on the goosebumps covering my skin from Hudson's strokes. He talks, keeping his cool, while he makes me feel like a puddle of goo. I never thought we'd be back in this place, and somehow this new chance excites me and feels different than it did back then.

It doesn't take away that his parents are still horrible people that like to make my life living torture.

"Are you okay?" Hudson leans in and whispers.

"Yeah." I nod. "Just got lost in my head." I turn to look at him, seeing worry reflecting in his eyes. I want to believe we can have a different outcome this time.

19
HUDSON

I'M NOT SURE WHAT thought crossed Lex's mind, but I'd rather have her shivering from my touch than tensing up. Instead of pushing, I pinch a toothpick in a meatball and pop it in my mouth. Toby is talking about a problem he had at work due to a mistake another accountant made, but my sole focus is on the woman beside me and thinking about how I can get her alone to steal a kiss.

"Excuse me." Lex stands and walks toward the hall that leads to the bathroom. It's like she read my mind.

"How's traveling?" Toby asks Tristan.

"It's great." Tristan goes on to tell them a story I've heard about five times already, so I stand and follow in Lex's footsteps. I wait outside the bathroom, and she jolts when she opens the door.

"Goodness, Hudson, you scared the bejesus out of me." She slaps my arm as I laugh.

"Sorry, didn't mean to. Are you okay? You said you were, but something's going on in that pretty head of yours." I circle my finger around her forehead.

Lex sighs and leans against the doorjamb. "I'm okay. I was just thinking, and my thoughts took an ugly turn, but I'm back to normal now." She smiles and holds her arms out.

"Tell me the ugly thoughts." I step closer until we're toe-to-toe. Wafts from her sweet perfume have been driving me crazy all night.

"I don't want it to get between us or ruin the night." She reaches for my hand and squeezes. "I'm okay. I'm happy and here with you."

My other hand goes to her waist.

"Are you sure?" I bend down to stare into those molten chocolate eyes.

"Positive."

"Good." I finally nod after seeing honesty swimming in her gaze. "Now, before we head back," I waggle my eyebrows and pucker my lips.

Lex giggles and leans up on her toes. Her warm lips press against mine, and I wrap my arm around her waist to keep her to me. Grateful I don't need mistletoe to kiss her, I allow myself to get lost in her.

She's so perfect. I'm determined to make her all mine again. Not just dates when I'm in town and text message conversations while I'm away—I want it all.

Lex slows the kiss and leans her head back, one of her hands squeezing my bicep. I release the hand she's holding and swipe the smeared lipstick from under her lip.

"You're gorgeous." I smile at her, eyes scanning every inch of her face.

"That kiss was..." She blinks her eyes as if she were in a daze.

"Dizzying?" I tease, seeing her reaction.

"Like I just stepped off a Tilt-A-Whirl."

I release a belly laugh and wrap my arms around her, kissing the top of her head. When she reaches around me and returns the hug, I sigh.

MEET AGAIN

"I hope I can keep making you dizzy. Just not so much that you feel you need to puke."

"Har, har." She looks up at me, her chin resting on my chest. I'm sure she can feel my pounding heartbeat. It's like a jackhammer making an entire house shake.

"This is okay, right? We are?" Her smile is small and nervous.

"Of course. I told you I'm not going to play games."

"But you're still your parents' son." Her nose scrunches. "Sorry. That was mean."

"They're mean." I shake my head and correct her. "I'm their son, but I'm not like them. Thankfully, my DNA doesn't match theirs when it comes to attitudes. You are what I want, what I've always wanted." I brush her hair away from her face so that I can get a clear view.

"Always been it," I whisper.

Her body sags against mine, and I tighten my hold.

"Let's go before they get the wrong idea." She steps back.

"As soon as you promise me, you're okay now." I lift my brows.

"Promise." She draws an X over her heart.

"Good." I drop a kiss on her forehead, and we head back to the living room.

All our friends pretend to look away, but they're not very good at acting. I chuckle under my breath and take my seat.

※※※

I knock on Lex's door and hope she doesn't mind my unannounced visit. After last night, I need to spend as much time with her as possible. She's been slowly letting me in, and I want to make sure I continue to knock down what's left of the walls keeping me from fully being in her life.

"Uhh..." Lex swings the door open. She's wearing a set of flannel pajamas that hide her curves, her hair's a knotted mess atop her head, and her eyes are swollen, and yet she looks beautiful.

"Hey." I slide my hands into my pockets and rock back on my heels.

"Hi." She clears her throat. "What are—"

"I wanted to know if you want to have breakfast." I beat her to it, interrupting her.

"Oh." She looks down at herself as if realizing she's in pajamas and back at me with her nose scrunched up.

"Did I wake you up?"

"No, I was awake, but my bed and I were having a love affair. It's just like you to get in the middle of it." She shakes her head in mock annoyance.

"I could say I'm sorry, but I'm not since I want to spend time with you," I wink.

Lex rolls her eyes. "It was a good one, too. I was so comfy." She scratches the side of her head.

"Well..." I look at her with raised eyebrows.

"Oh, sorry. Come in." She shakes her head as if not fully awake yet, and I chuckle. I think she lied about being awake.

I lean in and sense her tense. After last night, I didn't think she'd hesitate for a kiss on the cheek. I search her eyes and see panic. I smirk and brush my lips against her cheek and feel her body relax on a sigh.

"No need to get nervous." I smile.

"Well," she looks away. "I haven't brushed my teeth yet, soooo..." Her lips press together as red colors her cheeks.

Laughing, I pull her to my side. "I don't care."

"I do." She pushes away from me and walks away. "I'll be back." She calls over her shoulder.

"Take your time," I holler back, walking around her house. It's cozy and inviting. Bright colors decorate the space, perfect for Lex. It reflects her joyful personality.

I stand before a collage with different wall art hanging behind her sofa. The abstract outline of a dancer catches my eye. It suits Lex. I used to love watching her dance, be in her element. She was fantastic, and I bet she still is. I'm sure she's the best teacher with the amount of passion that fuels her career.

The pillow on her sofa reads, Chill Here, and I chuckle. Looking around her home gives me a glimpse into the Lex I don't know. The woman who grew up and moved on.

A shelf adjacent to the sofa houses books and a plant that has seen better days. Curiosity guides my steps until I'm pulling out one of the books. *Romance.* That doesn't surprise me. I riffle through the pages, feeling them tickle my thumb before placing it on the shelf again and grabbing another, taking in the colorful cover.

"I'm back."

I jolt at her sudden words and slide the book into its place on the shelf before turning around. A smile covers my face when I see she's changed into jeans and a sweater. Her hair is braided over her shoulder.

"Does this change in outfits mean you accept my invitation to breakfast?" My eyes scan the length of her body, appreciating the way her jeans follow her curves.

Lex shifts on her feet and twirls the end of her braid through her fingers.

"Yeah," she nods. "What kind of woman would I be to turn down a perfectly nice invitation that includes coffee?" She shrugs.

"You're right. You shouldn't turn it down, but only if it comes from me. Any other man will have to deal with the disappointment."

Lex laughs, walking toward me. "You're cute when you're jealous." She pats my chest as if I were a child.

"Jealous? No. Protective of what's mine? You better believe it."

"Yours?" She steps back and tilts her head to look me in the eyes.

"Mine." The one word comes out with finality, leaving no room for argument. I want Lex to know where I stand with her.

I wrap my arm around her waist, tugging her to me and dropping a chaste kiss on her lips. "I want this more than you know," I say with centimeters of space between our lips.

"It scares me," she whispers.

"I know, but I'm working hard to prove to you that I've learned from my mistakes. The biggest one was letting you walk out of my life without a fight."

Her bottom lip trembles right before she sucks it into her mouth, biting it down, likely to hide her emotions.

"We can go to The Bean for coffee and pastries or the diner."

"The Bean. I could so go for their apple tartlet."

"One apple tartlet and a latte coming right up." I smile and grab her hand to lead her toward the front door. Lex laughs and puts the brakes on.

"Hold on. Let me grab my purse and coat. It's freezing out there."

"Yeah, okay."

She laughs as she slides her arms through her coat and slings her purse across her body.

"You don't have a Christmas tree up yet," I comment, noticing the lack of one in her home.

"Ugh, I haven't had time to buy one between work and the workshop prep and a certain man trying to take up every free minute I have." She stares at me.

"I will not apologize, but I do know how to make up for it. After breakfast, we'll go buy a tree, and I'll help you decorate it."

"You will?"

"Of course. It's not like I'll be putting one up this year, so I can get my tree decorating out of my system."

Lex reaches for my hand and squeezes. "I like that plan."

I lift our entwined hands and kiss the top of hers. "Good. We've got a busy day ahead of us."

After breakfast, where a few people looked on at us with unmasked curiosity, we drive to the Christmas tree farm outside of town. We could grab one in the lot near the market, but nothing screams Christmas like cutting your own tree from a farm while there's snow on the ground.

Lex wears a gentle smile that makes her glow. She's been relaxed and happy all morning, making me feel like the king of the world. Knowing she feels that way when she's with me fills me with hope.

"This is so fun." She leans over the dash and stares at the lines of trees as I park. I'm glad there are still plenty to choose from.

"Let's go find you the perfect tree."

Her smile blinds me, but I wouldn't complain about losing my sight if I knew she'd be wearing that smile permanently because of me. She turns and steps out of my car. I take a deep breath and watch her for a second. When she looks at me over her shoulder, her eyes colliding with mine through the windshield, I know I'm in trouble. This woman has always had a special hold on me.

She must feel the connection, too, because she freezes, her eyes wide and unmoving. I smirk and step out of the car, taking my sweet time to get to her. Lex's eyes track me as I approach her, and I once again feel like a king.

"Ready?" I hold her hand.

"Yes." Her chest rises and falls with a heavy breath before I guide her through the lines of trees, each of us with a cup of hot cocoa the owners offered us upon arrival.

"There are so many to choose from." Her head moves around all over the place.

"We have plenty of time to pick one."

"Thank you for this." She pauses and turns to me.

"You don't need to thank me." I squeeze her hand. "Now, let's find you a tree."

We wander through the different trees, pointing out the ones we like. We're both prolonging the process. If Lex is thinking the same as I am, it's so we stay together longer, spending as much time as possible.

Children run around with their parents hot on their heels. Others are picking out and paying for their tree. I'm more focused on the woman beside me.

"Did you finally decide what you're doing for Christmas?" Lex tilts her head and looks up at me.

"I haven't spoken to my parents yet," I confess. After what Toby told me in November about how my parents tried to ruin Lex's chances of opening her studio, I haven't wanted to face them. I don't understand their motives, and it drives me insane.

"Oh, okay." She nods.

MEET AGAIN

"Let's pick out a tree. I think we have plenty to narrow down from." I smile.

"I like this one." She runs her fingers against the needle leaves. It's a full, medium-size tree.

"I think it's perfect for your place." I reach for her empty cup and stack it with mine to throw out. "Be right back." I kiss her cheek and head to the table at the entrance to ask for the saw.

Once I return, Lex smiles and claps her hands. I bend down on the ground, lifting a few of the lower branches so I can see the trunk clearly and start to saw it down.

"I won't lie, it's fun watching you use a saw on this tree. Quite the show. I wonder if I can gather some wood and watch you split it?" Lex's eyes shine with mischief.

"I'll buy an ax and unlimited wood supply," I challenge.

Lex holds the top of the tree to guide it as I finish sawing.

When I stand, I eye her with a raised eyebrow. She's fighting back a smile by chewing her lips.

"I'd do anything for you, even if it means standing in the snow, chopping wood while you watch from the window." I brush back a strand of hair, her mouth opening and closing wordlessly.

Then, I'm carrying her new tree to the owner at the check-out table, and Lex rushes behind me once she's gathered her wits.

"What are you doing?" Lex glares at the wallet in my hand.

"Paying."

"Absolutely not. This is my tree." She can fight me all she wants, but I'm buying her the tree.

"Right," I appease her and hand the man some cash.

"Hudson Remington." Her voice is firm and angry.

I look over at her with a smile. "Let me do this."

She opens her mouth to argue and shuts it again. She finally realized this was a losing battle. I smile triumphantly and get my change while the owner's son wraps the tree. Once it's secured on the roof of my car, I drive us back into town and toward Lex's house.

"You didn't have to pay." She crosses her arms in the seat beside me.

"I know I didn't. I wanted to. It's my treat."

"I can afford my own Christmas tree."

"I never said you couldn't." I glance at her and see her looking out the passenger window. I reach for her hand.

"Lex, I know you can afford it. That's not why I paid. I wanted to give this to you. Consider it payment to use as my own tree, too."

She rolls her eyes.

I squeeze her hand. "Are you gonna ignore me?"

"Maybe." I can see one side of her lips twitch.

"I guess I'll have to take the tree with me then."

"What?" Her head snaps in my direction.

"Ah, good. You aren't going to ignore me." I smirk and lift our hands, kissing the top of hers.

"Thank you," she finally says.

"You're welcome. Now, let's decorate this tree. I still need to buy Tristan a present, and I don't know what to get a man who travels the world for a living."

"I can help." She sits up straighter.

"I was hoping you'd say that." What I don't add is that I need a present for her, but I'm not using her help for that. I plan to make this Christmas special for her, and surprising her is the number one necessity to do so.

20
LEX

"Things seem to be getting serious between you and Hudson," Hope says as we look through the racks in Charlotte's, my favorite boutique in town.

"Did I tell you I caught them kissing?" Ellie smirks.

"What? No!" Hope's eyes widen and then look between Ellie and me.

I roll my eyes and move to another rack, leaving them behind.

"Yup. I went in to see her at the studio, and they were locking lips." Ellie's voice rings with amusement.

"Shut the front door. When was this?"

"The other night."

Hope nods slowly, smiling and waggling her eyebrows at me as if saying, *Atta, girl*.

"Whatever." I slide the hangers back until I find a sweater I like. Pulling it out, I place it in front of my body.

"That's pretty. It'd be great for the conference in New York," Hope comments.

"Yeah," I sigh. "In reality, I don't need it. I've got plenty of clothes to take with me." I'm not a frivolous spender, and my focus at the moment is getting gifts for my parents.

"I need to find something for my mom." I move around the store in search of something she'd like. I'm feeling uninspired, always getting her a top or accessories, but my mom is simple and doesn't need a whole ton of fancy things.

"What about this?" Hope holds out a knit sweater.

"It's nice." I shrug. "I feel like I've gifted her about twenty sweaters like that in the past."

"I know what you mean. It's hard to shop for my mom, too. What do you buy a woman who spends her life on a farm?" Ellie frowns.

"Does she need new boots?" Hope offers.

"Probably, but she's stubborn and likes her worn-in boots." Ellie grabs a dress and stares at it longingly.

"That's beautiful." I point to it.

"Yeah, but following in my mother's footsteps, I also spend my life on the farm." She places it back on the rack.

"Get it for the bachelorette party," Hope suggests.

"I could…" Ellie runs her fingers along the fabric. "Maybe I'll try it on."

"Well, I need to figure out what to get Toby. He's the only one I'm missing, and I have no clue."

"I mean, you're going to take his last name. I think that's a fantastic gift," I joke.

"Ha. It is. I wouldn't take just anyone's last name." Hope laughs and shakes her head. "Between the wedding and house hunting and work, things have been so hectic. I thought about a weekend getaway, but then we already have the trip to Winford."

"Are you getting Hudson a gift?" Ellie glances over at me.

"I have no idea. Are we at that point? What would I even get him?" I've questioned this for the past few days. Is it presumptuous of me to get him a gift? Would it be too much too fast?

"You can get him something small."

I look at Hope. "Any ideas?" My brows lift.

"We'll find something." She nods with the confidence I lack.

"Says the woman who doesn't know what to get her fiancé." I bump my shoulder with hers.

"I'm kind of relieved I don't need to worry about buying a gift for a partner," Ellie grabs the dress. "I'm going to try it on. Why not?"

"Atta girl," Hope cheers.

I continue searching racks until I find a long black and white glen plaid wool coat that my mom would love. It's classic with a modern twist.

"This is it." I hold it up.

"That's beautiful," Hope nods. "Your mom will love it."

"I think so, too. One down, one to go."

"You mean two to go," she winks.

I toss my head back with a sigh.

"Oh! You know what would be a cool gift!" Hope's eyes light up like she hit the jackpot.

I stare at her with furrowed brows and wait for her to continue.

"A custom candle with the scent of your perfume. Like that when he's in New York, he can turn it on and smell you."

I burst out laughing. "That is so strange. Smell me?"

"It's genius and something totally unique."

"It is unique, but it also sounds like something out of a creepy movie."

"Not if the scent is roses and…" She leans in and sniffs me.

"Hey!" I jump back.

"Let me smell you." Her voice is full of complaint.

"No." I bring up my shoulders and lean away from her. "I didn't even put on perfume today."

"Then it's your shampoo or body wash or something. You always smell good."

"I don't know if to be flattered or creeped out."

"Definitely flattered." She taps her lips. "It's like a combination of roses and..." she snaps her fingers as she tries to recall. "Mint," she calls out in excitement.

"Uh, yeah." My eyebrows lift.

"Make him a custom candle with those scents."

"That's weird. Here, smell me whenever you want." I throw my hand in the air. I don't even know if he likes my smell.

"I think it's great. Toby always comments on how good I smell. It's a guy thing. Besides, I think it's a great option for long-distance relationships."

I frown. Hudson and I are still dancing around in square one. As much as I want to jump onto square two, it disappears like it's taunting me. I don't know when we'll move to square two or three or fifty. He's hinted that he's making changes in his lives, but I don't know what those are and what they mean for us.

"Honestly, Hudson has money. We all know that. But what he can't buy is personal and intimate gifts like this. What's a shirt to a man who owns a closet full? But your scent...he can't get that anywhere." She points at me with raised eyebrows.

"Stop saying my scent. It weirds me out." I shiver and scrunch up my face.

"Don't you think a custom candle with the smell of her body wash or perfume, whatever she puts on, would be a great idea for a gift?" Hope stares at Ellie, who has returned from the fitting room.

"Oh, that is cool." She nods and looks at me with a wide smile. "It's sweet and personal."

I stare between my two best friends and shake my head. "I'll figure it out. How did the dress fit?"

"Great, but not sure why I need it."

"Sometimes, the best excuse is that we simply want it hanging in our closet." Hope smiles.

"You may be right." Ellie nods, staring at it. "Okay, I'm getting it."

After we pay, we walk down the sidewalk.

"Let's go into the antique store." I open the door, not waiting for them to respond. They know how much I love antique shopping. I look through the store, my eyes scanning like a hawk for any treasures I may find.

"Oh, I love this beaded purse." Hope holds the small purse.

"It's gorgeous." I smile.

"There are always so many treasures here," Ellie looks around. "Maybe I can find a gift for my mom here."

We each take our time. I scan the shelves and tables. Something about facing history makes me happy. So many amazing things are hidden in front of us, and if we pause to look, we'll find them.

"Oh, my goodness," Ellie shrieks.

"What?" I jump out of my aisle and look for her. Hope is already beside her with wide eyes.

"My mom is going to love this. I knew you were a genius shopping at antiques," Ellie stares at me with a huge grin. "It's an old edition of *The Secret Garden*. I doubt it's a first edition, but that's okay. This is my mom's favorite book."

"That's amazing." The green cover is in decent condition, and the artwork on the front is faded but not to the point where you can't make it out.

"Have you found anything?" Ellie looks at me.

I shake my head. "Give me a few, and we can go?"

"Take your time." Hope smiles, the purse she found hanging from her wrist.

I find a ton of things I'd love for myself, but I have nowhere to put them. Besides, my focus is on Christmas shopping, so I can't quite think about anything else and my stomach is growling. I walk back to where Hope and Ellie were standing and freeze.

"Darling, we're looking forward to your upcoming nuptials. Tobias is like a son to us, but I haven't received your registration yet." Mrs. Remington is talking to Hope, who has on a strained smile. I stay back, not wanting to face Hudson's mom. It'll be better for everyone.

"We're happy you'll be there. Invitations will be sent out soon," Hope nods. It's not the first time she asks Hope about the registry. It's becoming pushy.

As Mrs. Remington turns away from her, she sees me and narrows her eyes. Lifting her nose, she walks away with a sour look on her face.

"Ready to go?" I ask them.

"Oh, yeah." Hope nods. "Did you see her?"

"I did, but I wasn't in the mood to deal with her. I'm not sure what their problem is with me, but it's best for everyone if we have limited contact."

They both nod and walk to the register while I wait for them outside. I check my phone and see a message from Hudson. A smile instantly replaces my frown. We're no longer teens where our parents rule over us. The hint of worry that history will repeat itself still lives in the pit of my stomach, but I have to trust that it could be different if we're given a second chance.

I never interfered in Hudson's plans for his future—or, should I say, his parents' plans for his future, so Mrs. Remington can't argue with me there. Whatever choices Hudson makes are on him.

> Hudson: Hey, are you done shopping? Want to grab dinner?

MEET AGAIN

Lex: Hey, done for today though I wasn't too successful. I'm going to eat with Hope and Ellie

Hudson: Tomorrow you're mine. Have fun with the girls

Lex: Thanks *smiley face* Is Tristan around?

Hudson: I guess I'll have to eat dinner with my obnoxious younger brother

Lex: Don't forget Toby

Hudson: I'll give him a call

Lex: Talk to you later

Hudson: Call me when you're home *kiss emoji*

Lex: Ok

I pocket my phone as Hope and Ellie walk out of the store.

"I'm starving. Ready to eat?"

"Yes. I need some pizza in me, stat." Ellie licks her lips.

I laugh and nod. "Pizza and a glass of wine sound great."

"I agree." Hope loops her arms between ours, and we head to the restaurant.

Different ideas for a possible gift cross my mind. Maybe I'll take up Hope's idea to make him a candle. The sticker can have a special message from me or something. Definitely not, Smell Me, though. I'll have to do some research when I get home if I want to receive it on time.

After dinner, I get home with random ideas still spinning through my head for a gift for Hudson. Feeling nostalgic, I grab a box with memories and photos from high school.

A sad smile tilts my lips as I sort through the stack of pictures. Most include Hudson. When I see one of him in his football uniform, sweaty after a game, I run my fingers down his face. Tears cloud my eyes. It's been a long time since I've looked at these.

Picture after picture, memories surge through my mind like a rapid flood. An idea forms as I look at the photos, and I think I've come up with the perfect Christmas gift. If I can find someplace to do it on time. Otherwise, the candle may still need to be an option.

21

HUDSON

My fingers tap against the keyboard, but all I can think about is Lex. Unfortunately, I need to work so I can't see her until tonight. Being in Hartville has its pros and cons. The cons are dealing with my parents and having meetings more often with my dad.

I was hoping that being here for the holidays would allow me to slow down and do some research on the sports app, but that hasn't been the case. I'm also still working through what it is I want at this stage in my life and if my teen dreams are relevant.

A loud banging noise and mumbling come from the hallway outside my room. Taking a closer listen, it sounds like Tristan. I hop off the bed where I'm working and open my room door.

"They always want to control me." His hands are fisted as he pushes the door open with his shoulder.

"Who does?"

Tristan jumps and swings his head toward me. "A warning would've been nice," he bites.

"Look who's abnormally angry." I raise my eyebrows.

"Blame your parents for that."

"They're *our* parents," I remind him.

"Whatever. I would rather they not be." I follow him into his room.

"What's going on?" I know there's a reason Tristan traveled to town for Christmas, and I have a feeling it didn't go as planned.

"Nothing." He shakes his head, shoving clothes into a duffle bag without bothering to fold them.

"What are you doing?" I cross my arms.

"Packing," his voice is gruff.

"No, you aren't. You're staying for Christmas." I yank the bag from him.

"Nope. It isn't happening."

"Okay, you need to tell me what's going on." I toss the half-packed bag on the floor and sit on the bed. Tristan runs a hand down his face.

"Our parents are controlling, manipulative…" His words trail off, likely to not insult them despite whatever they did that upset him.

"We know this," I say slowly as if easing an angry animal.

Tristan drops onto the bed beside me, his hands covering his face as he takes a few deep breaths. When he looks up at me, I see a hint of vulnerability I'm not accustomed to seeing in him.

"I asked them about my trust fund."

My eyebrows shoot up. That's the last thing I was expecting. Tristan has always been adamant about not wanting or needing anything from our parents, especially money.

"I know, I know," he blows out when he sees my reaction. "But I have plans and need the money. I want to open my own non-profit organization and help humanity the way the companies I've volunteered for have. That requires a large sum of money that I don't have." He shakes his head, disappointment marring his face.

"The trust is yours next year when you turn twenty-five."

"Apparently, it's not quite as easy as that. I have to be settled. They added a clause to the terms that I wasn't made aware of. They don't want me to blow my money on traveling and not working." He scoffs. "They know nothing about the work I do, and they didn't even care to listen to my plan. It was dismissed as if I asked for a Lamborghini on my sixteenth birthday." He runs a frustrated hand through his hair.

"Do they want you to work at the agency?"

He shakes his head. "I'm not sure. That wasn't implied, just that I was settled down. I need a plan to get that money. It'll be worth it. I know it will be. Sorry, I don't want to wear fancy suits and hypocritically talk to clients. I've got other dreams, and they can't respect that." He looks at me and frowns. "No offense."

I release a heavy breath and shrug. "None taken. How much money do you need?"

"A lot, and I won't allow you to give it to me." He arches a brow.

"What if I become an investor?" It's something I can offer.

"I want to do this on my own. That money belongs to me. It's not my fault our parents don't agree on what I'll use it for. I bet if it *was* to buy a fancy car, they'd approve since it shows our family's opulence." Tristan stands and paces.

"I'll come up with a plan, though, that shows them I'm *settled,* whatever that means to them."

"You will, but you aren't leaving town. We'll have dinner with Lex and her family. Dad informed me yesterday that he and Mom are spending Christmas and New Year's in the Caribbean."

"I'm bummed." Sarcasm drips from him, and I have to hold back a laugh.

It was expected our parents wouldn't be here for the holidays. I think that's part of the reason we both decided to come. Well, Tristan obviously had ulterior motives, which I assumed. Heck, I did, too—a beautiful woman who's always known how to make me smile despite crappy situations.

"I could use a break from work. Want to go with me to pick up Lex's Christmas gift?" I stand from the bed.

"A gift?" he smirks. "What'd you get her?"

"Come with me, and you'll find out. We gotta drive to Dobson." When I went into the city to do some business, I came across a store that had the perfect gift for her.

"Vague." He grabs his coat.

"You'll see it in person. We'll grab lunch there, too." I walk back to my room and close my laptop before grabbing my coat and wallet.

"Let's go." I clap his back. Hopefully, this will help clear his mind and distract him from the disappointment.

"You were right. That is a cool gift." Tristan says once we're back in Hartville. He seems in a better mood.

"I think so, too. Combining the past with the present and reminding her of the good things we had going for us. I hope so, at least."

"Honestly, if she's willing to go out with you, she's giving you a chance. Trust that." He smiles. "Anyway, I'm gonna meet up with a friend who's in town. Remember Johnathan from high school?"

"Yeah, that's great. Have fun." I've got plans of my own after I hide this gift.

I stop at the market before heading to Lex's house. Tonight's about us. No interruptions or running into people we may know. I hope to spend more time talking to Lex and holding her close.

I knock on her door, carrying the paper bag from the market.

"Hey." Lex smiles, leaning against the door.

"Hi." She looks beautiful, her face fresh and her hair in a bun. She's wearing leggings and a long sweater, her feet in socks.

"Come in." She steps to the side so I can enter. I lean in and kiss her cheek, inhaling the rose scent that always surrounds her.

"What do you have there." Lex peeks into the bag.

"Goodies. I've got plans for us tonight."

"You do?" Her hands move to her hips.

"Yup. I brought some of your favorite things, and I have *The Holiday* queued up on my Netflix. Just need to log in through your TV." I lift the paper bag.

Lex stares at me with a stoic expression. She doesn't move or say anything. Her silence makes me second-guess this plan.

"You do still like *The Holiday*, right?"

"I do." She blinks rapidly. "I didn't think you remembered that."

Shaking my head, I place the bag on the floor by the door and hold her waist. Bending down to stare into her eyes, I smile.

"I remember everything." I pull her to me and wrap my arms around her in a tight hug. Her arms come around my back, and a relieved sigh leaves me.

After a few minutes, she steps back and smiles. "What snacks did you bring?"

"Popcorn, M&Ms, chocolate chip cookie dough because I know you'd rather bake them than eat store-bought and your favorite red wine."

Her eyes mist over. She tries to blink them away before I notice, but I see the tears welling.

"How did you remember all that?" She shakes her head, emotions clouding her face.

"I never forgot about you, Lex." I reach for her hand. "I was angry and confused as to why you didn't want to be with me, and it may have taken me a few years to understand your reasoning, but I get it."

"I wanted to be with you, but it was all on your terms."

"I know." My voice drops, and I step closer. My other hand holds the side of her face. "I didn't see it back then." We've spoken about this before, but I still feel like I need to tell her over and over again that I was selfish and blind but still loved her.

"We were young." She shrugs.

"I was selfish."

"That too." She nods and laughs.

"Ready for a night in?"

Her hand grips my wrist, and she brings my hand across to her lips, kissing my palm.

"Yeah."

I breathe out and grab the bag from the floor. Every time she lets me in a little bit more, I feel complete.

"Should we make the cookies first?" I look at her across from the peninsula in her kitchen.

"Of course." She raises her eyebrows as if that were a silly question.

I chuckle and grab the package from the bag, opening it. Lex grabs a cookie sheet from a bottom cabinet and preheats the oven.

"I also thought we could order pizza when we got hungry." I smile over at her as I break apart the cookie dough to place on the sheet.

"It's like all my favorite junk food."

MEET AGAIN

"I'm hoping that's the way to your heart." I wink. "You know, keeping the monster in your stomach fed and happy."

Lex laughs and playfully shoves my shoulder. "There are more ways to my heart."

"I know." I'm hoping to remind her about how we were while at the same time showing her how I've changed and grown up.

Lex grabs a piece of cookie dough and plops it in her mouth. "I think cookies are better raw." She licks her lips. My eyes follow the movement, and I clear my throat, looking away to gain my composure.

"Cake batter, too." I finally say.

"Yup. And brownies. I just love dough."

"It's got raw eggs." I shake my head.

"Don't some people put raw eggs in their smoothies or drinks or something? If we can accept that, then we can accept people eating raw dough and batter." She shrugs, set in her opinion.

"You do what you want, babe." I loop an arm around her waist and tug her to me, kissing her forehead.

"I will." She nods, her eyes blazing into mine.

I lean down to brush her lips when the oven beeps, alerting us it's preheated. We break apart, and I chuckle. We act as if we're still teens about to get caught kissing.

"The cookies should be ready in twelve to fifteen minutes." Lex turns to face me with her back pressed into the oven after sliding the sheet into it.

"I'll get the movie ready."

"I have Netflix connected to my TV if you want to search for it on there."

"Perfect," I smirk, giving her one more glance before heading to the living room across from the kitchen.

Sounds from the microwave echo through this part of the house, and I love being here with Lex. For so long, I believed it was an impossibility, and I have my best friend's wedding to thank for this. I don't think I would've had the courage to face her otherwise. Always an excuse to keep my distance.

My phone vibrates, and I fish it out in case Tristan needs something.

> Jameson: Hey how's the wooing going?

> Hudson: Great man

> Jameson: I'm glad. It's about time you got the courage to go after the girl

> Hudson: Thanks. How's Willa?

> Jameson: Great. Planning our first Christmas together and my grandparents are set on the belief that she's pregnant

> Hudson: Lol doesn't surprise me. In their eyes you're truly married

MEET AGAIN

Jameson: I know but I'm going to make it official soon

Hudson: Good for you. First you need to fess up to Grandpa

Jameson: It'll all work out

I smile at my friend's message. Jameson and Willa may not have been a real couple when they got married, but things have worked out for them.

"You're the best. Extra buttery popcorn and M&Ms. I split the popcorn between two bowls since I know you don't like chocolate candy mixed with the popcorn." She places two bowls on the coffee table, stealing my attention from my phone.

"Be back. Gonna grab the wine." She drops a kiss on my cheek as if she has been doing it for years. A huge smile covers my face.

"What?" she asks, noticing.

"Nothing. Want me to open the bottle? Sit, and I'll grab the wine." I move to stand. Her hand lands on my shoulder, willing me to stay put.

"I've got it. I'm going to check on the cookies."

"Okay." I watch her head into the kitchen. A half-wall blocks part of my view, but I still see her huge smile and excited body shimmying as her eyes squeeze shut. I chuckle to myself and lean back on the sofa, glad she feels the same way I do about seeing her.

When Lex returns and settles beside me, I wrap my arm around her shoulder and pull her close. I take a moment to breathe her in, allowing her warmth to envelop me. Kissing her temple, I reach for the bowl of popcorn with the M&Ms in it and place it on her lap.

"Thanks." Her voice is soft.

We get comfortable with snacks and wine while the cookies cool and get ready to watch a Christmas movie. I've never cared much for romantic comedies, but I'd die watching them if it meant having this woman by my side snuggled up close to me.

22

LEX

Hudson's back is to me when I walk out of the studio. I smile to myself, seeing that he's waiting for me to finish up work. The studio will be closed for two weeks, which will be a nice break. It'll give me the time I need to finish my choreography and presentation for the workshop.

I tiptoe toward Hudson, holding back my chuckle at his obliviousness, but I hear his harsh tone and halt.

"No. I told you Scott was handling those while I was away."

I step back, not wanting to interrupt or eavesdrop, but he must sense me because he turns around. His gaze is hard and intense. It's a contrast to the Hudson I've seen this past week and a half. I've gotten sweet Hudson, romantic Hudson, and funny Hudson. We went on a sleigh ride the other afternoon, and it was perfect. Now, I'm wondering if he's even going to want to grab dinner.

"I'll call you back." He hangs up the phone and keeps staring at me.

"Sorry," I say. "I didn't realize you were on the phone until I approached."

"It's okay. Nothing important."

I purse my lips and lift an eyebrow. "Right. That didn't sound important at all."

Hudson sighs, adjusting his winter hat on his head. "My dad's micromanaging all the way from the sandy beaches of the

Caribbean when I told him this week was nonnegotiable for me. I'm on vacation, something I never get to do."

He took this coming week off since Christmas is on Thursday, and I know he's looking forward to the time off. Since it's Friday evening, he's already off the clock.

"I get it." I smile. "Ready to go or..."

"Yeah." He nods, releasing a deep breath. "I've been looking forward to seeing you all day." When his hand seeks mine, I relax.

After Hudson came to my house with my favorite snacks to watch *The Holiday,* we had a turning point. Something between us just clicked differently than it had up to now. Being in his strong arms while we watched the movie made me dream of my own happy ending. If those two women could end up happily in love with men from different countries, then maybe Hudson and I could make this work living in different states. It'll still require one of us to make a sacrifice.

That and the fact that his parents don't think I'm good enough for him. Although, I'm starting to realize that Hudson cares less about his parents' opinions.

"Where do you want to go for dinner?" He looks over at me.

"I would love tacos. Want to go to the Mexican restaurant across town?" I give him my best smile.

He chuckles and squeezes my hand. "You don't need to smile for me to please you. We'll go wherever you want. I'm always down for tacos."

"Thanks." I lift his hand and kiss the side of it. "We can take my car."

"We'll take mine. The inn is around the corner." He tugs me closer, draping his arm around my shoulder. I cuddle into him, wrapping my arm around his back. His warmth makes me feel cozy as we get to the inn's parking lot.

MEET AGAIN

I could get used to nights like this where Hudson meets me after work, and we have dinner together. That would mean he lives in Hartville, and I'm not sure how much of a reality that is.

"Are you okay?" he whispers.

"Yeah." I nod, not wanting to alarm him. These are insecurities based on our history.

"Okay, good." He squeezes my shoulder and opens his car door for me.

The drive to the restaurant is quick. Hartville is busy. People are already in the holiday spirit and enjoying time off with family and friends. The energy around town is full of glee. It's my favorite feeling.

When we get to the restaurant, we have to wait a few minutes before we're seated. Hudson turns to me and pushes a strand of hair behind my ear.

"Are you done with your plans for the bach party?"

"For the most part. We do need to finalize a few dinner plans. You've slacked."

"I've been busy." He winks. "We can discuss it tonight."

"Sounds good." I smile. We've both been busy reconnecting, though I did already order the decorations for the suite.

"That reminds me. We may need your help. We want to decorate the suite when we arrive. Ellie is going to distract Hope so I can go into the room. Can you help me so it'll be faster?"

"I've got a better idea." His fingers lock with mine. "How about we tell Toby and Hope that we need to get out there earlier to make sure everything is ready? That'll give us a few hours to prep things."

"That could work. It's a short drive, so we can get there mid-morning and decorate. I wonder if they'll let us check into the room at that time."

Hudson smirks. "My friend runs the place, remember?" He quirks a brow.

"That's right. Hudson had to show off his connections," I deadpan.

"I was trying to impress you. It backfired." He squeezes my fingers.

"Yeah, I was still so angry at you." I smile.

"But I'm irresistible. Therefore, you were able to forgive me." A winning smile covers his face.

"You had to do some groveling." I tilt my head.

"I'll grovel for the rest of my life if I have to." He wraps his arm around me.

I stare into his eyes and smile. Being with him again makes me feel a certain way I've never felt before. Not that I've tried to date much since we broke up. I had other priorities.

"Your table is ready." A waitress smiles at us.

With my hand in his, he guides us toward the table.

"What can Tristan and I take to Christmas Eve dinner?" Hudson rests his arms on the table and looks at me.

"We've got it covered," I shake my head. "We cook way too much food as it is."

"We can't go empty-handed," he lifts his brows.

"Honestly, Hudson, we don't need anything." I shrug.

"I'll think of something. Your parents have been nice about inviting us."

"Excuse me? I invited you," I tease.

"Yeah, but I need to impress your parents now so they know I'm not some jerk who broke your heart."

"They don't think that. They understood we were in different parts of life, wanted different things." I look down at the front of the menu.

MEET AGAIN

"I've still got some making up to do, beginning with ordering you tacos," he gives me a playful wink, changing the mood.

"Make that three tacos and some chips and salsa, and it *may* do the trick," I tease.

"I'll see your chips and salsa and raise you fresh guac."

"Ah, you know the way to my heart."

"I'm trying," he nods with a smirk that makes him look way too handsome for his own good. His face shines, making him seem like his younger self, the guy I fell for in high school. He had boyish good looks, a big heart, and a sense of humor that always made me laugh with his terrible jokes and all.

"Let's order." He taps the table and picks up his menu.

I sometimes wonder what our life would've been like had we stayed together, and tonight is giving me an insight into that fantasy I used to get lost in before it all went down in flames.

"I hear Hudson is spending Christmas with you and your family." Hope smiles like the Cheshire cat. We're at her house for girls' night. I love nights like this, and with my hectic schedule lately, it feels like we haven't had time to spend together.

"Uh, huh." I nod, tucking my lips between my teeth.

"That's all you're gonna tell us?" Ellie's eyes widen.

"I feel like she's been too quiet about this relationship." Hope turns to Ellie.

"You know what'd get her to talk?" Ellie smirks.

"Sharing that picture from seventh grade…" Hope nods.

"Bingo!" Ellie's eyes turn to me. "Unless you want everyone to see you with that look of horror after we scared you at the sleepover, spill the beans, and I'm not talking the coffee beans."

That photo will haunt me forever. I was half-asleep when Ellie and Hope caught me by surprise on the way to the bathroom. The face I made is a cross between the painting of The Scream by Edvard Munch and some ridiculously twisted expression where my face muscles each ran a different way.

"You both are terrible. You know I'd tell you. I did invite him and Tristan to dinner since their parents won't be in town."

"Toby mentioned that. He had told him to come have dinner with our families, but Hudson said he already had plans with you."

"Sigh, I love a good second chance romance," Ellie's eyes droop like a love-sick fool.

"Anyway, his gift came in today."

"The candle?" Hope's eyes shine with optimism.

I grimace and shake my head. "That gets here tomorrow."

"Oh, my! You didn't tell us you were ordering it!" Hope shimmies around her house. "I knew it was perfect," she sings out.

"Anyway," I look at Ellie, ignoring Hope. "I was looking through my old memory box and found a picture of us in high school after one of his football games. I ordered him a t-shirt with our school team name and his last name and number on the back, like a jersey but more comfortable."

"That's so sweet," Ellie gushes.

"Really? It's not silly? I don't know if you remember that I had drawn a heart on his jersey with a sharpie and written good luck in the middle? I also had them add that detail in."

"No way, that's actually a very thoughtful gift," Hope settles down beside us again.

MEET AGAIN

"He's going to love it," she nods. "And the candle." She waggles her eyebrows.

I giggle and throw a cushion at her.

"What did you name it?" Curiosity sparkles in her eyes.

"Uhhh..." I look between them.

"Tell us," Ellie leans forward.

"So here's the thing," I stall.

They both look at me with raised eyebrows, their expressions mirrored.

"I looked up gift ideas and went down a rabbit hole of long-distance relationship gifts. It's like my computer spied on our conversation or something, and making your own candle was an idea." I couldn't believe it when I saw it.

"I told you I was a genius," Hope gloats.

"Genius, not so much since it seems to be popular," I shake my head, holding back my laughter, and Hope sticks her tongue out at me.

"This still doesn't tell us what you named the candle," Ellie stares at me with a curious gleam.

"It's nothing scandalous, but I don't know..." I trail off. "The lid says: If you miss me, smell me. And the label has an additional message, which reads: Light this when you're homesick of me."

"That's sweet," Ellie smiles.

"And you still got smell me in there" Hope fist pumps the air. "But so much better and more meaningful."

"Yeah, I thought so too. It was one of the options on the site. After the last few days, I don't think it's presumptuous to think he'd miss me."

"He totally will. I think it's sweet," Hope says.

"I think I'm going to give it to him tomorrow. He's coming over for dinner and mentioned a surprise, sooooo it could be a gift?" I scrunch up my nose.

It's been so long since I've been in a relationship, and Hudson isn't new in my life, but the feel of our relationship feels new. It's exciting and scary, and sometimes I wonder if I'm in over my head. We still have the same issues that tore us apart the first time, but I hope our maturity will make for a different outcome.

"Enjoy the ride, babes," Hope clutches my hand. "Trust and let go. You're amazing and deserve this happiness."

I nod, softly smiling as I avert my gaze. Internally, I'm squeeing like a teen in love. I can't believe my life has taken this turn.

23
LEX

Powdered sugar puffs around me, and I inhale it, causing me to cough. I wave a hand in front of my face and step back from the bowl. I'm pretty sure I'm dressed head-to-toe in butter and sugar. Maybe even some cocoa from the cake mix.

I huff and focus on making the frosting again, lowering the speed on the mixer so that the powdered sugar doesn't fly everywhere again. *Rookie mistake.* Once the butter and sugar are blended, I add cream cheese to the frosting and mix again. No red velvet cake is complete without cream cheese frosting.

Over the buzzing of the mixer, the doorbell rings. I keep mixing a moment more before stopping to answer the door.

"I'm coming," I call out when the doorbell rings again. I'm not sure if whoever's at the door can hear me or not, but they'll have to wait another second.

Seeing the frosting mostly mixed, I head to the door and pull it open. My eyes bug out when I see Hudson standing there dressed in a light green sweater and dark jeans.

"Uh…" I cross my arms and look down at myself and back at him in confusion. I know we didn't agree to meet at this time.

I'm still in my ratty pajamas. The more holes the shirt has, the more comfortable it is. My hair's a knotted mess at the top of my head, and I'm pretty sure I haven't put on deodorant yet today.

"Hey," Hudson smirks. "Were you having a fight with…" He tilts his head to examine me, "flour?"

"Powdered sugar," I grumble. "What are you doing here?"

"Well, I thought we could spend the day together. I didn't have anything to do since I'm on vacation and wanted to see my favorite girl." His smile is blinding.

"I'm...I-I need to shower," I announce.

Hudson laughs, deep and full, before stepping forward on my porch. He bends down to kiss my cheek, and I hold my breath. *Please don't let me smell. Please don't let me smell.*

"You smell sweet. Definitely sugar."

I nod in silence and look up at him. I would've preferred to be showered and dressed in normal clothes before he showed up.

"Come in. I'm just gonna go shower really fast." I keep my arms crossed as if that will hide the holes in my shirt.

"Take your time." Hudson walks into my house, and that's when I notice he's carrying a large bag.

I haven't even wrapped his gift yet, hoping to do it once I finish baking.

"It smells good in here. What are you making?" He turns to look at me.

"Red velvet cake with cream cheese frosting for dinner tomorrow."

"I love red velvet."

"I know." I nod with a soft smile.

"Is that my old Hartville High t-shirt?" Hudson raises an eyebrow.

"Be right back." I rush to my bedroom to avoid answering the question and look around like a madwoman. It is indeed his shirt, and I do love it, so I'd wear it and pretend it was mine and not his.

First, a shower. I turn on the warm water while I grab my towel and clothes. I'll wrap his gifts after. Thankfully, I got the gift bag and tissue paper already, so it'll be quick.

MEET AGAIN

After a much-needed shower and layer of deodorant before I forget, I comb my wet hair and squeeze the extra moisture with my towel. I'm not completely done up, but that's okay. At least I'm clean and hopefully smell better.

I walk back into the living room and find Hudson in the kitchen.

"Hey!" I call out when I catch him swiping a finger in the frosting.

"My hands are clean, and I couldn't resist." He licks his finger and walks to the sink to wash up.

"I need all the frosting for the cake, mister."

"I could eat that straight from the bowl with a spoon." He turns to me with a smile.

"That smile won't work in your favor. No more," I point my finger at him and wiggle it.

"Yes, ma'am." He salutes me, which causes me to giggle.

"You're ridiculous." I shake my head.

"That was my t-shirt." He tilts his head with a smirk.

"Fine." I throw my hands in the air. "It's so comfy."

"I just like knowing you still have it." He steps closer, and my breath hitches when his fingers trail along my jaw. His caress is featherlight.

"It's like a part of you didn't fully let me go because I know I never did." His confession is whispered and honest.

I sigh, nodding. Maybe I thought I had, but he was always in the back of my mind. Anger mixed with sadness made up my memories of him.

"I brought your gift." Hudson breaks the tense moment.

So I was right to assume.

"Oh, okay. I have yours, too."

"You do?" His eyebrows shoot up.

"Uh, yeah." My eyes round.

"I didn't know if you had gotten one. I mean, we didn't discuss this, but I wanted to get you something. I thought it'd be perfect for your living room when I saw the decor here." He's adorable when he rambles.

Smiling, I squeeze his arm. "Breathe."

Hudson takes a deep breath and smiles. "Open it up. Come on." He tugs my arm toward the sofa.

"Wait. Let me get yours." I speed walk to my bedroom and grab the bag with his gifts.

"I hope you like it," I say as I place it beside him on the sofa.

"I'm going to love it. I know how thoughtful you are with your gift-giving." One side of his lips lifts in a smile.

"Here, open it." He hands over a large square wrapped in paper. It's too thin to be clothes, and curiosity gets the best of me.

I rip the paper without caution and stare at the vinyl record artwork with the lyrics to "Wanted" by Hunter Hayes printed around it. The center of the vinyl has a light pink label with the words: Our First Dance and the date it happened when we attended our first Homecoming Dance together in high school. I'll never forget that night.

My eyes meet Hudson's, and his smile is blurry behind the tears.

"I don't know what to say." I shake my head. My fingers trace the circular design over the glass.

"Do you like it?" he whispers.

"I love it." I smile through my emotions.

"I wanted to remind you of better times, times where I gave you all of myself selflessly. I also wanted you to remember how much I still care. My biggest regret is that you didn't feel the way the song says. You were and still are everything I want."

MEET AGAIN

At this point, the tears are trailing down my cheeks, but Hudson continues to put his heart out there.

"I hate the way my parents have treated you. I don't care what they think. I don't care what they say. You are the most beautiful woman I know, the kindest and strongest. Never forget that." His fingers wrap around mine and hold on tight.

Mute, I nod through my tears with a small smile.

"Here, open your gift. I'm warning you now. It's not as meaningful as this." Suddenly my gifts feel dwarfed in comparison.

"I'm going to love it. I know it." He rips out the tissue paper and grabs the candle first.

A booming laugh comes from him as he reads the label and then opens the lid. He inhales and closes his eyes.

"It does smell just like you." His eyes meet mine. "I'm going to have to buy this in bulk because I'll miss you a lot. Good thing is that two weeks after I'm back in New York, you'll be there." He winks. "I've got big plans for us."

"There's more." I lift my chin toward the bag.

When he pulls out the t-shirt, his eyes widen.

"Wow," he breathes out. "This is a blast from the past." He holds the shirt open.

"Do you like it? I thought it'd be a nice memory to have, but this is easily worn, unlike an actual jersey," I jabber.

"You even added the heart. I still have my jersey, you know?" He looks at me over the top of the shirt.

"Yeah?"

He nods and turns the shirt around. "This is...perfect." He smiles and leans forward to kiss my cheek.

"I'm glad you like it."

Hudson drops the shirt on his lap. His eyes pierce mine in a soul-searching stare. "I love it, Lex. You have no idea...to know that we're in this place again but wiser." He bows his head. "I dreamed of it but thought it an impossibility."

He sets the candle on my coffee table and tugs me closer to him until his arms are wrapped around me. He inhales deeply, and I'm so glad I showered before we exchanged gifts.

"I want this to work out more than anything." His words are low and gruff.

"We'll find a way," he assures me, yet my heart bangs chaotically at the idea of him returning to New York in ten days. I want to make the best of the time he's here, and I pray we can make it through this second time.

His parents don't like me. I'm not sure why, but I assume it has a lot to do with not being rich and from high society. They see marriage as a business deal, and well, I don't have anything to offer them in that matter. I'm also Hispanic, which I'm sure is an issue, though they've never voiced it outright.

Growing up, I was a minority in Hartville. My parents always worked hard and made our family proud. For the most part, they were welcomed, although some people always turned their noses down on us. Those aren't the people I need or want in my life. Unfortunately, Hudson's parents fit on that list. Unless he breaks away from them completely, which I'd never ask him to do, I don't see how we could move forward without it getting between us again.

"Hey," he tightens his arms around me. "I feel sadness. Don't want that, not today." His hands reach for my ribs and tickle me.

"Ahh..." I call out and laugh. "Stop." I gasp for air and try to break away from him.

A loud snort comes from me, which causes him to guffaw. It gives me the escape I need. Looking at Hudson laugh so freely reminds me of the boy I loved once. Despite the obvious dislike from his parents, we cared for one another like few teens do.

"That's better," he says when he finally catches his breath. "Now, any chance you made a smaller red velvet cake that I could try today?" His eyes light up with hope.

"Not a chance. You'll have to wait 'til tomorrow." I shrug with pursed lips, hiding my smile. "But, we could go to The Bean and have peppermint hot cocoa and one of their pastries. Or!" I lean forward excitedly, my voice loud. "We could get the peppermint cocoa and go to Sweetness for a slice of pie."

Hudson chuckles and shakes his head. "Fine, I'll be patient for the red velvet."

"Atta boy," I wink and stand, reaching my hand out.

Hudson looks at my face and down at my hand. A smile covers his handsome face, and he shakes his head. He holds my hand and stands. "Let's go, sugar girl," he teases.

I lean up and kiss his cheek before grabbing my things and getting ready to head out. The way he looks at me is on par with the way I still stare at my first pair of ballet slippers. It's a combination of nostalgia and, dare I say, love. It's warm and gentle, like sunshine on a spring day. He makes me feel that way, and I shake off my doubts and uncertainties and focus on the moment, having him in my life again.

24
HUDSON

"Are you nervous?" Tristan smirks as we stand outside of Lex's parents' house.

"Why?" My eyebrows pull together.

"Because you're facing the in-laws for a major holiday after getting back together with Lex."

"You're obnoxious." I ring the doorbell. "There's nothing to be nervous about." I stand firm in my resolve. I already came over on Thanksgiving. I'm sure Lex has updated her parents about our relationship.

"Hey," Lex answers the door with a wide smile. "Right on time."

I stare at her bright brown eyes and full pink lips. Her hair is down in loose waves, and she's wearing a short corduroy skirt with tights and a fitted black turtleneck. She's stunning. My heart goes rogue as I look at the woman I'm set on having for the rest of my life.

"Hi." I lean in and kiss her cheek.

"Hey, Lex." Tristan winks at her before giving her a hug.

"Come in. My grandmother was asking about you." She steps aside.

"Is Abuela here?" I smile.

"Yup, and she's already had a bit of sangria." Lex's nose scrunches up.

MEET AGAIN

Her maternal grandmother is a hoot. I haven't seen her in ages. She was away for Thanksgiving with Lex's uncle's family, so it'll be nice to see her.

"I haven't seen her in so long," Tristan says.

"Get ready for the third degree and strong opinions." Lex smiles as we walk into the kitchen.

"Hudson, mijo, you're here."

"Merry Christmas, Mrs. Morales," I tell her grandmother before giving her a hug. She looks the same only a bit older. Her white puffy hair has been styled like a cloud for as long as I can remember.

"I'm so happy to see you. Are you wooing mi niña?" Her question is low for my ears only.

I chuckle awkwardly. "I hope so."

As she leans back, her hands still gripping my shoulders, her wrinkled smile warms my heart. This family was my second home for so long.

"Good, good." She pats my hand. "She's a stubborn one, but you know that already. I think she plays hard to get."

I laugh at her comment, shaking my head. Lex has every right to be wary of this second chance, but I'm proving to her each and every day that she's it for me.

"Hi, Mr. Leon." I shake his hand.

"Hello, Hudson." He nods once, still not fully opening up to me. I understand it, but just like his daughter, I'll prove to him that I'm worth her love and affection.

"Hi, Bianca." I smile at Lex's mom. "I brought a bottle of wine."

"You didn't have to, but thank you." She takes the bag from me and places it on the counter near the sink.

"How are you?" Mrs. Morales smiles at me. "Is life in the big city all it seems?" Her charming accent makes me smile.

ABI SABINA

I've missed this. I've missed the woman standing beside me with a tentative smile. Lex was so much more than just a high school girlfriend. I always envisioned a future with her.

"It's hectic and demanding," I chuckle.

"Nothing like a slower pace," Mr. Leon says.

"That's true," I nod.

"And my beautiful niña, to make you want to take things slower." She winks conspiratorially.

"Abuela!" Lex yells with wide eyes. Her face turns a deep shade of red as she stares at her grandmother.

I let out a deep laugh. "That's also true," I nod and wink at Lex.

"Oh my goodness." She covers her face and turns to her mom while mumbling, "No more sangria for you."

My laugh only grows louder. When her eyes collide with mine, they hold me captive. After the past couple of weeks and the gift I gave her last night, she shouldn't feel embarrassed. She knows what I feel for her.

"It's true, Alexa. That big city can't offer him you, and you're the best thing he could have," Mrs. Morales lifts her eyebrows in a challenge—one I don't intend to take.

"It's true," I nod.

Her grandmother starts talking in Spanish, and I'm lost. Tristan looks at me with raised eyebrows, and I shrug.

"Don't worry, boys, she's just letting Lex know that she's the elder in the family and can have sangria whenever she wants." Mr. Leon laughs and leans back in his seat at the table.

"Sounds more intense," Tristan comments.

"That's just the Cuban flare—loud and passionate. Don't let it fool you. She'll be laughing in a second." Right on cue, Lex says something to her grandmother that has her chuckling.

"Can I get you something to drink?" Bianca looks over at us.

MEET AGAIN

"I'll try some of that sangria," Tristan smirks at Lex's grandmother.

"Good choice." She nods.

"How about you, Hudson?" Lex looks at me.

"I'll have some as well." Normally fruitier drinks aren't my favorite, but this seems to be popular.

We all have a drink before dinner. The house smells of saltiness and garlic plus a combination of herbs. It makes my mouth water. Knowing Lex's family, dinner will be delicious. Cuban food is always great, and her mom's got a knack for cooking.

As Tristan tells them about his time abroad, I allow myself a second to feel this moment. We never had this type of gathering in my house. Everything had to be perfect. Drinks were practically served before guests arrived. It was stuffy and calculated and suffocating. It's part of what I love about Lex and my friends. Their families were different. They all felt like home, not a made-up picture to impress others.

Not to mention the woman who stole my heart back then always made me feel safe and wanted. Something I wish she would've felt reciprocated. It makes me question why I chose to stay in New York instead of fighting for what I truly wanted—a life with her, a career I enjoy, and a lifestyle I could be proud of. Family obligations down the gutter.

I smile at Lex when I catch her looking at me. A sweet and shy smile lifts the corners of her lips before she takes a sip of her drink. I reach for her hand under the table and lock my fingers with hers—her body trembles, causing my grin to widen.

She's stolen my heart once again, although I question if she ever returned it after our break-up four years ago.

Her thumb brushes against the side of my hand, and I look at her. Her expression is full of peace and happiness and intensity—a myriad of emotions that captivate me. Sparks travel between us, and I wish I could grab her face and kiss her.

"Lex?" She blinks away and looks at her mom.

"I'm sorry."

"When do you leave for the dance conference?"

"Oh, January thirteenth."

"I'm so proud of you," her grandma beams.

"We all are," her dad nods with a huge smile.

I squeeze her hand, knowing I'll have time to myself with her while she's over there. No interruptions. Well, except her job, but I'll work around it.

"And you'll be there to show her around," her grandmother smiles widely at me.

"I will," I nod.

"And continue the wooing. In my country, the man would have to woo the entire family." She sighs wistfully. "Your abuelo would come spend hours in my house, talking to my parents," she looks at Lex. Love reflects in her eyes.

"Anyway," she claps her hands. "Times are different now, but I still believe in tradition, mijo," she glares at me.

"Ooookay, Abuela. I'm cutting you off." Lex tries to quiet her with burning cheeks while Tristan laughs.

"Let's eat." Bianca stands from the table in the kitchen, giving her daughter an out. "Everyone to the dining room. Hudson, will you take the bottle there?" She hands me the bottle of wine I brought.

"Of course. What else can I help with?"

"We've got it covered," Lex smiles.

"I insist." I stare into her eyes, not backing down.

"Me too," Tristan claps my shoulder.

"I do need a strong man to carry the pork to the table, but don't tell my husband," Bianca says conspiratorially.

Mr. Leon huffs and shakes his head. "I'll pretend I didn't hear that." He kisses the side of Bianca's head.

"Strong man at your service," Tristan flexes his biceps.

I shake my head and roll my eyes, but Lex giggles. Lifting my brows, she bites down on her smile and shrugs.

"I like your muscles better," she winks and sways her hips as she moves around me to the stove. I stare at her as the pressure in my chest expands.

"Why don't you help an old lady to the table?" Mrs. Morales holds her arm out.

"Sure," I nod and give her my arm. With the bottle of wine, I guide her into the dining room.

"My granddaughter looks happy. Thanks to you, mijo." She pats my forearm with the arm looped around mine.

"I'm happy with her."

"Good, good. All I want is to see her happy." I don't miss the warning undertone in her comment.

"It's all I want, too. I can assure you that."

She nods, seeming pleased with my response. We enter the dining room, and I pull out her chair so she can sit.

"Thank you." She smiles brightly and adjusts her glasses.

Right behind us come Tristan with the pork shoulder, Lex with a covered ceramic dish, and her mom with another one.

"Take a seat, take a seat," her mom demands as she places the dish on the center of the table.

Lifting the top, steam swirls around us. Black beans and rice accompany the meat. It's been way too long since I've had a Cuban meal like this, always having had it with Lex's parents.

"It smells delicious. Thank you." I smile at them. They may not realize it, but if they wouldn't have invited us, Tristan and I would probably be eating some crappy junk food or reheated dinner we got earlier in the day in one of our rooms at the inn since everything is closed tonight.

"Of course. We always have room at our table for friends," Bianca smiles.

I nod, looking at Lex across from me. She must sense my mood because the smile she gives me is full of understanding.

We eat and talk, loud chatter and joking taking place all around the dining room. After dinner, Tristan and I help Lex clear the table and bring dessert. I pause before entering while my brother takes his seat again.

"I'm going to pretend you made this red velvet cake for me." I arch a brow as I look at Lex.

"Hmmm...think what you'd like," she shrugs coyly.

"Oh, I will. Thank you for tonight, by the way."

"You don't need to thank me." She shakes her head with a small smile. "I would refuse for you and Tristan to be alone on such an important holiday."

"I wouldn't want to spend it with anyone else. I need you to know that." I stare into her eyes.

"I do." She squeezes my arm with her free hand as she balances the plate with the cake in her other. "Let's go overindulge in sweets and regret it tomorrow."

Chuckling, we head back to the dining room and place the dessert plates on the table.

"It's not pumpkin flan, but it is cream cheese flan, my specialty." Bianca smiles warmly and begins slicing the flan while Lex cuts the cake.

As much as I'd like to steal a kiss from Lex, I'm enjoying spending time with her family. Thankfully, no one mentions my parents throughout the evening. It's like a spoken understanding that we shall not bring up. I can only imagine such a tight-knit family doesn't understand how parents can leave on vacation for the holidays without considering their children, but our nucleus is far from the true meaning of family.

When it's time for us to go, I shake Lex's dad's hand and hug her grandmother and mom.

"You boys come back tomorrow for lunch. Both of you," Bianca winks at us.

"We'll be here," Tristan promises, slinking his arm around my neck. "Thank you again." He gives her another hug.

Tristan waits for me by the car while I stand on the porch with Lex.

"I'll see you tomorrow." I hold her hand.

"Goodnight." She smiles.

"You're staying here?"

"Yeah, that way we can wake up together and exchange gifts."

I step closer to her. "Good, good. Tomorrow night, if you're free, spend time with me."

She nods, and as I inch forward, Tristan hollers, "It's cold as heck. Unlock the car, lover boy."

"I'm going to kill him," I whisper.

Lex giggles and places her hand on my chest, over my beating heart. "Go on. I'll see you tomorrow."

I nod, walking backward. I almost slip on a patch of ice and push my arms out to find my balance. Lex laughs, holding her middle.

"Watch where you're going," she yells.

"Ha, ha." I shake my head in embarrassment but smile. This feels like a new beginning for us, one I wished for many times.

Once I'm pulling out of her driveway, Tristan says, "Her family is the best. It's worth visiting Hartville just to see them. Sometimes I wish ours was like that, but I gave up on that dream a long time ago."

ABI SABINA

Silence settles in the car, each of us in our own heads. He's right. I gave up on having a close relationship with my parents when I was a teenager.

25

LEX

The days following Christmas have been full of me finalizing my workshop presentation and practicing the choreography nonstop until it's engraved in my mind like a timeless dedication on metal.

I've spent time with Hudson as well. He tends to show up at the studio while I'm working. We have lunch or dinner depending on the day, sometimes both.

Having this undisturbed time with him has allowed my hopes to get the best of me, and saying goodbye to him in two days will be hard. My heart swells when I'm with him, and the fall of not seeing him every day will hit hard. However, I can't seem to use that as enough excuse to stay away. I'm in deep—we both are.

At least we have tonight. New Year's Eve is always a bittersweet holiday for me. The start of a new year is exciting, but ever since I broke up with Hudson, I have wished I had someone to celebrate it with. Christmas is about family. New Year's is about friends and love, sharing intentions for the coming year, and making plans with someone special.

It may not be that way for everyone, but it was one day a year that I missed Hudson. It reminded me of another spin around the sun that I'd live out my dreams and leave behind the ones we made together.

I take a deep breath, and towel dry my hair before blow-drying it. Ellie and Hope are coming over to get dressed together and help me set up for our New Year's Eve gathering. This year it's my turn to host, and I've been excitedly making all kinds of appetizers despite everyone bringing something to share.

As I'm preheating the oven for the baked brie, the doorbell rings. I skip over with a wide grin and swing the door open. Hope and Ellie squeal and hug me simultaneously. I wrap my arms around them as we laugh.

"Come in." I step away from the door. "It's freezing out there."

Between my heater, my cozy sweats, and thick socks, I hadn't thought about the weather. It's been snowing on and off since before Christmas, making the holidays feel extra special. Of course, that could have something to do with Hudson, too.

"Brrr...yeah. I think the temps have dropped." Ellie scrubs her arms in an attempt to warm up.

"They said it would be an intense winter."

"Really?" I lift my brows at Hope.

"Yeah, as if we never get cold weather here," she shrugs and snorts.

Laughing, I close the door and usher them into my room. "I was just preheating the oven before working on my hair."

"Are you finally curling it?" Hope smiles.

"Yeah. Any chance you wanna be the bestest best friend and do it for me?" I smile eagerly, hoping she's unable to turn me down.

"I resent this. Just because I don't know how to use that thing," Ellie points at my wand as if it's offensive, "doesn't mean I'm not the bestest best friend."

"You're right," I hug her. "You're the bestest, too."

"That's better," she sighs. "I shouldn't get judged based on my lack of beauty skills. I was born and raised on a farm, and my mother isn't exactly a pro with getting dressed up. Not enough to teach me."

"That's why you have us," Hope throws her hands in the air. "We'll make you look like a knockout."

"I'm not sure why. It's not like I'll meet some handsome stranger and make eye contact and fall in love," Ellie frowns with a deep sigh.

"It's not for the man you'll meet someday. It's for you, babes." Hope wraps an arm around her.

"I know, I know. I'm just emotional today. Ignore me." She waves her hand in the air and smiles. "Let's get ready."

I exchange a look with Hope, but she shrugs and turns on the wand. I grab us some water, and we're soon a flurry of activity between doing our makeup and hair and preparing the food.

"Oh my goodness, yessss." Hope dances around my kitchen. "Your mom made her crema de..." Her hand makes a circular motion as if prompting me to speak.

"De vie," I tell her. It's the Cuban version of eggnog spiked with rum, and it's the most delicious treat. We only have it this time of year, and it's a hundred times better than regular eggnog.

"I'm so excited." She bounces around.

Her excitement is contagious. I feel like dancing around all over my house. I put on music, and we all start yelling to a Kip Moore song as we move around the kitchen. Once the food is plated, we'll get dressed to avoid any disasters. It wouldn't be the first time I dirtied my outfit because I didn't follow my gut instinct.

Soon, we're getting dressed. I smooth my short velvet dress over my hips and look in the mirror. The long sleeves will keep me warm, and the V-neckline is flattering, showing the right amount of skin while keeping it conservative.

"I love the deep green color this dress has." Hope touches my shoulder.

"Me too."

She's wearing a black sequins skirt with an ivory sweater that has some shimmery threads, and Ellie is wearing the black dress she bought when we went shopping.

"Let's take a picture before everyone gets here." Ellie dances in response to Hope's suggestion.

"I'll set up my phone," I say.

I hook my arms in each of my best friends' and smile as the camera on my phone counts down. We take a series of pictures, laughing and dancing and making silly faces. My friends are the best in the world, and I'd be lost without them.

The first person to arrive knocks on the door, and they make sure everything is set as I walk over to answer it. I smile when I see Toby looking dashing in a dress shirt, gray slacks, and charcoal wool coat. He's holding a paper bag.

"Babe!" Hope leaps toward Toby, almost knocking him off his feet.

"Easy there." A deep chuckle washes over me, and my head snaps behind Toby to find Hudson with a wide grin.

His eyes meet mine, and his expression shifts. Time pauses between us as we stare at one another, and my breath hitches. He looks handsome. Gorgeous, even. His hair is combed to the side in that modern style men wear now, where the top is longer than the sides. His face is covered in the perfect amount of stubble, and his eyes are green like a Christmas tree twinkling with lights.

An array of emotions travel through me seeing him at my doorstep on New Year's Eve. We may have spent Christmas together, but I still pinch myself to make sure it's not a dream.

MEET AGAIN

"Uh…we're gonna go inside because this is getting awkward." Hope's voice rings with amusement, but I don't bother looking at her. My eyes are fixed on the man before me.

"Hi." His gruff voice makes me melt.

"Hi." I smile, blinking away the daze that's taken over.

"You look stunning," Hudson steps forward, grabbing my hand at my side and brushing his lips against my cheek.

"You look…" Words are lost as I take him in. He's wearing burgundy tailored pants, a light gray dress shirt, and a black wool coat.

"Handsome?" His eyebrows wiggle.

My eyes meet his again, and I slowly nod as if I took Benadryl, and my reactions are drowsy.

"Ah, you're speechless. Good, good. I was going for that reaction."

Shaking my head, I laugh. "You look so handsome." I nod and wrap my arms around him in an embrace and kiss his cheek.

His hand lands on my lower back, and all feels right with the world. The way I feel with him gets better and better each time I see him. Safe and cared for mixed with wanted and beautiful.

"Come on." His whispered command tickles my neck.

"Yeah."

Before I can fully step away, he cradles my cheek. I close my eyes, inhaling his spice and woodsy cologne.

"I'm so glad I'm here."

"Me too." I blink my eyes open.

He grabs hold of my hand and closes the door behind us. "I brought dessert from Sweetness."

"What'd you get?" My eyes light up at the thought of the best bakery in town.

"Surprise." He taps my nose playfully.

"Whatever," I stick my tongue out and laugh.

"Look at you two." Hope smiles over at us from behind the kitchen counter. Toby stands on the other side, staring at her. It's endearing to see how much he loves her.

"You make me sick," Ellie jokes.

"Nice to see you, too, Ellie," Hudson winks at her.

"I really hope more people come, so I'm not the fifth wheel here."

"Yes, Jody is coming," Hope says of her cousin.

"Tristan, too. He had to do something and is running late," Hudson announces.

"Sounds good. I invited Cassie also." Cassie is the tap teacher at the studio and my only employee.

Soon after, more people arrive. Chatter fills my house as people have appetizers and drinks. Music plays from my tablet. It's the perfect evening with close friends. Everyone has been catching up and laughing. A soft smile creeps on my face as I observe my friends in my living room while I plate some desserts and grab the crema de vie my mom made.

I squeal when strong arms surprise me when they wrap around my waist, and I look over my shoulder. Hudson stands behind me with a crooked smile.

"Are you having fun?" I nod in response.

"Good. You know that we're close to midnight."

I nod again.

"And I'm going to want a New Year's kiss."

"You've hinted at it," I turn around and wink, draping my hands over his shoulders. Despite having distance between us, I can feel his warmth.

"Good. Wanted to make sure you didn't misunderstand my intentions." The way he says this makes my breath catch.

He emphasizes intentions, his eyes blazing into mine so I can see the honesty swimming in them. He makes me feel whole and cared for. In the past, we didn't have luck, no matter how much we wanted to have those good intentions. This time he's making it a point to let me know exactly what he means.

We're both wearing our hearts on our sleeves, and knowing he's also being vulnerable in this relationship makes it less scary for me.

"Want me to help you serve the champagne?" He smirks.

"Sure. I could use some help opening the bottles."

"I'm your man."

"Yeah, you are," I sing out and instantly regret it when I realize it was loud enough for Hudson to hear.

He tips his head back and laughs, a throaty full-belly laugh that makes me smile. I'd embarrass myself over again to see this side of him. The side I remember from when we were younger, not the man preoccupied with family obligations and torn between me and said obligations.

Despite the heat filling my face, I laugh along with him.

"Didn't mean for you to hear that."

"I'm glad I did." He wipes the corner of his eye before grabbing the bottles of champagne from the fridge.

"Ohhhh...look at her dress!" Hope points to the television where Sutton Wright, a country artist we love, is performing in New York City.

"It's gorgeous." The shimmery fringe dress and cowboy boot ensemble is the perfect country chic outfit for tonight.

"This is my dream outfit," Ellie comments, practically drooling.

"Do you wish you were there?" I look at Hudson. He could easily be spending the night with friends in some upscale bar or standing in Times Square watching the ball drop live.

"I wouldn't trade this for the world." A sweet smile creeps up his lips and makes my heart bang wildly.

While everyone is admiring the performances on the TV, I'm admiring the man in front of me.

"Let's hurry," he says, breaking the spell.

I nod and grab the plates with cookies and cupcakes, setting them on the dining table so everyone can grab what they'd like. Then, I serve small glasses with the crema de vie while the popping of cork creates background music.

"This is delicious." Ellie grabs the small glass and tilts her head back after taking a sip.

"It is." I nod, sipping my own.

"I think I'm gonna come spend every holiday season here so I can eat and drink at your house," Tristan says. "Better yet, tell Mama Leon I'm moving in." He laughs.

"She'd probably love that," I throw back.

My mom loves entertaining and having people over. She'd be over the moon.

"Good, I may need a place to stay."

I look at Hudson and silently ask for clarification, but he shrugs.

"He's been vague about things lately."

I nod and drink more of my sweet drink before grabbing a mini red velvet cupcake. All of the food today has been amazing. I'd much rather have snacks like this than a full meal. It allows me to eat everything I want and not settle for just one dish.

"It's almost time," Jody claps.

Everything becomes a flurry as everyone calls out in excitement. Ellie and Cassie squeal. Jody dances around.

"I'll grab the champagne." I move back into the kitchen to find Hudson already serving the glasses.

"Thanks, babe." I kiss his shoulder and grab two, so I can hand them out.

MEET AGAIN

Time passes so quickly as we all prepare for the final countdown. Excitement bounces off the walls as if we were kids again. We may be a small group of friends, but it feels like my house is full of love and happiness.

I don't need to look back to confirm Hudson is behind me. I can sense him, tingles moving down my spine. His arm wraps around the front of my shoulders and pulls me toward him, kissing the top of my head.

"Ten... Nine..." People start to count down, and Hudson turns me so that I'm facing him.

My eyes collide with his, intense green swimming with emotions that penetrate me.

"Eight..."

The rest of the countdown fades as I keep my eyes trained on his. Unspoken words pass between us. Everything I loved about him crashes back into me at warp speed. The way he made me feel. The way he'd protect me and make me laugh, and help me study for math when I thought I'd fail my exams.

He was everywhere in my life, and then he was gone.

Now, I'm back in his arms. He's back in my life. We're getting another go-around, and I don't want him to leave for New York the day after tomorrow. The thought of it makes my chest ache. I've gotten so used to seeing him every day these last few weeks. Even when he was first here and I didn't want to see him. He was an odd vision in Hartville when he came for the engagement party. Then, he became a fixture I got used to seeing, no matter how much it annoyed me.

It changed. Somehow he seeped back into my life, and here we are. Tears well in my eyes, and my attempt to blink them away is futile. The seconds slow down as his thumb brushes my tears away, and he leans his head down.

"I love you, Lex. I always have." His lips land on mine before I can fully comprehend his confession.

My pulse takes off in a marathon sprint like the Tasmanian Devil when he tornadoes. More tears fill my eyes. I grip the back of his shirt and cling on to this moment, the perfection of it, the gentle way his lips brush against mine, and his stubble scrapes my face—his warmth and love.

I'm overwhelmed by this man, in a good way. In a complete way, that fills me up, and I feel like I'm going to burst at the seams with joy.

When he leans back and looks at me, a small smile tugs at his lips. I've been silenced. Mute. Ideas race through my head, but nothing comes out. Before I have a chance to react, I'm pulled away, and he's pulled into a hug by Tristan.

Hope and Ellie hug me, and someone else—I think Toby—whistles loudly. I find Hudson across the living room and smile.

He loves me.

I jump up and down with my friends and then let out a loud whoop. They may think it's because of the holiday, but Hudson gives me a knowing smile. I want to run up to him, have him catch me, and drop kisses all over his face.

First, I need to tell him I also love him.

26

HUDSON

"I'll see you in ten days." I squeeze Lex's hand and tip her chin up so she can't divert her gaze. I want her looking at me. We shared a lot the last couple of days. The last few weeks, really, but after I confessed my feelings for her on New Year's Eve and she reciprocated after everyone had left, I knew things had changed.

"I know." A sad smile finds its way to her lips.

This moment was unavoidable. We both knew it'd come to this, but that doesn't mean I'm ready for it. It's the hard truth that one of us will have to sacrifice in our current life if we want our relationship to progress and have a future. As much as I thought I'd have time to do research on any other type of career, I've been busy soaking up every second with Lex.

"I'll call you. We can video chat so I can still see your beautiful face and the smile that lights it up." I brush my thumb across her cheek.

She nods somberly.

"Baby..." I whisper, pulling her to me and wrapping my arms around her.

When her hands clutch my back, my heart splinters as if an ax has just gone through it. Leaving her is reminiscent of when I left for college. That was a turning point for us—not in a good way—but history doesn't always have to repeat itself.

Smoothing my hand down her back, I make promises I intend to keep.

"Ten days, and you'll be with me again."

"For a short time," she retorts. "Are we playing a losing game?" Her round eyes look at me, tears filling them.

"No." I shake my head adamantly. Life isn't as cruel as to give me a second chance with the woman I've always loved and have it take her away from me again. The pain would be too great. I won't give up, not this time.

"How are you so sure? Your job is over there. My studio is here. It feels very much like deja vu."

"Because I'll fight for you." It's my one regret that I didn't fight for her when I should've. I just let her slip away.

Not this time.

Her smile isn't convincing, but I'll show her with my actions.

"I love you. Remember that when you begin to doubt this." I sweep a hand across the side of her face, swiping away her hair so I can get a clear view of her.

Lex makes my heart beat to a different rhythm. Upbeat, excited, positive. Like listening to your favorite songs from childhood and reminiscing about how great your life was back then. She shines light into my life. I'm no longer living only to close deals and sell real estate. I want to make her proud.

"I love you, too." Her fingers brush through the back of my hair, and I close my eyes. The sensation tickles me, causing me to shiver. It's such a caring touch. Something I haven't felt since the last time we were a couple.

"You and me, Lex. That's all that matters." I press my lips to her forehead and inhale her rose scent.

"Besides, when I miss you, I can now smell you," I joke, chuckling through the heavy emotions coursing through me.

She snorts and lifts her eyes to mine. "I thought that'd be such an awkward gift. It was Hope's idea, and I laughed so hard, set on not giving it to you."

"I'm glad you did. It'll feel like you're there with me." I smirk and inhale exaggeratedly to prove my point.

Lex scrunches up her nose and pushes back. "Weirdo."

"Nah…" I shake my head and pull her to me.

My phone rings, breaking apart the moment.

"It's probably Tristan." I fish it out of my pocket and see my dad calling. Ignoring the call, I let my phone fall back into my pocket and smile at Lex.

It's hard walking away. I've loved spending as much time with her as I have. Both of us being off work allowed us to truly reconnect.

"Go on." Her hands land on my chest.

"I don't want to." I screw my face.

Being in Hartville the last few months, even if for short periods of time, has given me time to reflect on my life. It's true that I enjoy selling houses. It's exciting, but I did have other dreams. However, I haven't made much progress with the sports app Toby and I discussed.

I'm not sure where to begin. It was a pipe dream when I was younger since I studied business and real estate instead of computer science. For so long, my path was carved for me that I didn't even know what I wanted to do.

"I don't want you to go either, but it's inevitable. We're prolonging it, which will only make it harder." Lex is the reasonable one out of the two.

"Whatever," I roll my eyes playfully.

She chuckles and kisses my cheek. "Call me when you arrive. Drive safe. The roads are wet."

"Always, and always." I peck her lips. "Tristan will keep me company."

"Good. Tell him I said bye and not to take so long to return to our slice of the world."

"Will do." I hug her. "I'm going to miss you, Lex. More than you'll ever know. Please don't give up on us."

Her arms tighten around me as if imprinting herself on me. She's already imprinted in my heart.

"See you soon." I refuse to say goodbye.

"You will," she smiles. "Ten days and counting."

My hand trails from the side of her face to her shoulder and down her arm, and I give her hand a squeeze as I step back, holding on until the last second. She blows me a kiss and giggles when I catch it and save it in my pocket.

"I'll have it for later," I wink.

"Soon," she nods, determined.

I let go of her hand and open her front door. "We'll talk tonight."

The drive to New York is going to feel interminable. I'm grateful my brother will be with me. Even if he's obnoxious at times, I know he'll keep me entertained and distracted.

"We will. Now go before I trap you in here, and don't let you leave." I know it's a joke, but the idea is tempting.

Walking out of her house is one of the hardest things I've had to do. I want nothing more than to build a life with Lex, but I need to figure out how to make that happen.

Lex

I stare at Hudson's retreating form and watch his car drive away. I stand by the door, the cold air seeping into my bones long after his car has disappeared from my street. My throat hurts from holding back my tears. My eyes sting from the cold and the tears filling them. My lips tremble from the impending tears.

I knew this would happen. I can't pretend it's a surprise, but that doesn't mean I can't be sad about it. Hudson and I have always been traveling on two different roads. We've met at an intersection, but eventually, we need to continue on our paths. Is crossing every so often enough to make this relationship work? I don't know, but I'm certain I love him.

People risk a lot for love, right? At least go to war for it, battle it out to see if it can survive.

Closing the door, I drag my body to the living room and drop on the couch. I hug my knees and stare until my gaze blurs.

Screeching ringing fills my living room, jolting me from my dazed state. I look around and find my phone with the screen lit up. Hope's name flashes and I have the temptation to let it go to voicemail. I fling myself after it at the last minute, rolling off the couch face first.

"Ow," I call out. My body lands on the floor with a thud. The corner of the coffee table stabs my side, but besides that, I'm safe from any injury.

"Hello?" I breathe out.

"What are you doing?" Hope's question is full of confusion. "Are you running?"

"No. I went to reach for the phone and rolled off the couch like a fool."

"Are you okay?"

"I'm fine. Thankfully no one witnessed it, so my ego is intact." I stand, hold my side with my other hand, and get back on the couch.

"How are you?"

"Eh...I think I'm gonna grab some cookie dough and watch Christmas movies."

"Oh, Lex. Want some company?"

"I'm okay. I'd rather be alone, to be honest." I am still processing. Half of me knows this is temporary. The other half doubts our situation will ever change.

"Call me if you need anything, even if it's just someone to sit silently beside you."

"Thanks, but don't worry." I curl my legs under me and lean into the armrest.

"I'm gonna worry, but I'll respect your need for space."

"Thanks."

After hanging up, I slide down on the sofa until I'm lying in the fetal position and clutch one of the cushions to my chest. This feels like an ending, and I do not approve of that emotion. Closing my eyes, I trap the tears and take slow deep breaths.

I slow my racing mind and go to the kitchen to grab cookie dough. Nothing beats eating raw cookie dough. I don't care how many people tell me it'll give me a stomach ache. It's worth it. Then, I turn on my television and search for a Christmas movie that will make me feel equal parts happy and sad. I could use a good cry.

The day passes between movies and junk food (thank you, pizza delivery guy). By the time my phone rings again, I am stuffed to the brim and feeling about as bad as I'm sure I look.

I stare at it for a few minutes, my reactions slow like molasses. My eyes snap open when I realize it's a video call. From Hudson. When I look like... Well, I haven't checked myself out in the mirror, but I'm sure it's not a pretty look.

I cringe and answer the call, my desire to speak to him greater than my pride.

"Hey..." His greeting trails off as his smile fades and his eyebrows pull down over his eyes.

"What's wrong?" His expression turns into one of concern.

"Nothing. Why?" I play it cool, but I'm not fooling him.

"You don't look like nothing's wrong. Talk to me? I know this is hard, but we'll make it through this patch."

"I know. I'm just emotional." I sigh, leaning back against the sofa and attempting a smile. I grimace when I see myself in my camera. My hair's a mess. My eyes are red and my face is blotchy. No wonder he reacted the way he did.

"You made it home safely?" I change the subject.

"Yeah. We hit traffic, making the ride longer, but I'm not sure why I was surprised. Everyone's returning home from vacation today." A wide yawn takes over.

"True."

"What have you done today? Besides missing me, of course." His confidence travels through the screen.

"Watch movies, eat junk food..." I shrug. And definitely miss him, but I don't need to voice that. He can read it on my face.

"I miss you, too."

I nod silently, sensing another wave of tears threatening to crash on me.

"Tell me something, anything." I lift my legs to the coffee table.

"Well, I've got an opening tomorrow for a condo. I already told you that," he chuckles. "Tristan is still set on making my parents give him his trust without conforming to their demands."

"That'll be interesting." I lift my brows.

"I know. I'm kind of afraid of what he'll come up with." Hudson shakes his head. "It's on him, though. Honestly, he deserves the money. It's his fund."

"I agree, but your parents have rules for it." Not that I agree with those rules. Tristan wants to use the money to do something good in the world and leave his mark. I would think any parent would be proud of that, even some stuck-up ones like the Remingtons.

"I know," Hudson sighs. "But let's talk about us." He waggles his eyebrows. "I've got so many plans for when you're here."

"It's just three days, Hudson. And I'll be at the workshop." I don't know how we're going to be able to spend so much time together regardless of being in the same city.

"I know, but we'll make it work. We'll do the cool New York stuff, not all the touristy stuff."

"I wanna see some of those so-called touristy things," I argue.

"We will, but there's so much more to show you. Leave the planning to me. Just email me your schedule." Determination lights his eyes. "Besides, you get in on the twelfth and have that entire afternoon to spend with me."

He has a point. Since the workshop is early on the thirteenth, I'm traveling the day before. A smile takes over. I can't help but love the way he wants to do this, show me the area, make it special.

We spend the rest of the evening talking until we're both yawning nonstop. After a prolonged goodbye similar to the one we had in person before he drove off, we hang up, and I get ready for bed.

One day down, nine to go. I can handle that.

27

HUDSON

"Hudson." My dad's firm tone makes me roll my eyes. I run a hand down my face and lean forward on my desk.

"I've been calling you since yesterday." His intonation is accusing. He called me twice. The first time I was at Lex's house saying goodbye. The second time I was video chatting with Lex and not about to hang up with her to speak to my father.

"I had two missed calls, and it was impossible to get back to you. How can I help you?" I lean back in my chair. The springs squeak as my weight pushes it back.

"I need you to go to Texas this month. I've got some properties for you to scoop out. You'll have to fly out on the tenth and stay for some meetings until the fifteenth."

I sit up, the chair almost rolling from under me. "Excuse me?" There's no way I'm traveling during those dates.

"Are you not listening to me?" He bites.

Moments like this are when I question why I work for my father.

"Of course I am, but how am I just hearing of this?"

"It just came up," he clips.

"Well, I've got some things going on those dates. Scott can go." My jaw tightens.

"No can do. You need to go. You're the Remington. Scott will handle other affairs." He keeps his words measured but direct.

"What is this for? What properties?" Since I haven't heard about any Texas properties, I'm curious as to why the urgency.

"They're vast pieces of land. A developer wants to buy them, and he's willing to pay big money to get what he wants. And he wants us to handle it."

"Like I said, I've got a few things going on those days." I refuse to back down and miss this opportunity with Lex.

"Change them. This is business, and it always comes first." His harsh tone throws me back. My father is all about business. He wouldn't know actual friendship or love if it slapped him in the face, but this is beyond his normal attitude.

"What's going on?" I press.

"Nothing, but I want this deal closed. You know that after the holidays, things slow down, and I don't want to miss this opportunity. My secretary will send your travel information later today."

Before I can argue, he hangs up. What in the world? I stare at my office door in confusion. Being away from the office has never been an excuse for my father not to send me work-related updates. If he knew about this deal, why didn't he bring it up before?

I get back to work but feel unrest. My hand reaches into my desk drawer, blindly grabbing my phone. I open my messages and write a text to Lex. I don't know how I'm going to tell her about this trip. I'll wait until I have all the details before saying anything in case it can be changed. If not, I'll book Scott a flight myself and send him instead. I'm tired of the puppet games my dad tries to pull.

Hudson: Hey babe

MEET AGAIN

Lex: Hi

Hudson: What are you up to?

Lex: Going over my workshop presentation

Hudson: You're going to do great

Lex: How's work? I wasn't expecting to hear from you so early in the day

Hudson: Boring and I miss you

Lex: Lol I miss you too

Hudson: I'll call you during my lunch break before you start teaching

Lex: Ok

I set my phone on my desk and sigh. Talking to Lex for a few minutes, even mundane things through text message, makes everything better. Tension rolls down my shoulders, and I close my eyes for a beat.

"Napping on the job. Maybe I *should've* asked Dad for a position here." Tristan laughs when he walks into my office.

"What are you doing here?"

"Tell me what's on your mind. I can be your personal therapist." He smirks and sits on the chair across my desk, folding his hands together.

I scratch the back of my head and stare at him. "Dad called telling me he needs me to go to Texas from the tenth to the fifteenth, right when Lex will be here."

"Really?" He lifts his eyebrows.

"Yes, and when I told him I couldn't, he basically told me I had no choice. Normally, I'd hear about meetings like this more than a week before." I shake my head, rubbing a hand across my cheek.

"I think I know why." Tristan's eyebrows lift slowly. He leans forward, his elbows on my desk.

"Elaborate." I wave my hand to hurry him up.

"Mom called me. She had questions about our holidays. She wanted to know how we spent the day, where we had Christmas dinner and if we went to their house and had Mary cook for us."

"Why would she say that?" She never even offered for us to go to their house and eat there. I thought Mary was off those days.

"Right," he shakes his head in anger. "I didn't want to give much away since I know they aren't fans of Lex, but apparently, she already knew. She then told me to give her all the details I knew about you and Lex in exchange for my trust fund. She'd heard Lex was going to be in New York for the conference since word had spread around town."

"That..." I trail off. My fists clench on my lap, and my teeth threaten to crack under the pressure of my bite.

"Yeah," Tristan nods pensively. "She thought I'd turn my back on you for some money. I sometimes wonder if we were adopted."

"Same." Disgust fills me. "I don't get it. I'm working the job they wanted me to do. I went to the college they approved of. Why can't they let Lex go?"

"The answer is simple: She's not good enough in their eyes. She's not rich or from their high society groups. She's of Hispanic descent, which for them is a lower standard."

"It's bull," I say tightly.

"I know that. Sorry to say, so long as you have any tie to them," his gaze sweeps around my office in a pause, "you're going to have to put up with this from them. Do you want to fight tooth and nail about everything in your life?"

"No." It's an easy response.

"Then, you've got some thinking to do, big brother. Beginning with if you're going to Texas or not." He slaps my desk. "I thought you should know what Mom had to say, though."

"It makes sense why Dad was so set on this trip." I need to be smart about this, not allow my anger to guide me.

"As soon as you mentioned it, I knew it had to be a scheme."

I take in my brother and his shaggy wavy hair that makes him look like a surfer, but I know better than to assume he's all play and no responsibilities. However, I know how much he wants that money to build his own dream.

"You really turned down the trust fund for my privacy?"

"Of course. Besides, that money will legally be mine when I turn twenty-five in a few months, so I have some time to plan a way for them to release it to me. I'm not backing down, and a little bribe wasn't enough for me to betray you." His smile is genuine.

"Thank you, Tristan."

"Just remember when I need some business advice in the future." He chuckles, leaning back in his chair and crossing his ankle over his knee.

"You got it," I laugh. "Thanks for letting me know."

"Anytime. Wanna grab dinner after work? I have a few things to do but should be done by six."

"Sounds good," I nod.

"Great. And you're buying since I don't have my business yet," he throws over his shoulder and laughs on his way out of my office.

Shaking my head at his antics, I get back to work before having to go to the condo showing this afternoon. Before that, though, I plan to call my dad's secretary and make sure she doesn't book any flights, or my father will be upset about losing money.

♡♡♡

"I'm proud of you." Tristan claps my shoulder before lifting his hand and calling our waiter over.

"It's not the full plan, but at least I made my point. I'm not going to stand by and allow him to interfere in my personal life.

MEET AGAIN

Just because I work at the agency doesn't give him a right to dictate who I see outside of work." I shake my head, jaw tight with tension.

"Atta boy. I'll stand by your side." Tristan laughs.

"What can I get you?" The waiter finally stops at our table. This place is packed, and all I want is a warm meal so I can go home and talk to Lex.

"I'll have the jerk chicken," Tristan orders.

"The steak for me." I hand the waiter my menu.

"Great." He nods and walks away.

"I wish I could spy on Dad to see his reaction when his secretary tells him she didn't make any reservations." Tristan's smile is mischievous.

"Same," I chuckle. "I'm sure he'll be blowing up my phone. Heck, he might even come down here." I shake my head.

"Hopefully, that won't be the case."

"I can't be held accountable for what I say if he does," I shrug.

"Don't blame you. I'm surprised by your self-control. I would've already confronted him."

"Is that how you ended up in your current predicament with the trust fund?" I lift my brows.

"Something like that, but in my defense, they had already said they'd only give me the money once I proved I had matured and was settled down with a serious job, preferably in a relationship." He never mentioned the part about a relationship.

"What?"

"Yeah," he snorts. "Apparently, having a girlfriend would make me less likely to take off. It's their way of controlling." He shakes his head in annoyance. "And we both know that they won't approve of just anyone."

"I'll help you in any way I can," I offer.

"I'm already counting on that," he smirks. I'm afraid of what plan he'll come up with, but I'd do anything for my brother. My parents aren't being fair.

"So, what are you planning for Lex's visit?"

I tell him my ideas and the places I want to take her and ask him for suggestions as someone who isn't a New York resident.

We talk about the showing I had today and the likelihood of the condo selling at the owner's asking price. Then, I get more information about Tristan's ideas for his non-profit organization. It's been so long since we've had this much time together, and it makes me realize how much I miss having my brother permanently in my life.

By the time we finish eating and get home, I'm ready to change and call my girl. It's been a long day, and all I want is to hear her sweet voice, see her smile, and listen to her speak. I turn on the candle she gave me and press her contact on my phone. Then, I settle into bed, crossing my legs at the ankles, and prop my phone on a pillow using a stand.

"Hey," Lex answers with a huge smile.

"Hi, how are you?"

"Good. Are you in bed already?" She narrows her eyes as if that'd give her a better view of my space.

"Yeah," I chuckle. "Wanted to be comfy, and I turned on your candle. Soon, my room will smell like you, and I could pretend you're here."

"Hudson..." she sighs. "Almost eight days."

"Can't get here soon enough," I tell her.

Right now, I could use her warmth and peace in my home. I could use a hug from her, a kiss. I want to be close to her, breathe her in. I miss her more than I allow myself to realize. My priority is getting my career on track so I can decide what direction I want it to take. If my father is this adamant about keeping me

MEET AGAIN

away from Lex, he definitely won't be on board with me moving back to Hartville and managing the office there.

28
LEX

THE STRESS FROM THE last week crushes me, and I blink my eyes to stay awake. I'm almost in New York City, and the drive has been interminable. Mostly because of my tiredness and anticipation to see Hudson.

The days passed rather slowly as I started up work again and spent my evenings video chatting with him. As nice as that is, I would catch myself looking out the big window at the studio expecting to see him, turning my head when the door to the coffee shop would open in case it was him. It was disheartening, but I'll see him in less than an hour. I just need to battle New York City traffic first, which gives me anxiety going from all the movies and shows I've seen.

I drive down the highway that rounds the city, and I stare in awe. These aren't skyscrapers; they're universe scrapers. *Wow.* The monstrous buildings create an outline in the sky a few miles before me, and the ocean ripples to my left.

"Take the next exit." My navigation app informs me.

"Oh, cannoli..." I switch my turning signal, focus on the road again and not the city that lies before me. My fists grip the steering wheel as horns blast around me. I go slow, not wanting to get lost or in an accident.

No one lets me get to my exit, and my heart thunders.

MEET AGAIN

"Do you want me to stop in the middle of the highway until you let me pass?" I yell inside my car as if the offending drivers moving past me could hear me.

I'm going to get a massage after this drive. Finally, a kind soul lets me pass, and I swerve onto the exit, slamming on my breaks when I see the line of cars in front of me. My breath swooshes out of me, and I slump back in my seat.

My navigation app keeps directing me through the flow of traffic—right and then left, straight for point four miles. As if I know what distance point four miles is.

"I just want to arrive at my destination." I have never driven in such a busy city before, and this is like a no-mercy, dive-head-first first experience. Goodness gracious, I wonder if I could convince Hudson to drive me out of the city on the way back home.

My phone rings, and I accidentally answer it on Bluetooth.

"Can't talk right now." I sound panicked to my own ears. It's probably my parents checking in.

A deep chuckle makes me pause, and I glance at the screen before looking back to the road.

"Lex, are you okay?"

"No. I am not okay. Next time, remind me *not* to accept a job like this in a city like this with traffic like this." I breathe out.

"I take it you're in Manhattan." His voice is light and joyful.

"Yes, but if you don't hang up right now so I can listen to my GPS, I might end up in Queens."

He continues to laugh at me.

"Byeeee," I give him a warning before hanging up.

"Your destination is on the right." I snap my head that way and sigh when I see my hotel.

"Thank you, Lord," I breathe out. Now, where do I park?

I slow my roll, craning my neck to look for parking. The website had mentioned a garage, but I don't see an entrance. I pass the hotel in my unsuccessful search.

Great. I could've taken a train or something. Who cares if I'd have to wake up extra early to go back to Hartville.

You cared because you wanted more time with Hudson.

Yeah, I'm definitely going to ask Hudson to drive me out of this city. I'll pay for his cab back to the city or his train or subway, whatever. I circle around the block, almost going in the wrong direction, and spy the valet for the hotel. I pull up to it and lower my window.

The young guy is already coming around.

"No, no. I'm not valeting. I'm staying at the hotel, and the website said there was a garage. Do you know how I can get there?"

"We don't have a garage. We're only offering valet." His eyebrows furrow. I could've sworn I read that on their website.

"Great," I mumble. "How much is it per day?"

"Sixty dollars."

My eyes bug out. "Is there any street parking around here?"

"No." He seems unamused. "If you're not going to park, I need you to move out of the line." His lips press together, and I look in my rearview mirror. I have three cars behind me waiting to valet.

"Fine." My phone rings again.

"Hello?" I answer, feeling bad for hanging up on Hudson.

"Babe. Look up." I lift my gaze and find him standing a few feet in front of me, one hand in his pocket. He looks older in a suit, a fancy black wool coat over it.

"You're here." He's like a savior. I think I even see the sun rays peeking out from behind the clouds to shine down on him.

"Of course. Drive up a few feet. Don't valet. I've got a parking spot in my building."

"Are you sure?"

"Positive."

I sigh and call out the window. "My boyfriend's here. Sorry." I don't look at the valet driver out of embarrassment and drive toward Hudson. I smile when Hudson opens the door.

"Let me drive."

"Oh, thank goodness. I love you." I wrap my arms around his neck and press my lips to his cheek.

He chuckles and hugs me. Everything feels right again. The stress of the drive almost dissipates. *Almost*. I am definitely going to need more than one hug to overcome this disaster.

"Come on." He squeezes me one more time and steps back.

With him in the driver's seat, I can relax. The muscles in my neck and shoulders are tight and coiled. A massage would definitely be a great cure.

"I'd ask how the drive was, but I think I got an idea." Hudson laughs.

"Stressful. I'm tired, and I hate driving places I'm unfamiliar with. Can I turn right, or is it one-way? Stop and go. Just so much unknown." I shake my head.

"We'll get you checked in the hotel a little later. Are you hungry? Thirsty?"

"I could go for some coffee if that's what you're asking." I smile.

"I've got the perfect place then. We'll drop your car off and walk to a coffee shop near Central Park." His smile lights up his face. The way he glances at me is full of happiness, and it makes my heart burst like a balloon during a gender reveal party while confetti falls all around me as I jump for joy.

I can't believe I'm in New York City and spending the afternoon with Hudson. What world am I living in? I'd pinch myself if my fingers weren't stiff from gripping the steering wheel.

"We'll go to dinner later. I want to take you to so many places. Are you sure you can't stay an extra day?" He lifts his eyebrows.

"I don't know." I shake my head. At first, I didn't consider staying longer than the conference days. Hudson and I weren't a thing when I got invited to host a class, but the workshop does end on Friday, and I could extend my stay and make a weekend out of it.

"I'd have to see if the hotel has a room available."

"You can stay at my place," Hudson says quickly.

I lift my brows and tilt my head.

"I have an extra room." He adds hastily. "Think about it."

"Okay. Let me come down from the drive so I can think clearly." It would be nice to add the weekend and have a more relaxed stay with him.

"Is that Central Park?" I point out the window when I see greenery in the middle of concrete.

"Yup. If you're up for a cold stroll, we'll walk through it one afternoon."

"Yes!" My eyes light up.

"I'm glad you're here." His hand reaches for mine on my lap, making my skin tingle and my heart pitter-patter.

"Me too." I smile over at Hudson, who's focused on the road ahead with a peaceful expression.

"We're here." He taps my knee.

I look up in time as he pulls into a parking garage. Excitement soars through me, and I lean forward on the seat, looking through the window. Curiosity about Hudson's home fills me. I can't wait to see it.

"Excited?" He teases.

"I am," I nod. "I have to know if you live in a bachelor pad or some minimalistic high-end place." I arch a brow.

"You'll have to find out for yourself. Come on." He opens his car door with a smug smirk.

I follow him, leaving my suitcase in the car.

"I'm nervous." Hudson runs his hands down his thighs in front of the elevator.

"Why?" I lean back.

"I don't know. It's a part of me you don't know yet. I can't help but wonder if you'd approve or not."

"Hudson." I reach for his hands. "Why would you think that?"

"Because I'm not the man you thought I'd become when we were younger."

"You are. You're still funny and kind and a hard worker. Yeah, you have some new qualities that have developed, like much more persistent than when we were younger, but that worked out in my favor in the long run." I wink and clutch the lapel of his coat.

"Show me your home, and then take me to coffee."

"Yes, ma'am." He salutes me and presses the elevator button.

Laughing, I hook my arm with his. "Don't call me ma'am."

"I know. I realized after I said it that it didn't work well. You should be called beautiful, amazing, sweetheart."

We step into the elevator.

"Keep going." I wave my hand to encourage him.

Hudson chuckles and wraps his arm around my shoulders in a protective hold. It doesn't take long to get up to his floor. We walk to his apartment, and I don't miss the expansive wall space between each door on this floor.

ABI SABINA

When he opens the door, and I step in, my eyes widen. It's nothing like I imagined. I walk through the small foyer into a vast living room with huge windows. An ivory leather sofa sits to my right, with an enormous television mounted on the wall and a marble coffee table between the two. A charming bar cart sits against another wall. It's contemporary with a hint of vintage that adds charisma to the style.

"Wow…" I breathe out when I turn and see an ornate white fireplace with wall-mounted bookshelves on either side.

"Hudson, this is amazing." I find his eyes across the living room. He looks at me with a softness I've come to get used to, and it makes me feel so loved.

"You like it?"

"It's beautiful."

"Let me show you the kitchen." He walks toward me and then guides me to the kitchen.

"Whoa," I whisper.

While marble countertops, gray cabinets, stainless steel appliances, and a round wood table off to the side. It's a dream and much bigger than I'd expected. Clearly, this apartment isn't a regular one found in any old apartment building.

"Stunning." I shake my head and look at him.

"I'm so glad. Let's go get some coffee and show you around a bit. I'm trying to convince you to extend your trip." He waggles his eyebrows.

"Yes. I could use some coffee."

"You're going to love the place I have in mind." He links his fingers with mine and leads us to the coffee shop.

As we walk down the road, my eyes bounce around everywhere—brick buildings, glass and steel buildings, ornate buildings that look European. People walk around despite the cold and wet climate.

MEET AGAIN

Turning left, we walk across Central Park. To think that blocks of greenery exist in the center of this concrete jungle is fascinating.

"Hopefully, there's a table available by the window so we can have a view." Hudson squeezes my hand and opens the door to a fancy-looking coffee shop.

Amber Rose is printed on the door, and large glass creates the structure.

"Sounds good." The small shop is bustling with people as we stand in line. The menu reads regular coffee options and some I've never heard of.

"What do you want?"

"A latte." I smile up at Hudson.

"Go grab that table, and I'll order." He whispers, and I follow his line of vision and nod. "Hurry, or someone will steal it," he adds.

"Ay-ay, captain." I tease and speed over to the table, dropping my purse on the top before sitting. I hear a sigh and look up to find a woman frowning.

Close call.

Staring out the window, I see people dressed in all styles walking in front of me. Central Park is across the street, with looming buildings creating a backdrop behind it. I look over at Hudson, and he seems so at ease here. I can see how he fits in. And I wonder what that means for us.

29
LEX

AFTER CHECKING IN TO the hotel yesterday, Hudson took me to Chelsea Market, where we ate the best tacos ever (though I'll never tell that to the owners of El Jefe in Hartville) and walked around looking at the different shops. It was amazing, and I was sad to say goodnight to Hudson at the end of the evening.

Even after waking up in Manhattan this morning, it still feels surreal to be here. My stomach flips as nerves pulse through me. I've spent weeks preparing for today, and I'm scared I'm going to blank out, forget the choreography, or throw up in front of everyone. Or all three plus some bonuses I can't even think of at the moment.

At least it'd make me memorable. I cringe at that thought and take a deep breath.

I look at myself in the mirror again and nod at my reflection.

"You've got this, Lex." I high-five myself in the mirror and then laugh as I stare at the ceiling. I'm so ridiculous.

Grabbing my bag with all my notes, I look at the directions on my phone and get ready to follow them. The school shouldn't be more than ten minutes away if I don't get lost.

When I step out of the hotel, I pause. So many people are already buzzing about this early in the morning. It's a stark contrast to Hartville. We may not be a tiny town, but we're by no means a city, let alone one of this massive size.

MEET AGAIN

I take a deep breath and focus on the directions. I want to arrive early, so I have time to talk to Michelle and settle in.

A deep sigh escapes me when I see the school in front of me. "Thank goodness I didn't get lost."

My heart pounds like an angry hammer as I walk inside. I look up at the high ceilings before searching my way around the hallways.

"You're here!" A loud squeal surprises me.

I smile when I see Michelle rushing toward me with open arms. Her long hair is half-up, and she's wearing a pencil skirt and blouse.

"It's so good to see you." Her smile is genuine.

"You too. Gosh, it's been so long."

"I know. How are you? How was your trip here?"

My eyes widen, and she laughs.

"I know, driving in this city is crazy. I'm so glad they have great public transportation." She waves her hand in the air.

"Anyway, let me show you around. You have a room where you'll teach. It's set up with chairs already and a laptop for you to project your presentation."

"Great. Will I be able to move the chairs when I teach the choreography?" We walk down the impressive hall with totally modern architecture. I look around in awe, passing a flurry of people who excitedly wave at Michelle.

She smiles at all of them but keeps her attention on our conversation.

"Yes, you're set up in a classroom, so during a break, they'll come and help you clear the room. It's all lined out in the schedule." She flips through a stack of papers and pulls one out for me. "Here."

I read through it, taking in the different times.

"You'll have time to participate in one of the classes if you want. Let me know which one you choose that fits with your teaching schedule."

"Thanks. I'm so excited about that." I read through the schedule. Mine is highlighted for me already, which I'm grateful for.

"I'm nervous," I admit.

"Don't be. You're a pro. It's going to be amazing. People are excited about your topic and learning how to blend dance with business. It's unrealistic every dancer will make it professionally, and they love the idea of knowing what to do in case they'd want to teach or run their own studio."

"That's good to know," I exhale.

"You're going to do great," she gives my arm a gentle squeeze. "We can catch up during lunch."

"Sure."

I step into the room I'll be teaching in and stare at all the empty chairs. I pinch myself and jolt. Not dreaming. This is my real life. Despite my doubts, I'm proud to experience this opportunity. I set up my presentation on the laptop and turn on the projector.

Soon people start filtering through the door. I smile and introduce myself to each of them, taking the opportunity to get to know them a bit. I have from seasoned dancers to those just starting their careers.

With expectant eyes on me, I formally introduce myself, sharing about my dancing, my studio, and personal tidbits to break the ice. I relax as people laugh at my jokes and begin to interact with my presentation.

This is more than about me standing here and lecturing. I want them to share their ideas and experiences and ask questions.

"What made you decide to open your own studio?" A young woman asks.

"I wanted to share my passion with others. When I was young, my town didn't have a dance studio, and my parents sacrificed to take me to a nearby town that had one. If I could give something to my community and share my love for dancing, I'd take the opportunity. It was always my dream." I smile at the girl.

"You never wanted to attend a dance school and pursue a professional career?" another woman asks. "Michelle says you were the best in your class growing up."

"I admire people who take that route. It takes a ton of dedication, hard work, and determination. Ultimately, I wanted a different lifestyle. This works for me, but that doesn't mean dancing professionally shouldn't be someone else's dream." I nod.

I continue with my presentation. My topic is broken up into three parts so I can spread it out each day, and I have time to really expand the information and answer questions.

When it's time to dance, the students spread out. Their excitement is palpable, and I cross my fingers that they like it. With counts of eight, I show them the first part of the dance with the music before breaking it down and teaching it to them. By the time it's lunch hour, I'm tired, hungry, but happy.

"How'd it go?" Michelle grins.

"Great. These students are amazing."

"They are. Some are alumni. We wanted to make this conference go beyond our students to other dancers. We have people from all over the country."

"That's so amazing. It seems like you're doing great things."

We stand in line to grab the catered buffet lunch.

"Yeah, I really love my job. I'm glad I took this route after performing. It fits me much more." Michelle hands me a plate that I gratefully take.

"How is life? Are you still with that guy you were dating?" I don't miss the way her eyes glance at my ring finger.

I shake my head. "Actually, long story. We ended up breaking up in college, but we recently got reacquainted and are dating again. He actually lives here."

"Ohhh...soooo my invitation was right on time." Her eyebrows dance on her forehead.

I shove my shoulder against hers and giggle. "We were not an item when you called. We had seen each other, but I wasn't quite ready. Things are going well, though." Thinking about Hudson makes a broad grin break out on my face.

"Seems like it by that smile. I'm happy for you."

"Thanks. How about you?" I serve myself some grilled chicken and salad.

"I've been seeing someone for a few months. Dating is hard, but I really like him." She smiles broadly.

"That's great." It's so nice to catch up with her.

"Thanks."

We finish serving our lunch and take a seat. Michelle introduces me to other teachers, and I meet the director of the school. Everyone is kind and welcoming, sharing about themselves and their careers. It's so much better than I imagined, breaking down the intimidation I felt when I first arrived.

I step away when I finish eating and call Hudson to let him know how it's going. I had a few messages from him, and knowing I can call him to share this with him is on a whole different level of surrealism.

When the day comes to an end, I'm exhausted and ready for a shower. I walk back to my hotel to do just that and wait for Hudson to finish work. He said he had plans for us tonight, and as tired as I am, nothing would stop me from spending the evening with him.

"How does pizza sound tonight?" Hudson drapes his arm around my shoulder and tugs me to him, kissing the top of my head.

"Amazing. I've always heard pizza is a must in New York."

"Good. I'm taking you to this small place. It's laid-back, and you can tell me all about your first day." His warmth envelops me in a safe cocoon.

"It was amazing, Hudson." I beam. I still haven't come down from the high of my first workshop. I'm tired, but I feel like I was able to impart some of my wisdom to other people. That's what I've always wanted.

"I'm so happy to hear that. You see, nothing to be worried about." He squeezes my shoulder and smiles at me.

"I was so nervous," I chuckle. "But the people attending are great. They asked a ton of questions, shared their own stories. They've loved the choreography so far, too. Oh! And I'm taking one of the classes—trending music and dance moves to keep up with the times."

Hudson quietly chuckles beside me, and I turn my head to look up at him.

"What?" I cross my arms.

"I love how excited you are. It's endearing." He pulls me toward him in a quick motion, making my steps falter and almost fall.

"Hey, now." I poke his chest.

"I love it," he repeats. "You look happy."

"I have the best job in the world." I shrug.

His smile slips as he nods.

"What?"

"Nothing. Ready for some amazing pizza?"

"Tell me it's extra cheesy." My mouth waters. My body has evaporated the grilled chicken and salad I had for lunch. When I work, my mind and body are so consumed by what I'm doing that I'm hardly hungry. It's afterward that I become a starved beast.

"Don't worry. It's just as you like it. We'll feed that growly monster." He pats my stomach, and a deep red covers my face. I didn't think he had heard it since there was noise around us.

We enter a small place, and I'm instantly hit with the salty goodness from the cheese, garlic, and spices. It's nothing fancy, and I love it. Metal tables and chairs with metal framing and cushions covered in red vinyl on the back and seat are crammed in the restaurant.

I tell Hudson everything about my day. He listens intently with a small smile. When they bring our pizza, my eyes widen, and I think some drool dribbles down the side of my chin.

"That looks amazing."

Hudson serves me a slice, and I don't bother waiting. I dig in. The crust is thin without being crispy. It has small pepperonis on it and basil leaves, and oh, my goodness... I chew my first bite and close my eyes. Thin strings of cheese stick to my chin, and I have the decency to cover my face and grab a napkin. Hudson sits across from me, his shoulders shaking in laughter.

"Best pizza ever," I comment after swallowing my bite.

"I'm glad you like it."

"Like it? I want to wrap up stock and take it back to Hartville." His eyes light up at my comment, and I take it as a sign that he's happy.

"How was work?" I ask, eating my pizza like the well-mannered human my parents raised me to be.

"It was work," he shrugs.

"Not a good day?" I press when I see the frustration lining his face.

"Nothing to worry about." He smirks, but it doesn't quite reach his eyes the way his smiles do lately.

I drop it, not wanting to ruin dinner. If he didn't have a good day, I hope I can make his evening better. We eat our pizza, keeping the conversation light in the packed restaurant.

"What's Tristan up to, by the way?" I look at him before taking another bite.

"He's around. He wants to give us time alone, so he's doing his own thing. We'll catch him soon. I'm being selfish for now," he winks, and butterflies go wild in my stomach.

When it's time for dessert, Hudson orders a tiramisu for the two of us with the promise that I won't be too full to indulge in it.

The way he's looked at me throughout dinner has made me giddy, like a teen girl who just received tickets to her favorite boy band concert. His gaze is deep and intense. His laugh is rich and warm. Could our lives have been this way all this time had we not taken different paths?

I shake that idea away. There's no point in focusing on the past. It's already done, and we can't change it.

Hudson reaches for my hand, linking his fingers with mine. I shiver at the contact and smile up at him.

"I can't tell you enough how happy I am that you're here. Stay through the weekend," his demand comes with a hint of pleading.

Hearing the emotions in his voice, the yearning, makes me nod my head slowly.

"Okay."

"Really?" His eyebrows shoot up, and his eyes widen.

"Yeah. I want to spend time with you. It's not that I don't." I turn our hands over so I can trace the lines on his palm.

"I just get nervous that we'll get stuck in this back and forth limbo," I confess, turning my gaze down to where our hands are.

"We'll figure it out, I promise." His words are full of determination and honesty. I simply nod, hoping he's right.

"You're my number one. Now and always."

My eyes lift to his and find fire blazing in them. I tremble, captured by his gaze. There's no denying the sincerity and fierceness coming from him.

"You're mine, too." I lace my fingers with his and lift our joined hands, kissing the inside of his wrist.

His fingers tighten around mine, and he clears his throat.

"I'm going to pay."

The tension between us is palpable. Emotions run high, desire to make things work mixed with fear that they won't. It feels a bit reckless, but I know Hudson won't give up without a fight. Not this time. And I plan to do the same. Four years was enough time to miss him. Now that I have him in my life again, I won't let anyone take him away. Not when we both want this.

"Ready?" His voice is gruff when he speaks after paying the bill.

"Yeah." I stand.

"Let's grab a cab," Hudson suggests when we walk out into the rain.

He hails a cab, and after unsuccessfully trying, the third cab stops for us. We sit side by side, our thighs pressed against each other. I'm hyperaware of him, of the way his fingers mindlessly brush against mine, how his chest rises and falls with deep breaths, the heat that moves through us. I wish I could kiss him right now, but I don't want an audience.

Hudson lifts our hands and observes them, maybe seeing the way they fit together. I've done that plenty of times.

"I love you so much." His words are quiet.

"I love you, too." I turn my head to look at him. His expression is serious. Gone is the funny guy. In his place is a man pouring out love and...longing.

"We're going to work out. Trust me." His lips softly brush the top of my hand, causing a shiver to run down my spine.

"I do."

His other hand cradles my face and brings his forehead to mine. We both close our eyes and take deep breaths. The only sound is the commercial on the radio.

Hudson tips his head up without inching back so that his lips barely brush against mine. "You're mine."

"We're here." The cab driver breaks the spell cast over us, and I blink my eyes, leaning back. My lips part as I breathe heavily. Hudson seems to be doing the same.

"Thanks." He clears his throat and opens the door.

Sliding out, he reaches for my hand and helps me out. I race to shelter under the hotel's awning while Hudson pays our cab driver. Then, he's stalking toward me with long strides.

"I'll walk you up." He whispers in my ear, wrapping his arm around my back in a half-hug.

I nod against him and lead the way, his hand in mine.

ABI SABINA

Hudson has always been the person to fill my heart with love and make me feel safe. For so long, I thought I was replaceable in his life, but he's showing me that was never the case.

30

HUDSON

Having Lex here these last couple of days has been amazing. I've loved showing her around the city, and since it's the last day of the conference, I have something special planned. Lex being here has provided the distraction I need, too. My dad didn't love the idea that I wasn't going to Texas. I'd guess it's because his manipulative plan backfired and not because of a deal.

I called the developer I was supposed to meet with, and he told me next month was actually better for him, but my dad had insisted we meet this week—more proof of his scheming. I'm over it.

When Tristan told me about our mom's bribe, I knew my parents had gone too far. My mind's been racing with ideas, all of them leading to the same conclusion—cut ties. I allowed them to mess with my life when I was younger, but not anymore. I learned from that mistake. Wanting distance from them only created a barrier between the woman I love and me. But being in Hartville won't make it easier.

With a chaos of ideas going nowhere, I grab my phone and send Lex a message.

> Hudson: Dinner tonight. I'll pick you up at the school

I put my phone down and smirk. She checked out of her hotel this morning and insisted on taking her bag with her to the conference instead of having me pick it up before she left. She's brave to drag a small suitcase through these streets. I wish I could see her. No doubt she'll get a few unimpressed comments.

Then, she's spending the night in my apartment. I didn't want her leaving after the conference and driving at night, but more than that, I didn't want to say goodbye yet. When I left Hartville, I knew I'd see her in ten days. This time around, it'll be three weeks before we go to the bach party. Too long for my liking.

A smile takes over when my phone lights up. I open up Lex's message, not focusing at all on work. I should call it a day.

Lex: Can't wait. I'll be done by 3

Hudson: I'll be there

I look over some properties I need to show next week, learning all the details. They're all luxury homes, like everything we represent. As nice as the commission is, it gets old dealing with one side of society.

Hopefully, time goes by quickly, or I'll sit outside the school and wait for Lex for two hours.

MEET AGAIN

"I need to shower and change before we go out. Should I dress up?" Lex smiles over at me, our intertwined hands swinging between us. I drag her suitcase with my other hand as we get up to the street from the nearest subway stop near my apartment.

"Hmmm...yeah, dress up tonight." We've gone to laid-back places the last two evenings, but today I'm bringing out the big guns.

"Okay. I'll be as quick as possible."

"No rush." I squeeze her hand and smile. I could see us living a life like this, being married, coming home together after work, having date nights. I want that.

"Good," she breathes out. "I really need to wash my hair." Her nose scrunches up.

I chuckle and look at her bun. It looks fine to me, but who knows.

"You have plenty of time, promise. We're going to dinner at seven and then a surprise."

"You know I don't like surprises." She turns her head and looks at me.

"This is a good one." I wink.

"I guess I'll have to deal with it," she shakes her head in mock annoyance.

"Good." I turn toward my building.

We walk up to my apartment in silence. A wide yawn takes over Lex, and she covers her mouth a second too late. Her cheeks turn pink.

"I could use a nap."

"Then you'll have a nap. We have time."

"Don't tempt me with a good time," her eyebrows dance on her forehead.

I unlock the door to my apartment and wait for her to walk in. "What's it going to be? A shower or a nap?"

"A shower, and then I'm going to nap while my hair air dries. It's perfect," another yawn interrupts her comment.

"Uh, huh." I nod, dropping my keys in the glass bowl on the table by the entrance. "I'll take your bag to your room. The bathroom has towels and soap and all the good stuff you need." I went to the store yesterday during my lunch break to buy shampoo, conditioner, and the soap she always uses.

"Thanks." She kisses my cheek before following me to the guest bedroom. As much as I'd love to hold her through the night, I'm giving her space.

"Anything for you." I've never meant something as much as I do those words. I'd do anything for Lex.

"Hey, there, stranger," Tristan walks out of his room with a wide smile. Thank goodness this apartment has three bedrooms. "How was the conference?"

"It was great," Lex gives him a sleepy smile.

"I'm glad to hear that. Hudson's been hogging you, but maybe we can all hang out tomorrow."

"That'd be fun." Lex looks at me.

"Yeah. Jameson and Willa want to meet Lex, too. We can all do something."

"Are these your friends you were telling me about?" Her eyebrows lift.

"Yup."

"Great," Tristan claps my shoulder. "I'm going to grab something to eat in the kitchen. I've been working for too long."

Lex raises her eyebrows, but I shrug. Tristan is being too secretive about some of his work, and I'm not going to get into it unless he wants me to. Chances are he's scheming a plan to get that trust fund on his twenty-fifth birthday.

MEET AGAIN

As I set Lex's suitcase by the foot of the bed, she takes out her bun. Mesmerized, I watch her hair cascade down her shoulders. It's messy and perfect. She's a sight for sore eyes. Stunning, perfect, all mine.

"Stop staring." Her eyebrows dip, and she screws her face.

"Never." I loop my arm around her and pull her to me. "I want to spend the rest of my life staring at you."

Her breath catches, her eyes dancing between mine.

"Go shower," I whisper. She nods silently and heads to the bathroom while I walk out of the room and go into the kitchen for some water. Having her here for the next two nights is going to be a challenge to my self-restraint. I could spend every hour kissing her.

♡♡♡

"Dinner was delicious." Lex rubs her stomach as we walk down the sidewalk.

"I'm glad you liked it. Charlie Bird is a must-try here." I'm glad she liked the restaurant. Her eyes lit up when she saw the original brick mixed with an industrial design.

"The scallops were to die for. And the burrata...goodness gracious." She licks her lips, and I laugh at her overreaction.

"I was hoping you'd like it.

"Loved it." She looks over at me with a lazy grin. It's the look of a fully stuffed woman, but I'm not done with her just yet.

"This isn't in the direction of your apartment, is it?"

I smirk at the way she's already orientated with parts of the city.

"Nope, I've got another surprise." I reach for her hand and look at her with a broad smile. I haven't been able to stop smiling. Forget my parents and their attempts to ruin my happiness. Forget my job and meetings and showings. She's all that matters. She makes everything better. She makes my stress melt away.

"Okay," she nods happily and follows along for the ride.

I stop in front of a small hotdog joint, ready to open the door.

"Uhhh..." Her caramel eyes round.

"Come on." I nod, holding back my smirk.

She nods and enters, standing quietly beside me. Her fingers twist together as she looks around the place. It's dated and smells like boiled hotdogs.

"What can I get ya?" The middle-aged man lifts his chin in my direction.

"Ten foot-long dogs and a pound of relish, please."

"Hudson?" Lex tugs my hand. "We ate." Her eyes grow like saucers.

"Yeah," I try to keep it cool.

"Right this way." The man nods and opens the door to the bathroom.

"What in the..." Lex stares up at me.

"Knock fives times," is all the man says, and I grab Lex's hand and pull her through the dark hallway.

"I'm so confused. This isn't a bathroom. What the... Ow." I hear a slap against the wall.

"Are you okay?" I stop and reach out for her. The hallway is poorly lit, giving me just a glimpse of her face.

"Yeah, yeah. I hit something, trying to reach out my hand. Maybe a lamp or something on the wall?"

MEET AGAIN

I chuckle and grab both of her hands, setting them on the back of my shoulders so she can follow blindly. When I reach a door, I knock five times and wait.

The door swings open, and music streams out of it. A dim room opens before us, and Lex gasps.

"Oh my goodness! Is this a speakeasy?" I find her mouth dropped open and eyes full of surprise.

"Yup."

"Good, because I was so confused when you ordered ten foot-long hotdogs. I was about to kick you without the man seeing."

I throw my head back and laugh. "Seeing your reaction was priceless."

After giving the doorman my name, we take a seat on a loveseat reserved for us. A small round marble table sits in front of us with a tea candle. The entire bar is inspired by the twenties with a retro decor that feels like you have entered a portal to the past. The waiters and waitresses are dressed for the era. Jazz music sounds from the speakers. The only thing that's proof of being in the present is the customers dressed in regular clothes and their smartphones.

"This is so cool." Her excitement pulses all around her.

"It is," I nod. "Let's have a drink, yeah?"

We both lean in close together and look at the drinks menu. I inhale her perfume, dizzy from her. She's better than any cocktail.

"The Mary Pickford sounds good. So does the Scofflaw," Lex looks up at me. Despite the low light setting in the bar, her face is illuminated.

"I'm going to have the Scofflaw," I tell her, unable to take my eyes off her. I'm mesmerized.

"So I can order the Mary Pickford, and you'll let me try yours?"

I nod silently. Anything she wants, it's hers. I reach out to hold her face, strumming my thumb across her cheek. As I lean in, a waitress speaks. I look up at her with a scowl for interrupting the moment, but the poor woman is just doing her job.

I place our orders and look back at Lex. She looks comfortable on the loveseat, her leg crossed over her knee. Her eyes scan the bar, taking in every detail.

"I'll have to admit that New York is different than I imagined. It's a mix of people and cultures. It's fascinating." She turns her body toward me.

"Yeah? It is a cool place to live." I can't deny I've had good times in this city.

"I can see that. It's interesting and full of history. Don't you miss nature, though?" She tilts her head, scrutinizing me.

"Upstate New York is a short drive, and it's gorgeous. It's nothing like the city and reminds me a lot of back home. Maybe I can drive us out there in the morning and hang out with my friends at night."

"I've heard that. Wouldn't it be like driving to New Hampshire, though?" Her nose scrunches up adorably.

"Nope. In two hours or so, we can be out of the city and in the countryside."

"Wow." Her eyebrows lift. I love that she's enjoying the city and giving it a real chance.

"We'll take a drive tomorrow." I tap her knee, excited about showing her more of New York and chipping away any preconceived ideas she may have. I can imagine us living this life.

Our drinks are served, and Lex comments on the beautiful presentation before taking a sip and closing her eyes.

MEET AGAIN

"This is so good." She smiles over her glass.

I want to bottle up the moment. I wish I could be recording it, save it for eternity. Every time I spend with her is special, but something about tonight makes it feel different. For the first time, it feels like we're already living our forever.

I refuse to let my thoughts about our reality interfere. Not tonight. Not when we're this happy. Nothing will ruin this moment. I wrap my arm around her and lean her against me. Kissing the top of her head, I feel lightness fill my chest. For so long, I felt like I was running a race with no direction. I finally found my guiding light.

31

LEX

My body feels light, buzzing with goodness. I can't get over how great it feels to be here, to be with Hudson. Last night was amazing. When I saw the hotdog place, I was so confused, but the speakeasy was such an incredible experience. We laughed and danced. Feeling his arms around me as we swayed to the soft jazz made my eyes water.

I'm excited about exploring the rest of the state today with Hudson and Tristan. I love being outdoors and exploring nature, even if it is freezing. Each season provides unique beauty to our world.

My phone rings on the nightstand, and I reach for it as I finish sliding my arm through my sweater sleeve.

"Hello?" I breathe out when I see that it's Michelle.

"Hey, Lex," she answers.

"Hey, what's up?" I fix my sweater so that it sits right on my body.

"Not much. We didn't get a chance to talk yesterday afternoon, but I wanted to thank you again for coming to the conference."

"I should be thanking you," I laugh. "It was an amazing experience, and I made some great contacts." I took the liberty to socialize and network with peers. I talked about my students, their dreams, and was encouraged to tell them about the programs in the city for those interested in pursuing a

MEET AGAIN

professional career. I know Sarah is, though a few other students have talked about it.

"That's actually why I'm calling..." Michelle stalls. "I know you have your studio, and it's your baby, but my school has an opening that I think you'd be perfect for."

My body drops on the bed. My heart stops, heat (not the good kind) filling me. I grip the messy sheets beside me. Words are gone, my voice lost.

"Hello?" Michelle giggles. "Did I shock you?"

"I'm not even qualified." That's the best that comes out of me.

"You have the teaching experience. It's a Modern One class for incoming students, and you definitely have the capabilities and knowledge. My boss was impressed with your choreography. Of course, you'd have to interview like everyone else, so it wouldn't guarantee the position, but I think you have a great chance."

She's speaking, but all I hear is the buzzing in my ears.

"Wow..."

"Yeah," she laughs. "I thought since your boyfriend lives in New York, you could be interested. It'd take your teaching to a different level, with adults preparing for a professional career instead of children. That's something to consider if you want."

"Can I think about it?" I love my kids. I can't just turn my back on them.

"Of course. If you're interested, send your resume sooner rather than later. I'm excited for you. Regardless of what you decide, this is a great indication of your talent and professionalism."

"Thanks." I nod to myself. "I'll get back to you."

"Sounds good. Have a safe trip back home." She happily says before hanging up.

I slump into the bed and close my eyes. A teaching position in a prestigious New York school? It's not Juilliard, but it's still a high-caliber school. Nerves land in the pit of my stomach like a ton of bricks. Do I want this? My immediate response is no. I love what I do. Is it a great opportunity, even just to interview for it? Of course. I'm not dense.

Knocking on the door breaks me from my stupor. "Yeah?"

"Are you ready?" Hudson's voice sounds muffled through the wood.

My heart pounds for another reason. How is he going to react when he hears about Michelle's call?

"Yeah." I jump to my feet. I scurry around the room, grabbing my scarf and gloves as the door opens.

"Are you okay?"

My head snaps up to look at Hudson. His eyebrows pull together, and he steps into the room.

"What's wrong?" He's instantly in front of me.

"Nothing," I shake my head.

"You're not a good liar." He cups my face, and my eyes flutter closed.

"I want to enjoy our day. We'll talk about it later."

"Nope." He shakes his head with persistence.

"Please," I beg.

"Talk to me. We've already had too much lack of communication in our past. Come on." He grabs my hand and leads me toward the living room.

"You were fine earlier when we had coffee, so what's going on?" His hand remains in mine.

"Michelle called me." I take a gulp of air and prepare to tell him the news. I know Hudson, and he's going to see this as a sign for us to be together, but it's not what I want. If it were, I'd be jumping for joy and emailing my resume right away.

"What did she say? Was everything okay with the workshop?" His eyebrows furrow, concern pinching his lips.

"Yeah, it was great. That's why she called. Her boss was impressed with my choreography. There's an opening at her school to teach modern dance to first-year students, and she thought I'd be great. She said I should send my info for an interview."

"Wow, that's amazing, babe." His face lights up, making me feel even more guilty.

"Why aren't you excited?" He leans back, scanning my face.

"I love my studio and my students and the classes I already teach. If I wanted this, I would've been excited from the moment she mentioned it. I don't feel that way." I shrug.

"You can have someone teach your classes during the semester and have your own in the summer months. This is perfect." He stands and paces. "You'll live here, and we can spend as much time together as we want without worrying about goodbyes or when we'll see each other again. My parents will be far away, so they can't meddle or be jerks." His beaming smile would look perfect on a billboard, but it doesn't captivate me.

"Hudson," I stop him. "This isn't what I want."

"It's the right opportunity." He leans back in disbelief. His eyebrows pull down, and his green eyes darken in confusion.

"It's not right if it doesn't feel good to me. Do you want me to end up resenting you for giving up my dream?" I throw my hands in the air. This feels like deja vu.

"You're not giving it up. You'll still have it. It'll buy me time to figure out my next steps."

"What are you talking about?" I shake my head. "Never mind. I thought you had changed, understood and respected my career choices." Tears blur my vision. "You're the same person."

"I don't want this life." I fling my arm in the air.

"You mean the life I have?" His jaw ticks.

"You know what I mean."

"No, please elaborate. Explain all the ways my life disgusts you." His nostrils flare.

"It doesn't disgust me!" I toss my head back, a cynical laugh escaping me. "Nothing about you disgusts me, but I love what I do. You told me you respected that and understood why I wanted a studio in Hartville, but your words and actions right now are betraying that." I turn around, giving him my back and staring out the huge windows with views of tall buildings.

"Does it make me selfish to turn this down? Maybe. Maybe we're not meant to be together and are just chasing a teen fantasy." I turn around, tears streaming down my face. I push them away angrily.

"Don't say that." He steps toward me and pauses. "Lex," he pleads.

I shrug, unable to speak. My lower lip trembles and I look away.

"It could be temporary. Why won't you even consider it?" He trails his fingers through his hair, tugging at the roots.

"Because I don't want it. I wouldn't force you to do something just because the opportunity presented itself."

"I'd do it. If it meant I could be with you, I wouldn't doubt it. Your actions are speaking volumes as well, Lex." His eyes blaze with anger.

"I'm going to go."

"No."

"Yes, Hudson. I need space."

"Don't leave like this." The way he looks at me breaks my heart. I thought we could have this again, blend our lives.

"There's no reason for me to stay. History seems to always repeat itself, and we aren't safe from it."

"Lex," he calls after me. Sobs wrack my body as I walk into the bathroom and lock the door. I lean against it and slide down, clutching my knees.

Was I naïve to believe this time was different? His parents would probably have a good laugh at our failed attempt.

When I finally pick myself off the floor, I get back into the room and hastily pack my bag. My eyes are puffy and red. My reflection finishes breaking what's left of my heart. I keep my head down and walk through the silent apartment. There's no sign of Hudson. I swallow back my tears and grab my car keys before heading to the garage.

I sit in my car for a long time, a mess of thoughts clashing together. We had it all, and at the snap of a finger, it's gone, just like four years ago.

I wipe my eyes and look up. Hudson stands by the open elevators. His gaze pierces me before he turns and enters. Another sob moves through me.

I need to get out of here. I need to go. I pull out, recklessly leaving the garage and driving onto the busy streets. Unlike when I first arrived, I'm driven by anger and frustration instead of fear and nerves. I open the GPS on my phone and see the town name we were going to visit together. Not ready to drive the six hours to Hartville, I turn on the navigation and follow it. Maybe I can start a new life there.

I snort and shake my head. *Ridiculous, Lex.*

My emotions are haywire the entire three and a half hours it takes me to arrive in Chapel Falls. An hour into the drive, I had to put my phone on Do Not Disturb because it wouldn't stop ringing and pinging with messages. It was interrupting my GPS directions. It took an extra thirty minutes than it should have since I had to slow down and wipe my eyes throughout the drive.

I feel empty by the time I park near Main Street in this quaint town. I numbly walk along the sidewalk, seeing the town without really looking at it. People stare as I pass them. I can only imagine how horrible I look. My eyes must be bloodshot by now. One person smiles sympathetically, and it takes everything in me not to break down right there.

"Are you okay, dear?" An older woman looks at me with furrowed brows.

I nod, choking on my cry, and keep walking. How can one phone call ruin an entire relationship? Maybe it didn't. Maybe our relationship was already fractured with uncertainties, and the phone call shined a light on them.

I look up and take in the center of town. *Wow.* It's beautiful and magical. Starting over in a place like this sounds nice, but escaping your problems isn't realistic. I'll enjoy the time I have here, at least. Chapel Falls is unique, with snow piled on the sidewalks and stores lining Main Street. I walk into different ones, looking around. It helps to clear my mind and focus on something other than my heartache.

Waves of emotions roll over me throughout the day. I wander up and down the small quaint town. I see a gazebo in a small square and take a seat on a bench in the frigid cold. At least the weather is helping numb me. If it freezes my tears, that'd be great. I don't want to feel anymore. I don't want to think or hurt.

We were supposed to get things right this time. Everything pointed to a successful relationship. We seemed unbreakable, but Hudson seems to still believe that I can easily change my career path to suit us, suit *him*. I know relationships should be give and take by both partners, but I don't want to give up my dream. I don't want to turn my back on my studio. This isn't just about teaching dance; it's about being a part of my community.

Maybe he's right in saying that my decision speaks volumes, but I love Hudson. I really do. I'm just not sure I love the life he says we can have.

I grab my phone to check the time and see a ton of calls and messages. I forgot I turned on Do Not Disturb.

Hudson stopped calling and writing to me about an hour ago. He probably gave up, realizing I was right. We're destined for different roads.

Hope has called a ton of times and sent over thirty messages. I read through them, my body trembling with repressed cries.

Lex: I'm ok. Took a detour and will be home soon

Hope: Thank goodness you responded. I was about to send a search and rescue team for you. Where are you? What kind of detour? Hudson is worried sick

Lex: I'm not ready to talk. I'll be home tomorrow

Hope: Where are you?

Lex: Hope, please. I checked in, let you know I'm alive

Hope: Ok. Call me when you're ready

I don't respond. Looking up and seeing how the sun is beginning to set already, I hope there's a hotel or inn I can stay the night. Driving at night is not my cup of tea.

As I walk back into the center of town, I see a coffee shop I spotted earlier and walk in. A barista should know about a hotel. The interior is charming and adorable. Brick walls, colorful art, and mismatched chairs and tables fill the space.

I attempt a smile when I walk up to the young barista, but her eyebrows furrow.

"Oh, darling, are you okay?" She looks at me with careful observation.

I nod and avert my eyes, looking at the menu behind her on the wall.

"Can I have a chai latte, please?"

"Sure." She continues to stare at me. "Would you like something sweet?" Her smile is kind, crinkling the corners of her eyes.

"Just the chai," I shake my head.

"I'll tell you what, a chocolate chip cookie on me. It's our famous recipe."

"Thanks," I choke out.

"No need to thank me. You look like you could use some sweetness." My watery eyes betray me.

MEET AGAIN

I pay for my latte and hesitate. When the barista lifts her brows, I dive in. "Do you know if there's a hotel or an inn with availability for tonight?"

"Chapel Hills Bed and Breakfast. The name isn't unique, but the building is historical and a dream. Let me call and check if they've got a room for you." She's so helpful and kind. I watch as she dials the number and asks someone named Donna. She whispers something, likely about my state, and nods.

She smiles when she hangs up and looks at me. "You've got a room booked."

"Thank you," I sigh. "I'm parked here on Main Street. Is it far?"

"Nope. It's a block down. Your GPS should get you there, and she's got parking so you won't have to lug your suitcase in the cold."

"Thank you so much," I say again.

"No problem. I'll get your order for you."

I stand by the end of the counter until she hands me my latte and cookie. Taking a seat, I sip my drink and close my eyes. So good. It's cozy and feels like home. Another wave of emotions slams into me, and I lower my head and trap the tears with my closed eyes.

A scalding shower sounds great right now, so I can cry freely and wash away the day. I wave at the barista and head to my car. It's going to be a restless night, but it's better than arriving in Hartville wearing heartbreak for everyone to see. Once again.

32

LEX

"You have to tell us what happened." Hope continues to insist. After two days of asking for space, she and Ellie disregarded my wishes and broke into my house. Literally broke in. When I got home from the studio, they were sitting on the couch in the dark and nearly gave me a heart attack.

"Hudson already told you." I roll my eyes, keeping my arms crossed as a barrier.

The days since I arrived from Chapel Falls have been challenging. More than challenging. I've been living like a zombie. Try as I might to put on a smile and be present, my students can tell I'm not myself. As excited as I was to tell them about the conference, especially my teens, I've barely been able to get it out. Every time I try to, I think about the job offer.

"So you don't want that job?" Hope pushes.

"No." I shake my head. "Maybe it makes me a terrible person?"

"You're not a terrible person," Ellie says, squeezing my arm. "We all know how much the studio means to you."

"Yeah. Don't feel guilty because you love your job." Hope smiles sympathetically.

I nod, my lower lip trembling. Doubt has been pounding against me as I replay my argument with Hudson. Well, more than an argument—our break-up. Did I make the wrong choice? Should I sacrifice my studio for love? So many questions that have no real answers.

"Oh, babes." Hope reaches over and hugs me. Her arms are tight as she soothes me. Ellie joins in, both of them knocking me over on the sofa. I snort and finally wrap my arms around them.

"I'm such a fool. I should've seen this coming," I say through tears.

"None of us saw it coming. Not even Toby. He mentioned that Hudson was looking at a career change or something."

"What?" I lean my head back and look at Hope.

"That's what he said," she shrugs.

"That doesn't make sense," I shake my head. If that were true, he wouldn't have insisted I interview for the teaching job in the city.

"I don't know, but you'll overcome this." Her smile is sad and unconvincing.

"I just want to go to sleep."

"It helps to talk about it."

I look at Hope and shake my head. "I don't want to. I want to sleep. I want to forget about it. I want to unlove him."

"Sweetie," Ellie presses her lips together.

"No," I say firmly. "I appreciate you both. You know I love you like sisters, but I want to be alone now."

"Okay," Hope nods and stands. "We'll go."

Ellie opens her mouth to protest, but Hope reaches for her arm.

"Come on. We'll call you soon." Hope drags Ellie from my living room.

I don't bother walking them out or locking up. I remain on the sofa, staring at a blank spot on the wall. Beside it is Hudson's Christmas gift, taunting me. I don't look at it. My eyes remain on the spot until they become tired, and I slide down on the couch, clutching one of the cushions to my chest.

Everything we lived and spoke about the last few weeks seems to have evaporated faster than rain in a desert. We were so close, but when it came down to it, the truth unraveled. *How did Lorelai Gilmore overcome heartbreak?* Probably by drinking copious amounts of coffee.

The next few days drag. The pain in my chest doesn't lessen. Despite knowing it'd be long-distance, I miss Hudson. I miss talking to him and his messages and his smile. I've been tempted to write to him, but what would that fix? We're still dealing with the same issues, and I'm still angry at his instant disregard for what I want simply because a new plan fits what he wants.

Knowing I'll have to face him in a couple of weeks makes me nauseous. Hope would kill me if I bail on her bachelorette party, but I wonder if I can get away with it.

I reach for my phone in between spoonfuls of cookie dough ice cream. The few messages he's sent stare back at me.

We need to talk.
He's sorry.
He misses me.
Am I sure I don't want the job?
Call him.
He loves me.

MEET AGAIN

That last message makes my chest shake with a repressed cry. I throw the phone across the sofa and hide my face in the cushion. I'm glad I have a weekend to rest and stay in.

I still need to call Michelle to thank her and decline the offer to apply for the job as soon as I have the energy or three cups of coffee. Being with my students this week has just cemented what I feel. They're my family and what I wake up in the morning inspired to do. Those kids have become more than students through the years, and I can't—won't—leave them on impulse.

But at what point do I put my relationship with Hudson first?

I stand and grab some coffee. It may be noon, but it's coffee time all day long in my book. The bachelorette planning will keep me distracted for the rest of the afternoon. Everything needs to be perfect, including me, if I'm going to face *him.*

Hours later, someone knocks on my door. I ignore it as long as possible until the knocking turns into incessant pounding and doorbell ringing, creating the most obnoxious playlist.

I swing the door open and lift my brows when I see my grandma. *Oh, boy.*

"Let me in." She doesn't wait for a response, instead pushing past me with a heavy bag. "It's freezing cold." My grandmother has been living in the United States for years, but her thick accent is still in place, and I love it.

"Hi, Abuela, how are you? Great? Oh, wonderful." I murmur to myself sarcastically.

"If you're going to speak, say it loud enough for me to hear." She lifts her eyebrows. She's feisty today.

"What's wrong? Boy problems. I don't know why. Hudson is a great man who cares about you." She sits at the counter and begins taking things out of the bag. Containers with food. Her coffee maker.

ABI SABINA

According to my grandma, an American coffee maker does not make real coffee. It has to be made in an Italian press, grabbing the first *colada* (brew) and mixing it with two tablespoons of sugar until the rest of the coffee finishes brewing to create *espumita* (foam). And *ta-da*, you have Cuban coffee that will keep you awake and going for hours. It's the best, to be honest.

"Talk to me, mija." My grandma softens her voice and smiles. "Pastelito?" She hands me a cheese and guava pastry, and I practically moan. We may not have Cuban pastries in town, but my grandma makes the best.

I take a big bite, messy scraps of crispy dough falling on the counter unceremoniously. I chew slowly to buy myself time.

"We broke up. It's the same as before. He wants me to give up my dreams just so we can live in the same city. I'm so confused, torn about choosing him or my career." My eyes water and I take another bite of the pastelito.

"You know how much I love ballet. I'm so proud of you." I nod at her words, her hand gently holding mine. My grandmother danced ballet in Cuba before she had to leave the country. She never danced again, but her passion lives in her and through me. She taught me the basics when I could hardly walk. From there, she guided me as I reached different stages of my career.

"Love is also important. Do you love Hudson?" Her brown eyes gaze at me meaningfully.

"I do."

"Is there a way to make it work?"

I shrug. Do I move to New York even if it's not what I want, just so I can be with him?

MEET AGAIN

"I'm afraid I'll end up resenting him," I speak the fearful truth and wipe my nose with the back of my hand. Abuela hands me a napkin. "Thanks," I mumble.

"Cafecito time." She claps her hands with a smile and stands, opening the Italian press and preparing the coffee maker.

While she works, she looks at me and continues speaking. "Love is about sacrifices. Look at your Abuelo and me. Do you think I wanted to leave my family in Miami and move here?" She waves her hand in the air and lifts her eyebrows. Her face says it all.

My grandfather found a job a friend of his recommended, and they moved to Hartville. Back then—and even now—Cubans were a minority in this area, but it worked out for them. They made amazing friends who became family and built a life for themselves. My uncle was already in college, so he was able to stay in the city. That only fueled my mom's resentment. She was in her late teens when she moved, and she rebelled because my dad was in Miami. Their families were friends, and my parents started dating in high school. He eventually moved here to be with her, and they got married.

"I know it was hard."

"But it worked out," she nods with resolve.

"Are you saying I should sacrifice my studio to move with Hudson?"

"I'm saying that relationships take work and commitment and sometimes sacrifices, but only you know where you'll be truly happy. Is he enough, or do you need your studio as well?"

"In an ideal world, I'd have him and my studio." I know how selfish that sounds, but my grandma points it out anyway.

"And he gives up his career?" She lifts her brows, the clanking of the spoon against the stainless steel cup where she's mixing the coffee and sugar fills the silence.

"No, but he's been unhappy. Or so he said." I slump back into my stool.

We really had it out before I left. I don't think we ever yelled at each other that way, not even when we broke up the first time. I hate that. I hate that we left things the way we did.

"You've got some thinking to do." She tilts her head.

"Yeah," I sigh. Maybe it's a good thing I haven't called Michelle yet.

My grandma spends the rest of the day at my place, making me eat more food than I can fit in my stomach and drink coffee. By the time she leaves, I'm in a food coma, and all I can think about is vegging out on the couch. I wonder what Hudson is doing right now.

33
HUDSON

"You still haven't heard from her?" Tristan says incredulously over the phone.

"Nope." I run a hand through my hair. "I messed up big time, and now she won't even talk to me."

"What are you going to do?"

"I'm not sure, but she can't avoid me on the ski trip." Unless I can get to her first. It's just my luck that work has me traveling and unable to drive to Lex and make her face me, talk things out so I can apologize for being a jerk.

I got excited at the prospect that we'd finally be together. I should've known. But why won't she take this job? Or at least try. Does she care so little about me and our relationship that her studio is more important?

These thoughts have plagued my mind for days. They make me angry and sad and guilty. I haven't been on top of work, and clients are noticing when they have to repeat the same question.

"I think it's time you take a hard look in the mirror and decide what you want to do. If you ask Lex to move to New York only to quit your job in a month, that will create a bigger wedge between you. The job they offered her wasn't temporary or to substitute. It'd be bad form to accept only to quit a few months to a year later." When did I think Tristan would be the voice of reason in my life? Never, that's for sure.

"You're right, little bro."

"I know I am."

"Always so humble." I roll my eyes.

"Why be humble when I can be proud." He laughs.

I lean back against the bed frame at the hotel I'm staying in. I'm tired of traveling, of pretending to care what these entitled clients think is a good buy just because they're in competition with their friend and want to burn money on a home that won't be a good investment for them.

I'm just tired and in a terrible mood, wanting to see Lex.

"You've got some thinking to do, and I'm going to bed." He's been working on his non-profit plan and traveling to meet with people. I'm proud to see he's fighting for what he wants despite the financial roadblocks.

"Thanks for checking in. Bye." I hang up.

Unlike Tristan, I'm not fighting for what I want. I'm stuck, expecting things to work out without me taking action.

I look over my notes. Something about the sports app is just not feeling right. I enjoy selling homes and finding people a place to build memories—people like Hope and Toby, who are starting off a new chapter in their lives. It's rare that I work with those types of families, though. They don't provide the hefty commissions my dad wants.

How can I work in real estate while doing it the way I love?

Wheels start turning, and a plan builds in my mind. My pen scribbles on my notebook, writing down everything that comes to me. One of these will stick and become an expandable plan.

What I know for sure is that I already screwed up with Lex once. I won't forgive myself if I don't prove to her that I've changed despite what she currently believes.

34
LEX

"Are you sure you don't want me to drive out with you to decorate?" Ellie asks with wide eyes. The last two weeks have flown by as I've focused on work, choreographies, and finalizing the plans for the ski trip.

"I'm sure. I'll be okay. It's a short drive. Stay and drive with Hope. We can't let her drive up there alone or with the guys. She needs her friends."

Regardless of whether Hudson is helping me or not, I'm going early and decorating the suite. Hope deserves that and more. I won't let my failed relationship ruin the happiest time in her life.

"Call if you need anything. Take pictures of the room before she arrives."

"I will. I'm going to let you go. If I leave now, I'll get there with plenty of time to decorate." It'll take me longer to do it on my own, and I hope the resort is okay with letting me get in early. I called, and they said they would, but sometimes things don't go as planned.

Like your relationship with Hudson.
Shut up, subconscious.

"Byeee." Ellie sing-songs.

I take a deep breath and grab my bag. I wish I were as excited as she is. My priority at the moment is getting to the resort and decorating the suite so that Hope has the best bachelorette party ever. Thankfully, I don't ski, so I'll be able to hang back at the resort and minimize my interaction with Hudson.

It takes longer to pack my car than planned, and when it's full to the brim with bags, I begin my two-hour drive to Winford. My emotions are haywire. I should be doing this drive with Hudson. I should be doing a lot of things differently. This wasn't in our plans. Breaking up, him insisting I move to New York. He was working through his own changes.

The way he threw in my face that I didn't want this relationship to work hurt more than anything. How could he doubt my commitment?

I blink back tears and focus on my even breaths. I can't take any detours today. I have a mission to accomplish, and nothing will deter me. Turning up the volume, my mind concentrates on the songs playing, and my eyes remain on the road. One breath at a time, everything will work out.

By the time I pull up to the resort, my shoulders are tight, and my hips are stiff. All my stress is pocketing in different parts of my body. I stretch my arms overhead, and a wide yawn takes over. When the valet chuckles, my eyes widen, and I cover my mouth. A moment too late, apparently.

"Sorry," I say.

"No worries. We'll help you with the bags and park your car." Another man opens my trunk after wheeling over a cart.

"Thanks." I nod. My stomach growls, and I stare at the man, hoping he didn't hear. All it does is make me think of Hudson calling it the growly monster, and my shoulders drop.

I help the porter by grabbing my own suitcase and thank him for his help. No doubt this would take me forever to get up to the suite. We enter the resort in silence, and he patiently waits while I check-in. Thankfully, the room is ready for me as promised.

MEET AGAIN

My stomach growls again in the silent elevator with the porter. Fire burns up my neck and face, no doubt making me red like a tomato. He chuckles quietly, covering it up with a cough. *Not smooth, mister.*

I count up the floors as they appear on the small screen. How long does it take to get to the eighth floor?

Finally, the doors open, and I bolt out of there before the porter and press a hand to my stomach as I head toward the right.

"This way." The porter calls out after me

"Oh, right," I speed walk to catch up to him.

A few feet down the corridor, he stops by the door.

"If you need anything, please let us know. We're at your service."

"Thanks." I smile, confused as to why he's saying that when we're still in the hall.

I open the door and step in, freezing. I glance back at the number and confirm it's the suite assigned to us. Why is there a box of pizza on the coffee table? The porter smiles and begins wheeling the cart inside. I'm forced to step in as well so that he doesn't crash into me, and my heart stops when I find Hudson leaning against the wall with his hands in his pockets.

My head snaps back at the porter, who's already piling my bags near the entrance without concern.

"Hi." His deep voice washes over me.

"Hi." My beating heart echoes in my ears, whispering hope into my being.

Hudson leans off the wall and slowly steps toward me. I hold my breath.

"You look beautiful." He breathes out.

I'm stuck in place, staring at him. The thump of the door closing behind us is muffled by my continuing erratic heartbeat.

"What..." I shake my head.

"I'm sorry." He doesn't let me finish. "I'm so sorry, Lex. I messed up big time." He stands mere inches from me, and the scent of his cologne invades my senses. His heat envelops me, and it takes everything in me not to close my eyes and sag into him.

"When you told me the news, I became blind with excitement. I disregarded your feelings and dreams when I'm the one that's unhappy. I shouldn't have said the things I did. I know how much you care." He reaches for my hands.

"I love you more than anything. I'll grovel, beg, plead for your forgiveness. I just want you back in my life." He drops to his knees. His hands remain in mine, his lips turned down and eyes full of sadness.

I bite back, holding in tears. Shaking my head, I drop to my knees. We're equally at blame, and both said things we shouldn't have.

"I'm sorry, too." A tear rolls down my cheek and the corner of my lip. "I-I got so upset, the past still lingering. I love my job, but I love you more. Of course, I do. Us, our relationship means everything to me." I tilt my head and look at him.

"I don't get to pretend my stubbornness and emotions didn't get between us as well. I just need you to understand that my studio is my dream. It's what I've always strived for. Teaching at the college level doesn't allow me to share my passion the same way I can with younger students in my own place. I get to decide how I teach and how I run my business. It gives me freedom." My lips press into a tight line, Hudson's eyes never wavering from mine.

His hands squeeze mine, and he nods. I take a deep breath, ready to say the rest of my piece.

"Moving away to not have to deal with your parents isn't a way to live. That's escaping a situation, not facing it, and healing from it. You need to for your own sake. Forget theirs, but you need to heal." I move one of my hands over his heart. It's beating as rapidly as mine.

"You're right." His words are low and hoarse.

"I don't want to be right. I want to be happy." I drop my hand from his chest.

"I want to make you happy." His head falls forward.

"I was happy with you. So happy." I hold his chin and lift his head. He leans into my touch, warming my heart. In this moment, he looks so much like the teenager I fell in love with all those years ago.

Without responding, his strong arms wrap around me. I fall forward into him but don't complain. His scent surrounds me. His warmth and love create a bubble around us. When I hug him, he releases a heavy breath.

"I'm sorry," he whispers into my ear.

I shiver when his breath tickles the top of my neck.

"I'm sorry, too." I tighten my hold around him.

"I've missed you so much. Talking, seeing your face, video chatting."

I bury my face into the crook of his neck and shoulder, breathing lighter than I have the last few weeks. Hudson pulls me closer until I'm flush against him, resting me on his thighs.

"I love you." He leans his head back to look at me, brushing away my hair from my face.

"I love you, too, but…" I bite my lower lip and look away. "We're still in the same situation."

"No, babe. We're in a whole different boat. Actually, we're not even at sea. We're firmly on the ground." I push my head back and look at him as if he's grown two heads.

"What?"

Hudson's deep laughter vibrates against me.

"I've done a lot of thinking these last few weeks. Losing you propelled me to make decisions and take action."

I sit back on my heels and stare at him with raised eyebrows.

"How about we have some pizza? It's not stock of it, but I figured a box of the pepperoni would be a good start." He gives me a dazzling smile. I swear it twinkles under the light.

"Wait. Is that pizza from the place I loved? What was it called?"

"Roman's Pizza."

"That's right." I nod.

"It's cold, so we'll have to microwave it." He frowns.

"I bet that pizza even tastes good cold." I stand and hold my hand out. "Let's eat and talk."

After heating the slices of pizza, we sit at the small round table in the suite. I stare at Hudson, still confused.

"You know I've had my issues with working at the agency."

I nod silently.

"I felt lost as to what I wanted. I actually enjoy selling homes. I kept trying to bring in older dreams from childhood into the present, but it wasn't the same," he shakes his head. "I'm not the same."

"That's normal," I encourage him.

"Yeah. Anyway, I want to work in real estate, but in a different way."

"How so?" I pick at the pizza crust.

"Eat so that it doesn't get cold again, and I'll explain." He lifts his chin toward my plate and takes a bite as if proving a point.

I eat and listen.

"I want to sell homes to people looking for a place to build memories. I don't want to worry about huge commission

MEET AGAIN

rates and push aside people only because they aren't seeking million-dollar properties." He stands and grabs water bottles from the small fridge. I trail his movements. He demands attention. His tall frame, strong body, and confident strides are difficult to avoid.

"I spoke to my father and turned in my resignation. He wouldn't have it at first," Hudson laughs dryly. "I'm done. It's time I live my life the way I want. That includes you."

My eyes widen, shock clouding my expression.

"I know," he shakes his head and smiles. "I never told you, but my mom tried to bribe Tristan with his trust fund in exchange for him telling her about our relationship. At the same time, my dad schemed a way to have me traveling to Texas the days you were in New York."

"What?"

"Yeah," his jaw ticks. "I told him that wasn't going to work, and I changed the meeting. I don't want them controlling my life anymore, and if I continue to work for the family business, I'm allowing them to."

"What are you going to do?" I'm stunned he finally stood up to his parents.

"I found a small office. I'm branching out on my own. Hudson Homes. I want to find homes for people who appreciate it. Families, young people just starting out. Help them create memories they'll treasure."

"Wow," I breathe out.

"In Hartville."

"What?" I screech.

"It's time I start my life with *you*. If you'll have me."

Disbelief freezes me until I repeat his words in my head and snap out of it.

"Of course." I stand, the chair falling backward. I don't bother to fix it and round the table. Hudson laughs, pushing his chair back.

"Is this really what you want? I witnessed you in New York. You fit there."

"It's what I want. These last few months, I've realized how much I miss Hartville, my friends. The office is small, and it'll take me some time to get started. I did promise my father I wouldn't take any of his clients. It's not the type of clientele I'm aiming for anyway."

"That's very loyal of you."

His hands move to my waist.

"We'll make this work. A real chance. No selfishness or demands or resentment. Clean slate."

"I like the sound of that." I nod, searching his eyes for any sign of sacrifice on his part.

"You promise this isn't you giving up because you feel guilty and want to please me?"

"I want to please you, but no, this isn't about that. I've had time to think. Tristan talked some sense into me, too. It's what I want. I also want to work on merging technology with my business. An app where people can view a home as if they were present. Like a walkthrough instead of photos. It'll take lots of work, but I'm excited about the idea."

"That would be amazing, especially if someone's moving to a new city." I hold on to his shoulders.

"I think so, too. I have a friend from college who might be able to help." He nods. "We're okay then?"

"Yeah." I take a deep breath. "We're definitely okay."

"Good. Let's finish our pizza and decorate this suite." He pulls my head down and drops a chaste kiss on my lips before giving me the most amazing smile in the world. This one does twinkle all on its own.

My heart soars, my own smile covering my entire face. This is not what I was expecting, and I'm still trying to wrap my head around it—Hudson in Hartville. I love the sound of that.

35

HUDSON

I wasn't sure Lex would hear me out. I was terrified and banking on cold pizza and the hope she still cared enough to give me another chance. They say the third time's the charm for a reason.

When I saw her in the suite, I swore my heart was going to race out of my chest. She looked sad and stunning. As soon as she noticed me, her face morphed into an adorable confused expression.

My heart slowed when I realized she was hearing me out. It began to beat rapidly again when she forgave me. Seeing the excited wonderment on her face when I told her about my career change reaffirmed my decision. Although I needed to make this switch for myself, it impacted her in a way I was hoping would help unite us.

It was the right choice, and I've never felt as light as I have since I told my father I was quitting. I thought he was going to have a coronary. My mom has been calling me nonstop. I haven't answered any of her calls, though I know it'll be hard to avoid them living in Hartville.

The bach party has been a success so far, especially having Lex by my side. We've skied. Well, all of us except Lex. No luck convincing her. As much fun as I've been having, though, I wish we were in Hartville together, alone. I love my friends, but after reuniting with Lex, I want to spend time with her, talk to her, and hold her in my arms. Kiss her without any reservations.

A hard clap lands on my shoulder, and Toby chuckles. "You were lost in thought there." He shakes his head with a knowing grin. "Glad things worked out."

"Thanks. Unfortunately, my parents are still in denial or plotting my demise. It's going to be interesting living in the same town with them again as an adult."

"And dating Lex."

"I already dated her before while living with them. They won't get in the middle of us." I shake my head adamantly.

"Now that you've made choices that benefit *you* and not them, I believe you." Toby lifts his brows.

"You didn't believe me before?" I inch my head back, eyebrows furrowing.

"I believed you loved Lex, but you had this guilt-filled idea that you had to take over the family business. Some kind of loyalty I never really understood, to be honest." Toby frowns.

"Me neither, but I did feel that way." I scratch the side of my head and stare off.

What is it with wanting to please parents even when you disagree with everything they represent? Is that part of being someone's child? Blind loyalty?

"Anyway, tonight we'll have some drinks, eat some great food, and forget about the rest. I'm getting married!" Toby yells across the bar at the resort.

Laughing, I shake my head and wave at the bartender. The girls had spa day today. Meanwhile, we had a long day out on the slopes, so we're all having dinner at the resort. Now I just need Lex to hurry down.

"What can I get you?" The bartender stands before me. I order us all a round of beers and head toward where Toby and the rest of the guys are standing at a hightop.

"Beer coming up." I smile at them.

"Speaking like a true best man." Toby chuckles but stops midway and widens his eyes.

I follow his line of vision, and my mouth dries.

Lex is glowing. She's wearing a short satin V-neck long sleeve dress. My eyes trail up her body, slowly appreciating her curves until I reach her smile. Red lipstick makes me hold back a groan. I don't care who's around us. I stalk toward her and wrap my arms around her.

"You look stunning, beautiful. Wow..." I breathe out and stare into those chocolate eyes. "You always do, for the record, but..." I shake my head.

"Thank you." She wears a shy smile.

Her hands move to my chest, over my baby blue dress shirt. "You look handsome."

"Thanks, babe." I kiss her cheek.

All night, I keep my eyes on Lex. I can't look away. While she eats, drinks, and laughs, I wish we were in Hartville. After dinner, we go back to the bar. I grab Lex's hand and pull her to me, keeping her close as I move us to the soft music.

Her smile wins me over. When her fingers brush the back of my hair, I close my eyes and lean my forehead to hers. Everything seems perfect for once in my life, and I clutch on to this feeling.

"When are you officially moving to Hartville?" She leans back and looks into my eyes.

"Soon," I promise. "I'm finishing up a few things at the office next week, and then I'm all yours," I smirk.

"I like the sound of that." Her lips twist into a smile.

"Yeah?"

"Uh, huh. I need someone around to feed my monster stomach and bring me coffee when I'm working."

"Hold on. Am I just your food and coffee delivery man?" I raise my brows.

Lex rolls her eyes up thoughtfully. "Yeah." She nods, and a huge smile breaks out on her face before she laughs.

"You, sir, are the man I love. We could be on a deserted island having to fish with branch spears we carved, and I wouldn't want anyone else by my side."

"I like the sound of that. Well, not the deserted island without food but having you by my side." My arm tightens around her waist, keeping her close to me.

"Same," she rubs her nose against mine.

I keep her close the rest of the night. I plan to keep her close for life.

I'm finally back in Hartville for good. I stare around the apartment I rented and the mess of boxes. It's much smaller than my condo in New York, which is expected, yet this feels homier.

"Knock, knock." I turn toward the open door and smile when I see Lex standing here holding a tray with coffee cups and a paper bag.

"Hey." I grab the tray from her hands and kiss her softly. "Welcome to my new home." I extend my free arm around as if showcasing a prize.

"I love it," she nods, walking in and looking around.

"Me too."

"I'm here to help. Toby and Hope will be by later after a meeting for their wedding."

"Thank you. Tristan should be here this afternoon, too." I place the tray on the countertop and smile.

"No need to thank me. Put me to work." She claps her hands.

"Breakfast first?" I lift my brows.

"Ah, yeah. I brought some pastries from The Bean. There was a new barista."

"Really?"

"Yeah," Lex shrugs. "Anyway, pastries, coffee, and work."

We do just that. Opening boxes is overwhelming, but Lex tackles each one with determination. Once my kitchen is clean and stocked, I wipe my forehead with my t-shirt. It's cold as heck outside, but this apartment and unpacking are making me sweat.

"Let's go have lunch before Toby and Hope arrive. I need a break."

"Are you sure? We can order something?" Lex looks around at the opened boxes spilling with my belongings.

"I'm positive. If I stay in here, I'm going to go mad."

Her sweet giggles make me smile. "Grouchy and hungry. That's a deadly combination." She saunters over to me.

"Come on, let's get you fed." She quirks a brow, and it makes me want to kiss her silly. Unfortunately, I don't have time for that right now. I'll be able to spend as much time with her as I want once this place is in order.

"Let's grab subs from the deli. It's not far from here, and I could use a walk."

"In the snow?"

"It's not snowing right now. Besides, isn't that your favorite?" I angle my head and raise my eyebrows.

MEET AGAIN

"Yeah." She nods. "But if I slip on a patch of ice, I'm bringing you down with me."

"Wouldn't expect anything less." I laugh and reach for her hand, dragging her out of my apartment and into the cold outdoors. A deep breath fills my lungs.

"I need to buy some artwork for the walls, make it my home. My apartment in New York was plain, so I didn't have any to bring with me."

"We can go to different stores. The antique shop might have some cool options." She gives me her best smile.

"You and your antiques," I laugh.

"Excuse me." My head snaps up at the familiar icy voice.

I stop, staring at my parents on the sidewalk. Lex's hand tightens around mine, and I love that she doesn't let go as if we were caught doing something bad.

"Hudson," my father nods.

"Dad." I keep my expression serious.

"I see you've decided to downgrade in all aspects of your life," my mother's face sours as her eyes scan over Lex.

I scoot to block her and stare at my mom. "If choosing to love someone who accepts me unconditionally is a downgrade, then I should've downgraded a long time ago." My jaw ticks, fire blazing in my veins. I take a deep breath and remind myself that she's my mother.

My mom scoffs in response and rolls her eyes. "Soon, you'll realize she's not good enough. You need someone who is going to take your career to the next level. She probably convinced you to quit and move back."

"With all due respect, Mrs. Remington." Lex moves and stands next to me, her chin lifted. "I've never wanted to get in the way of Hudson and his family. Quite the opposite. Many times I told him to express how he felt so that you could be a family. Time and again, you've proven you care more about your appearances than him, and it saddens me because I know how special it is to have loving and supportive parents." I squeeze Lex's hand, and she glances at me.

"Hudson is a hardworking man. He's kind and loyal, which is why he went to work for you in the first place, but *soon* you'll realize that not everything in life is money and social class. You're right. I'm not rich, nor do I have the connections you may have, but I love him with every ounce of my being. That, to me, is more important because I'll support any decision he makes, even if it means sacrificing our relationship. His happiness matters to me."

I release her hand and wrap my arm around her shoulder, kissing the top of her head. Gratitude and awe fill me for the woman by my side. I look at my parents' serious expressions and frown.

"I hope one day you'll realize that all I ever wanted was to have loving parents present in my life. I hope you one day accept my choices and Tristan's. More so, I hope you accept the woman I love because, despite everything, family is important to me."

With that, I walk around them and head to the deli.

"Are you okay?" Lex whispers.

"Yeah, more than okay."

"They'll come around. I could tell." She smiles at me.

"Maybe, maybe not, but I've got you, and that's all I need." I kiss her temple and thank the Lord he brought her back into my life. Lex is the woman who's always owned my heart, despite distance, time, and space. It's her. It's always been her. *She's* my family.

MEET AGAIN

♡♡♡

Want more of the Meet Cute series?

Tristan's story is coming in 2022 in ***Meet Fake***!

My parents think they can manipulate me into being the robot they deem acceptable to society by withholding my trust fund, no matter that I want to use it for a good cause. I'll do anything to get that money on my twenty-fifth birthday, even if it means striking a deal with the new barista, who is in a financial bind. It's the perfect deal. How difficult could it be to pretend to be in love with a virtual stranger? Easy, peasy.

Continue reading for a sneak peek. Scan this code to grab your copy!

♡♡♡

Thank you for reading Meet Again! If you loved Lex and Hudson's story and want to share the love, you can leave a quick review on Amazon so other readers can find this story.

Connect with me through my Abi's Sweet Reads email where I share all the bookish news, behind-the-scenes, and book recommendations. Scan the code on the next page to sign-up and receive a free novella, *The Set Up*.

SNEAK PEEK
Meet Fake
SAGE

ONCE WE FINISH, TRISTAN and I stand by the door, looking at each other.

"Thanks for your help. I could've done it on my own, but we definitely got it done faster."

"You're welcome. It was good to feel productive and useful." His lips press into a straight line.

"I'm sure you're plenty productive with your job." I wave at his messenger bag.

"Sometimes. I just need a few more things to work out in my favor."

"I get that, " I nod.

"Actually," he shifts on his feet, gripping the strap on his messenger bag. "I actually wanted to ask you something." His eyes avoid mine.

My heart races. Is he going to ask me out? He's handsome and all, but I don't have the energy for dating.

"This is awkward, and I don't want you to take it the wrong way." He looks at me again, his eyes serious.

"Do I have something in my teeth?" I rub my tongue along them.

Tristan lets out a guffaw and shakes his head. "No. I would've told you that a long time ago. Friends don't let friends go the entire day with food in their teeth."

"Friends?" I lift my brows. "I met you yesterday."

"But I helped you clean, so technically we've fast forward."

I shake my head and put my hands on my hips. "What do you have to say?" We're getting off-topic.

"You seem like a cool girl, er, woman." I wave my hand to hurry him up. "Okay, okay," he chuckles.

"Here's the thing. How do I say this without sounding like a jerk?" He looks up at the ceiling. "Like I told you, I'm working on opening a nonprofit organization. It's a dream of mine. Of course to do that I need money, which I technically have."

"I'm not following." I shake my head. My eyebrows pull low over my eyes. Tristan scrubs a hand down his face.

"My parents have a trust fund for me. I have the money in that fund for my business, but they have recently decided that I will not get that money when I turn twenty-five because they don't agree with my lifestyle or what I want to use it for. It's a long story, and they aren't ideal parents," he shakes his head in frustration.

"That's unfair. You're going to use it for an amazing cause."

"I agree," he nods. "But in my parents' eyes, I've been traveling the world and wasting time. They have no idea all the work I've done nor care about it. It's not up to par with their fancy life. They want me to prove I've matured and settled down, thinking I'm going to blow the money on traveling some more."

"Okay..." I'm not really following. Maybe he needs to vent to someone and a virtual stranger is the easiest person to let all your problems go.

"Right, so I won't be getting a desk job or working at the family business. It's not for me, and that money *is* mine. You mentioned yesterday something about losing your job, which I don't understand since you just started this week, but that's

MEET AGAIN

beside the point." He refocuses on what he wants to say while my cheek blaze with embarrassment.

"I have a proposition for you. I need to prove to my parents I'm settling down. You, it seems, need money. If I show them I'm in a committed relationship, they'll think I'll use that money for something they deem acceptable. We can pretend to be in a relationship for the next two months, and once I have my trust fund, I'll give you a cut."

My eyes widen and I step back. Is he serious? Words have left me. My brain shut off. Tristan looks at me expectantly.

"Say something? Even if it's no."

"What?" I shriek.

"I know this is totally out of left field and not a normal request."

"This is beyond abnormal. This is crazy." What kind of person asks a stranger to pretend to date in exchange of money?

"If I weren't crazy with desperation, I wouldn't even think about it. My parents have tried to bribe me to tell them about my brother's relationship in exchange for the money, but I wouldn't do that to him. They don't approve of his girlfriend, so he recently cut ties with them. All I'm left with is this option. I know it's insane, and we don't really know each other."

"We don't know each other at all," I correct him.

"I beg to differ. I know you like to read and draw. You're good at serving coffee and always smile at customers. You know I love to be outdoors and have a passion to help people."

So that's what this is about. Help the poor barista who needs money. I shake my head.

"I don't know."

"Think about it. The money would be a big chunk."

I look at him incredulously.

"A hundred thousand," he blurts out.

"You're crazy!" I yell.

"I can afford it... As soon as I have that money in my bank account."

"Goodness gracious, how much is even in that trust fund? Don't answer that," I lift my hand. "It was a rhetorical question."

"Think about it. No pressure. If you decided you can't do it, I'll still consider you a friend." Honesty rolls off him. Who is this guy?

Find out what happens next in Meet Fake!

THANK YOU!

THANK YOU FOR READING my book! I'm so grateful for your support. Having readers to share my stories with is everything I could dream of.

It takes a village to publish a book, and I owe a ton of gratitude to an amazing team! Thank you to my editor, cover designer, Just Reads promo company, betas, ARC readers, and bookstagrammers who have encouraged me and supported Meet Again since I started sharing about it. PHEW, it feels good to have you in my corner!

To all the authors I've met and those I already knew who have provided friendship and support—THANK YOU!

A special thanks to Kirsten Oliphant/ Emma St. Clair for answering questions when I was beginning to dip my toes into this genre and being such a support in this community.

ABOUT ABI SABINA

Abi Sabina writes sweet closed door romance full of swoon, sass, and humor. She traded in the big city life for small town living when she moved to Spain.

She hasn't wrangled herself a country boy yet, but she writes books based on charming heroes and small town charm. (And she throws in the city setting every so often.)

She loves coffee, country music, and the mountains. Her goal is to write stories that make you feel, smile, and cheer on love.

Made in United States
Troutdale, OR
05/01/2024